ALSO BY JOSÉ DONOSO

The Boom in Latin American Literature:
  A Personal History   (1977)

Charleston and Other Stories   (1977)

The Obscene Bird of Night   (1972)

This Sunday   (1967)

Coronation   (1965)

Sacred
Families

Sacred Families

Three Novellas
by José Donoso

Translated from the Spanish
by Andrée Conrad

ALFRED A. KNOPF
NEW YORK
1977

THIS IS A BORZOI BOOK
PUBLISHED BY ALFRED A. KNOPF, INC.

Library of Congress Cataloging in Publication Data

Donoso, José, (Date)
Sacred families.

Translation of Tres novelitas burguesas.
I. Title.
PZ4.D6849Sac3   [PQ8079.D617]   863   76-45455
ISBN 0-394-40222-7

FIRST AMERICAN EDITION

 Assistance in the translation of this volume was given
by the Center for Inter-American Relations.

for Gene and Francesca Raskin

Contents

Chattanooga Choo-Choo

THE THIN STREAM of oil Sylvia was pouring over the escarole shone pure gold in the light of the flaming charcoal that was reducing itself to embers in the fireplace. Ramón puffed on his pipe, waiting to broil the chops. The terrace was open to the darkness of the hills, clotted here and there with clusters of ancient chestnut trees—remnants of a forest cleverly exploited in the layout of the housing development to conceal the other units that rose up around the modernized country house at its center. A moth, fat, soft, clumsy, struck against the patch of Sylvia's shoulder left bare by her peasant blouse. She didn't feel the blow, to judge by the golden thread that continued to fall unperturbed over the salad. It was as if her perfect back were made of some kind of plastic, polished and inert. But the gentle collision must have triggered a hidden mechanism beneath her skin, because in almost reflex response to the moth's assault, she said, "What a shame Magdalena couldn't come—she's so nice. You might have settled on one of the houses today . . ."

I felt the idyllic tone of the afternoon, spent looking at houses in the project, abruptly change key with Sylvia's remark, the way milk suddenly, for no good reason, separates or turns sour. At first, I thought a note of irony had crept in again to what Sylvia was saying about Magdalena; that the sudden souring must spring from my natural diffidence toward women who are new converts to Women's Liberation in an ambience where it is still considered daring, women who monotonously repeat their catechism about "poor creatures" who are victimized by their husbands and their own cowardice, who feel obliged to stay in town with the children on weekends. But no, this was not what had turned the tide, rudely changing pleasure into alarm. I felt that Sylvia was invoking Magdalena's presence over and above theory and sarcasm: Sylvia needed support, or help, or protection; against what dangers, I did not know. What protection could she need in this delightful world of ours, where evil did not exist because everything was taken for granted? Everybody knew Sylvia and Ramón were perfect; their impeccably structured relationship was admired by all as being (in one direction or another) beyond love; trite as it is these days to dwell on such details, it is still worth mentioning. No, Sylvia's words about Magdalena disclosed no insecurity regarding the relationship between my wife and our children as compared with the relationship between Sylvia and her son, now in the custody of his father, entrenched in the prosaic conventions of Madrid society. Insecurity was irrelevant, because Ramón was Ramón del Solar: he took the pipe out of his mouth, leaned over the fire that lit up his face like a sorcerer's, and blew out the flames, leaving a mass of glowing coals.

"The chops," he said.

As she passed them, Sylvia persisted. "And Magdalena's taste is so marvelous . . ."

Had she tasted it? Maybe because she was passing the meat as she said this, it flashed through my mind that she meant a "taste" of Magdalena's that only I knew; the idea made me retreat before the anthropophagous Sylvia. But of course she meant a different kind of "taste": the "taste" that governed our visit to the houses that afternoon, providing us with a common language; a "taste" related to aesthetic judgment, ordained by the social milieu in which we lived. This was what so rudely soured it all: Sylvia could not possibly regret Magdalena's absence that night, for the very simple reason that she barely knew us. This harping on her good taste, on how much we needed her, this repeated praise that betrayed a somewhat limited sensibility (since evidently for her the language of suggestion was not enough) was an irritating exaggeration that detracted from future possibilities, given the fact that the four of us had first met the night before, at Ricardo and Raimunda Roig's cocktail party. No doubt Sylvia and Ramón had heard as many stories about us as we had about them. But it was absurd, a travesty, to pretend that the immediate liking, the bare promise of friendship, the possibility of sharing not only a sense of humor but aesthetic judgment, had had time to grow beyond an embryonic affinity. For the present, although Sylvia wanted to pretend otherwise, she and Ramón were two-dimensional to us, with hardly more depth than the rest of the people crowded together as if on a large, strident poster at last night's cocktail party—just as we were to them, no doubt.

It could be argued whether or not Ricardo and Raimunda Roig were the center of a certain Barcelona world. It could even be argued—in fact, it was, with a frequency that smacked of pure propaganda on the part of their detractors —whether they were beautiful, talented, intelligent, even whether they were honest about their aestheticizing, lefticizing positions. But this ubiquity of their polemic existence made them universally sought after, and everywhere they went they were followed by a retinue, and in turn by the momentary favorites of these favorites, to whom night after night they opened the doors of their tiny top-floor apartment on Calle Balmes. Raimunda's legs were famous: not long and stylized like a model's, but well-turned, full, soft (so said the cognoscenti) to the touch beneath the dark stockings of winter or atop the naked tan of summer; too soft and rounded perhaps, almost pathetic, as if quivering on the brink of the catastrophe of one pound, one year too many. But those who had known her a long time said she had always been that way, with the deepest décolletés, the shortest affairs, and the smallest bikinis, with black cannibal eyes filled with the most insulting or the most insinuating black smile, depending on what she wanted to elicit from the person she was talking to, her voice scorched by gin. Although she tried not to show it, Raimunda had the brains in the family; she was the one with the nose for the unusual: the extraordinary neck or moustache, the Carole Lombard dress at Los Encants, the perfect model for her husband's photographs, picked to be attractive enough to sleep with him several times, but not attractive enough to take him away from her. Above all, Raimunda possessed a vast talent for starting rumors about herself, her husband, her lovers; rumors so delicious that later they could reap their own harvest in commissions from millionaire companies fascinated by the Roigs' incomparable techniques in photography and love. Despite those commissions, vicious tongues had it that the Roig Studio's real income came from material sold to the porno shops in Scandinavia, the U.S., England, Amsterdam, and Tokyo, since the domestic raw material—so to speak—for these things was so cheap and the Roigs so ready to explore the new, the exciting angle. Each trip they made abroad, always for specific reasons (Jerry Lewis, *Bomarzo, Hair*), brought them back to Barcelona with more perfect cameras, filters, and lenses, with fur coats more scandalously disheveled, bought for a king's ransom in Portobello Road; or they would buy a country house in Ampurdan to remodel. Of course, it was easy to get out of Spain with a dozen rolls of erotic stills and even, it was said, actual movies of orgies starring the more intimate visitors to the Calle Balmes attic.

"Ugly people are always evil; you have to be careful not to get mixed up with them. If a woman has short legs or bad skin or is overweight, I run, not just because I'm repelled but because I'm terrified she's going to do something perfectly bitchy to me."

That was the most memorable thing Ricardo Roig had ever said. However, he passed judgment constantly, on anything and everything; his words moved with the voracious energy of a fire that consumes and razes and then passes on to the house next door. In spite of his vehemence, a clear, coherent thread ran through it all—sub- or supra-rational, depending on one's opinion of Ricardo—which in some way united all his enthusiasms and his dislikes, a sagacity that functioned in spite of the equivocations and excesses, and was often proved right. The presence of his profile (of an antique ugliness in the style of Antonello da Messina), of his short-cropped hair, his somber turtlenecks, his filthy fingernails, was enough to make a restaurant fashionable, to introduce a painter, to give a model her entrée, to condemn a style of interior decoration. What was said about the two of them (naturally) was that they were snobs, superficial, I can't stand them, they're always saying the same things over and over, those pointless witless arguments between him and Ramón . . . what they need is a courtful of sycophants, intellectuals posing as lightweights, and vice versa . . . But the ones who protested the loudest were the ones who ran fastest to the attic when they were invited; forgetting their moral and intellectual pretensions, they "dressed down" in the least conventional thing that had been stored at the bottom of a trunk for just such an occasion. If they could not attract attention, at least they could pass and be able afterward, in conversations with friends who had no access to the Roigs' world, to modify the opinions of people who did not claim the Roigs' acquaintance.

We, who did not belong to the Roigs' world at all, were invited every once in a while to the attic (Magdalena's beauty had attracted them like two flies, while wine was being served after some lecture on a boring book) and we rubbed elbows with several of their friends and enemies. I have always admired people who know how to create an aura, transforming things and appropriating them as if by witchcraft, debatable though the quality of that magic may be. Magdalena and I were delighted to go to Ricardo and Raimunda's. When we arrived that night, everybody was sitting around on cushions, on the rug, reclining against armchairs or each other. The soprano sax coming out of the stereo whined and skittered through the crosscurrents of laughter and conversations that I could not hear but could see sketched on the faces of acquaintances who shot some greeting or other at me. Raimunda grabbed me to hand me a glass—No, no, water, Raimunda, wait, no, I'm on Valium and if I have a vodka so early I'll short-circuit—and guided me through the crowd which, as usual, was six times larger than could reasonably fit inside the attic. Flash! I closed my eyes and opened them again.

"Lovey!"

"Kaethe!"

"It's been ages!"

"Yes, ages . . ."

While I stooped to kiss the tiny, perverse photographer with the Shirley Temple curls, the Little Lord Fauntleroy suit, and brains addled by McLuhan, I looked around for Magdalena. In the distance, made three times more distant by the number of people, I saw her standing comparing her sequined hot pants with an identical pair on another woman. The woman talking to Magdalena was extremely tall and slender and stood as if her body had been put together according not to any anthropomorphic and mimetic principle but rather to a fantastic and expressive one, an exaggerated abstraction of elegance, symbolic at best. Her elbows bent backward, her head was minute, her torso almost absent, and all of this was balanced on the thinnest of legs crossed with the same complete disregard for anatomical credibility as a stork striking a calculated pose. And yet her body was not the most extraordinary thing about her. *That* was her face— perfectly artificial and with a surface as smooth and even as an egg, on which were distributed a pair of large dark eyes lacking both expression and eyebrows, two patches of color on the cheeks, and a dark mouth near the lower end. Kaethe said she must go give Magdalena a kiss, she was divine in her hot pants, like a chorus girl.

"The only thing missing is a top hat. With sequins too, of course," she added.

I told her to wait a moment, because the hot-pants twins were about to start something in the middle of the room, and I didn't know who the other one was.

"You don't know her? That's Sylvia Corday, Ramón del Solar's friend . . . you know that whole story. Yes, she does look as if she's made of plastic modules—just like a mannequin in a window. They say she doesn't have a face, or at least not any features. Where's her nose, for example? Nobody's ever seen it. Not even Ramón, apparently. Every morning she sits down at the mirror and invents her face, paints it the way one would paint a still life, or a portrait . . . naturally, *after* Ramón has put her together piece by piece so she can, well, I don't know, bathe, and all those things. Sometimes you see Ramón for weeks at a time without Sylvia. You ask after her and he says she's in Cappadocia posing for *Vogue*. Cappadocia is very 'in' this season. We were thinking of organizing a charter with Raimunda and Ricardo. But it's a lie, she's never been further than Tarrasa. It's because he's fed up with her and won't put her together or make her up. He keeps all the pieces in a special box: all those weeks Ramón is resting and so is she. That's why she's so incredibly young, because during the weeks she's put away and disassembled, time stands still for her. Then when Ramón begins to miss her again, he assembles her and they go everywhere together. Isn't she the perfect woman? Ramón is cute, a little on the boy scout side, but cute. Of course she's a very ballsy lady."

This season everything was "ballsy" in Barcelona—it certainly was, to hear Kaethe say the word in her thick German accent with her air of a depraved little boy—just as everything this season was Forties: the fluffy hairdo Sylvia was wearing that night and the two women's sequined hot pants made them look like chorus girls out of *Vamps of 1940*. As if reading my mind, Sylvia and Magdalena raised their legs parallel, put an arm around each other's waist, turned their heads to the left in unison, and began to dance with a coordination so perfect that it seemed mechanical. When they stopped in the center of the circle that had formed around them, a spotlight was focused on them, everybody quieted down, and they began to gesticulate, emitting doll-like sounds that seemed to come from a hand-operated gramophone hidden behind a curtain.

> *Pardon me boy*
> *Is this the Chattanooga choo-choo*
> *Right on track twenty-nine?*
> *Please gimme a shine.*
> *I can afford to go*
> *To Chattanooga Station,*
> *I've got my fare*
> *And just a trifle to spare.*
> *You reach Pennsylvania Station*
> *At a quarter to four,*
> *Read a magazine*
> *Then you're in Baltimore,*
> *Dinner at the diner,*
> *Nothing could be finer*
> *Than to have your ham 'n eggs*
> *In Carolineeeeeer . . .*

They sang in the most vulgar American accent of thirty years ago, in the style of a period that we had been abruptly cut off from by the poverty-stricken years of isolation after the war; now, in middle age, we were living through an adolescence whose universal myths we had barely known about at the time of their creation. The two women's gestures and grimaces, the pursed, dark lips, the stridency, the hair floating with the dance, the glitter of teeth in sudden, broad smiles, were unquestionably those of the Andrews Sisters. Magdalena and I had hummed this song to the rhythm of Glenn Miller—and danced it in the days of Swing: it belonged to another geological era, now buried and forgotten. We had never discussed these people again. I would never have believed Magdalena, sober and rather timid by nature, capable of taking part in this nickelodeon revue. Still less of remembering with such monstrous precision the words of "Chattanooga Choo-Choo"; not only had I not heard the song, I had not even thought of it, in thirty years. What obscure convolution of the brain had stored these absurd lyrics? What circumstances unknown to me had fixed them there, in the gray attic of her memory, for three decades, to be resuscitated intact, exact, here and now, out of the blue?

Sylvia and Magdalena started in again like two dolls, raising their knees, stretching their legs and arms in unison, suddenly showing two profiles, two necks, two masterfully coordinated smiles. Ballsy, ballsy, Kaethe murmured in her impenetrable German accent, admiration overwhelming her usual speech affectations. But I was trying to resist my urge to hurl myself at Magdalena and dismantle her like a machine, to discover why and where she had hoarded that idiotic song, intact like that, perhaps related to secret things unknown to me and hidden throughout so many years of marriage. I must have been muttering, because Kaethe, standing next to me, worshipful, whispered Shhhhhhh! as if Caballé herself were about to sing. The two women, haloed by the spotlight, all glitters, gestures and grins, drew apart and paused to look at each other before continuing the song:

When you hear the whistle
Blowing eight to the bar
Then you know Tennessee
Is not very far,
Travel all along, go,
Got to keep 'em rolling,
Chattanooga choo-choo
There we go.
There's gonna be
A certain party at the station,
In satin and lace,
I used to call Funny Face.
She's gonna cry
Until I promise nevermore . . .
So Chattanooga choo-choo
Please choo-choo me home.

The spot dimmed on the two dolls. In the hullabaloo of applause and congratulations that followed, I found myself excluded, unable to understand the sudden autonomy of my wife, or to tolerate her capacity, until this moment unknown to me (I who thought I knew her completely), of transforming herself into an empty, vulgar Forties doll, of representing the reality of that period, naïve and cruelly American, to those who had not actually lived it: a legend incarnated in a style, a form, a fashion, an ephemeral song that would live again through the fad of a few months. I wandered around for a while unrecognized in the crunch of people, tinkling my ice cubes to pass for a vodka-drinker, until I heard Kaethe's angry voice at my back. I turned around rudely, banging my elbow into her. In the heat of the argument, not even looking to see who I was, she grabbed the glass from my hand and clenched her fist around it, as she spat an imprecation at Paolo. I held my breath to see whether she was going to drink it or hurl it in Paolo's face as punishment no doubt for one of his habitual indiscretions. She drank it in a gulp. The disgust on her face turned to accusation as she recognized me.

"You! How revolting! It was water!" she cried.

Paolo slipped away. The novel sensation of water in her throat seemed instantly to calm and revive her. She introduced me to Ramón, who begged me as a contemporary (of himself and "Chattanooga Choo-Choo") to menace Kaethe with obsolescence: next year the Fifties, the year after that the Sixties would be in style as Camp, and this acceleration of nostalgia meant that before she ever became "in," she would embody the absurd, the comic, the dead, although she had barely begun to blossom at the end of the last decade. In the middle of this discussion Kaethe was kidnapped by a boxer with a nose broken à la Picasso, the author of mystico-erotic poems soon to be published by the Roig Studio, illustrated with photographs of his torso. I wound up in a corner, nursing a real vodka at last, and talking to Ramón. He explained that since Sylvia was a model and this year everything was Forties, he had felt compelled to teach her "Chattanooga Choo-Choo" and all the accompanying mythology to help her acquire the style of the period (an asset in her profession). It had been almost like training a circus dog, he said. At first he thought she would never be able to capture the essential spirit, the recent past is the most passé, we let time go by before reviving past periods with a coating of idealization or irony, but young people today hurl themselves starving onto the cadaver of a past each time more terrifyingly recent, until soon there will be nothing left but to transform their own present into carrion in order to be able to eat.

The current of the Roigs' gathering shifted. Once interest in the Andrews Sisters died, the crowd focused on the boxer, who was defending Fidel Castro's disdain for "longhaired intellectuals" against the cautious dialectics of a blue-eyed, blue-bearded publisher while at the same time he allowed Raimunda and Kaethe to take off his T-shirt adorned with the face of Che Guevara so that we could all compare his splendid pectoral muscles with Kaethe's exiguous breasts. The television that was blueing the publisher's face was turned off, and little by little the music, the departures and arrivals, the rapid exhaustion of conversation, the displacement of centers of interest, made Sylvia and Magdalena drift toward our corner. The model's eyes, round as two balls, her eyelashes painted with all the meticulousness of a Betty Boop, were admirably vacuous as they searched for Ramón's approval. Only her telltale look could break the Forties aura that enveloped her and kept her prisoner of a fictional past revived by a fad. The ideal woman, Kaethe had said; whom one *teaches* "Chattanooga Choo-Choo." She wasn't a woman like Magdalena, who had stored the song along with God knows what other secrets and individual kinks in the depths of her memory, to which I had no access. Ramón spoke to Magdalena, who was no longer defined by the song or her period look; without asking for my approval, she had abandoned them, after stamping them with her own personality:

from outside the Forties, from a passionate present, she and Ramón debated Pacelli's maneuvers with the Nazis, whether there were three or four Andrews Sisters, whether they were white or black; then they remembered Mr. Chad, war photographs by Capa and Margaret Bourke-White, and styles by Penn and Hoyningen-Heune. To attract Ramón's attention, Sylvia interrupted:

"Since Ramón belongs to a different generation, he wants to become one of the Young by knowing what's Camp . . ."

"What the hell has that got to do with it? Camp has been dead since . . ."

Ramón did not finish his sentence, realizing that to do so would necessitate a whole string of explanations to her that he did not feel like making. Still clinging to Ramón she talked and laughed with Magdalena, who thought Ramón was leaving Sylvia on the sidelines—neither her words nor her presence made any dent in the conversation. To draw her in, Magdalena commented on the Afro wig Raimunda was wearing that evening. But our evocation of the Forties, only to be understood through the laughter of nostalgia, had so carried us away that Ramón suggested (since Ricardo got furious if any of us formed a separate group instead of throwing ourselves wholeheartedly into the turbulent tide of his gatherings) that the best thing to do was to sneak out and go somewhere for dinner and drinks and conversation. We went to the Bistrot and afterwards to have coffee outdoors at Las Ramblas, and later we wandered from one bar to the next. After that we sauntered on to a neighborhood somewhat farther afield, to criticize, in the livid night-glare of the street lamps, a steel-and-glass slab recently completed by Ramón's ex-partner. We discussed the huge public controversy stirred up by Ramón's modernization of his country house, then we decided to leave immediately to spend the weekend looking at the development where Ramón suggested we buy a house. . . . Yes, leave immediately, because we were letting the dawn creep in behind El Corte Inglés, which clearly could not be tolerated.

"The children . . ."

No, both Ramón and Sylvia affectionately insisted that our foursome must be prolonged, but Magdalena could not leave the children that weekend. She had promised to take them to a puppet show, and even though she really didn't want to go . . . Sylvia replied, "I'll telephone you when we get back from the country."

"Absolutely. We have lots to do together."

"Yes, and talk about these tyrants."

This conversation took place as the two women were leaning over to kiss goodbye, words spoken into each other's ear, though out loud, laughing, in a tone of joking conspiracy. Later when Magdalena was actually saying goodbye to me, she urged me to go with Sylvia and Ramón. "I'll go another day, maybe next weekend when I've got myself organized to leave the children with Mrs. Presen." She told me to pick out several possible houses, since I understood those things and mine was the taste that generally prevailed. Hearing this, Sylvia, who had settled in the front seat beside Ramón, her head resting drowsily on his shoulder, spoke in a low voice to Ramón while I gave Magdalena another goodbye kiss.

"The submissive little woman . . . she must be a real man-eater."

She said it in a particular tone of voice that in the heaviness of dawn seemed calculated to evoke an atmosphere of shared secretiveness, of sects; it had happened with Magdalena and now was happening again, more logically, with Ramón. In fact she was terribly wrong: Magdalena was not submissive. We simply had defined our respective duties, divided the labor. Magdalena did not devour me: she was a human being determined by outside circumstances very different from my own, with an awareness of this and of what needed to be done. I would have liked to explain to Sylvia, to make her understand that Magdalena in no way condemned her, that furthermore she knew nothing about Sylvia that was not already part of the well-publicized legend. That was why the next night, while Ramón broiled the chops over charcoal after a quiet afternoon among trees and hills and attractive houses, her insistence that the absence of Magdalena, with whom she had felt such affinity, was so sad, struck me as being something more than malicious. It's true she used the word *affinity* only two or three times all day; but I sensed that in her mouth the word was charged with more meaning than it ordinarily had, as if Magdalena's absence impeded the realization of some joint venture which this "affinity" would have made possible. But there in the sunlight, among the reflections of the chestnut leaves, it seemed irritating nonsense that this inconsequential, decorative doll should ally herself with a woman as substantial as Magdalena. It was only at nightfall, when she set the table on the terrace, lightly humming "Chattanooga Choo-Choo," that the moth's attack on her naked shoulder seemed to press a button setting numerous mysterious mechanisms in motion, and although the golden thread of oil falling on the escarole did not waver, she repeated, compulsively it seemed to me, that it was *such* a shame that Magdalena had had to stay with the children, that children were a bore, that her own child was with the Jesuits because the father had insisted on it, and perhaps it was a good thing after all; that Magdalena was one of the most ballsy women she had ever met, so with-it, so stylish, so . . . and she repeated the word *affinity* again. Now, in the light of the charcoal, with the night clear and warm outside, it sounded dangerous.

Ramón and I said nothing. Only the gentle sizzling of the meat on the fire kept the night's vast silence from my ears. It seemed to me that while he turned the chops Ramón was threateningly trying to catch Sylvia's eye. Now it was she who avoided his glance—in self-defense against Ramón's censure of her insistent repetitions? She hummed quietly as she concentrated on garnishing the salad with parsley and olives and lit the candles. Then she raised her voice and sang:

"... *please choo-choo me home!* There we are. I'm sure Magdalena would have arranged these wildflowers in the center of the table much more gracefully ..."

One more mention of Magdalena and she would lose Ramón, who was sick of it, or earn herself a cruel reprisal: Ramón, I was discovering, didn't care for real autonomy in Sylvia. Despite the couple's much-touted "freedom," he continued to be a gentleman of the old school in search of the modern "sex-object," whose liberation Sylvia embodied in the pages of the women's magazines. But still Sylvia risked losing him. For some unknown reason, she had to say Magdalena's name one more time. But in doing so, she realized she'd gone too far and that there is a limit to a man's tolerance for repetition. In the instant she said the word *Magdalena*, she looked at Ramón across the table (set with a style that Magdalena would never have had the time or patience for) and I saw her pathetic face, egg-shaped, beautiful, completely vacant: in the uncertain light of the flickering candles, it was no more than a surface on which to project various ideas of beauty.

"Ramón," she said.

He didn't answer.

"I don't feel at all well, I don't know what's the matter with me, I'm exhausted ..."

Still he didn't answer. Without looking at him she turned to me and said, "Would you be too crushed if I left the two of you alone together to eat? I'm drained and dying to go to bed after our night watch yesterday. It's not too little food, is it, just meat and salad? The fruit is luscious."

Realizing Ramón wasn't going to, I answered. "No, of course not. Anyway, I'm sure your salads are exquisite."

Sylvia already had her hand on the doorknob and turned it. But once more she couldn't resist. "I'm sure Magdalena's salads are much more original than mine." Then she disappeared.

I would have liked to ask Ramón, who was above all a

civilized man, what this obsession of Sylvia's with Magdalena was, what the basis of this much-touted "affinity" was, above and beyond their perfect synchronization in "Chattanooga Choo-Choo." But I didn't have time, because Ramón jumped up and ran after Sylvia, slamming the terrace door behind him, leaving me alone with the pieces of meat sizzling over the fire. A moth—perhaps the one that had attacked Sylvia's shoulder earlier, starting her on her litany—fluttered around the candles. Then I felt it graze my neck and gave it a slap before meditating on the dire consequences of smashing a bug that big and soft. I leaned over the terrace railing. The night was dark, perfect, conjured up specially to tempt possible buyers of houses in this development in the hills. The sky was like a green glass cyclorama with projections of stars, planets, constellations. Yes, I thought, resting my elbows on the railing, this *had* been a very pleasant encounter. At our age, sudden new friendships and the energy to pursue them are rare. And my desire to buy a country house had coincided exactly with Ramón's offer, as our taste had with his. This meeting at Ricardo and Raimunda's prophesied a very mature and yet very young—or at least very youthful—relationship; that is, until the damned moth had crashed into Sylvia's shoulder and set all her obsessive machinery in motion, accelerating it, making the repetitions insufferably frequent, until the word *affinity* had acquired a disturbing connotation that destroyed everything . . . at least for the moment. Anyway, Ramón would come back, and we could pick up the thread of a civilized conversation between two mature but still unjaded men.

But Ramón didn't come back. The chops began to turn black over the charcoal. I really was very hungry so I saved them from their hell and sat down alone at the table to eat. Magdalena's salads, though prepared with less ostentation, were actually better than this one of Sylvia's, which I began to cut up. Now that the meat had stopped suffering over the coals, the silence filled everything and I stretched out in a hammock near the terrace railing, bit into a pear, and day-

dreamed about buying a house here; thought about chestnut trees and the white trunks of walnuts; about being
Ramón and Sylvia's neighbor, which Magdalena would love
too, and the children . . . Was it really a myth that Sylvia
had a son? . . . It seemed impossible that her minimal body,
with its elegant head and neck, its attenuated extremities,
had given birth to anything . . . and I found myself wonder-
ing, but not with lust (a word totally inapplicable to her
person), about her arms and legs; her womb, which must be
useless; the generally antiseptic quality of her looks; her
highly polished exterior, so well finished, so different from
the juicy, fragrant, palpable substance of Magdalena's brown
body. Yes . . . this Sylvia was a strange person. Perhaps she
would turn out to be much more complex than I first thought.
Perhaps, like Magdalena, I too would find an "affinity" for
her . . . we would see how things developed. In any case,
nothing, absolutely nothing could sour this night, its fresh-
ness that could almost be touched with one's fingertips . . .
the luxury of that vast darkness inhabited by leafy trees
taking up the volume of the night.

I don't know how long I lay there, thinking. Basically
nothing disturbed me about Sylvia's attitude toward Magdalena, even though it implied a certain aggressiveness toward
me. But that could easily transform itself into a good,
friendly relationship. This potential aggressiveness of Sylvia's
didn't matter very much because it was as if nothing she
felt was substantive, but only adjectival, decorative, part of
the aesthetic ambience that surrounded her and Ramón. It
was only at first that she had seemed disagreeable, but not
now; now, her very artificiality had a kind of charm. Once I
reached this conclusion and decided it was an unimportant
problem that could easily be taken care of, I must have fallen
asleep in the hammock, thinking that nights would all be like
this in the house nearby. I could rest on weekends after the
oppressions of work, I could escape to paint. Then I heard
a car start. Jumping to my feet, I leaned over the railing and
shouted, "Who's there?"

The car backed up until it was directly below. Ramón poked his head out of the window.

"I have to leave," he said.

"But why? Is Sylvia all right?"

"She's asleep. I've had an urgent phone call from Barcelona. I must go at once, I'll phone tomorrow to . . ."

I didn't hear his last words because as he said them the car started forward, piercing the night with its lights, until it was moving fast enough to climb the hill that would take it to the expressway.

Telephone? But wasn't that exactly what had kept me from signing a contract on the spot for the house with the big studio, the fact that it was impossibly difficult to get a telephone in this development? Wasn't that what had kept me from suggesting Marta and Roberto as other prospective buyers? A slight uneasiness invaded me when I realized I had been left alone in a strange house, with none other than the fantastic Sylvia Corday. Obviously, Sylvia's trump card was her beauty. For many she might be sexually attractive, but for me, she was too abstract or symbolic. Not for a moment had there been the hint of a possible sexual adventure between the two of us. On the contrary, I thought, if at any moment Sylvia had shown a preference, it was decidedly for Magdalena, not for me. That might explain her slightly aggressive attitude toward me and her monotonous insistence on the necessity of Magdalena's presence . . . No, leaving Magdalena alone in this country house with Sylvia might not have been wise. What about their date to see each other when Sylvia got back? . . . I laughed at the absolute impossibility of what I was imagining. Anyway, Sylvia was asleep.

I knew where my bedroom was: they had shown it to me as we came in, pointing to pajamas and robes in the closets. Now that Ramón had left and Sylvia was asleep, I ought to do the same. I drank the rest of my cognac, stood up, and went downstairs to the bedroom floor. Inside my room, I turned on the tensor lamp on the night table, pleasantly focused for reading, and went into the bathroom.

Ramón insisted that all his houses, whatever their cost, have perfect bathrooms, that the effectiveness of the bathrooms was, in the last analysis, the definitive sign of an architect of quality. My bathroom, like those in all the houses we had visited in the development, completely fulfilled his requirements. But, I thought, it was a little like those dehumanized bathrooms in luxury hotels, with no old magazines on top of dirty clothes hampers, no half-empty bottles of medicine in the medicine chest, no little portable stove for emergencies, no amusing poster that would be taken down and replaced in a month. But it was populated with an oppressive abundance of chromium faucets for imponderable modern uses, with mountains of plush towels, tiles that were obviously proof against everything: heat, water, children, gymnasts, even scratches. At once I thought of Sylvia. Yes, Sylvia shared a certain quality with the luxury hotel bathroom designed by the best architect with no expense spared. All she lacked was one of those little paper bands sealing off everything, ensuring that what one is about to use is perfectly germ-free. No, Sylvia couldn't have any children, the child must be her husband's from a former marriage. The toothbrush glass, the cologne, fingernail scissors, talcum powder, everything was ready on top of the porcelain shelf next to the basin. And dangling from it—what refinement—one of those booklets of red tissue that women use to blot their lips so they won't ruin the fat, pristine towels.

Suddenly it occurred to me that I shouldn't have come. At this hour I ought to be wrapped in the perfumed embrace that joined my sleep to Magdalena's. I opened the little booklet as if to read it. The first page had not been used to blot lips: the perfect shape of a woman's mouth had been cut out of it. . . . I picked up the nail scissors on the countertop, examined them carefully, and saw that a few tiny shreds of red tissue were still caught in the blades. Elementary, my dear Watson. This would be amusing to show Magdalena, and nobody would miss it. As easily as people steal hotel towels, I dropped the booklet into my pocket, so that Magdalena could see the possibilities of refinement presented by a modern bathroom. After brushing my teeth with a new toothbrush, I went to bed. I left my jacket and pants on a chair, and as soon as I pulled the covers up I fell into a heavy sleep, without a moment of regret that Magdalena's mortal, carnal presence was not in the bed to protect me.

Only when I found myself sitting up with my finger on the lamp button did I realize I had been awakening slowly. The sensation that there was a strange presence in my room had been insinuating itself into my dream and had finally drawn me out of it. It wasn't a noise. It was more as if something clumsy, like a moth, were beating blindly and defenselessly against the furniture; the tables and chairs its body did not have the strength to overturn were injuring its vulnerable surface. It had to be the moth. Awake now, with my finger still on the lamp button, I went on listening to—or rather feeling—that desperate fluttering. I pressed. The beam of light from the bedtable was directed right at my chest, where the book one was supposed to read at night would have been. The rest of the room remained in shadows arranged in varying concentrations of dark furniture; the light curtains moved slightly because I had left the window half open.

But was that the curtains, moving, floating? A gust of air just barely stirred the folds of cloth, and a ghostly figure broke away.

"Sylvia!"

She didn't hear me. Of course. How could she hear me without ears? That was the first thing I was surprised and horrified to notice she was missing . . . and yet I *wasn't* surprised. It never crossed my mind that her ears had been cut or pulled off, just that Sylvia wasn't wearing them and as a result couldn't hear me. . . . But she must be aware that the bedside lamp had been turned on. Still groggy, my eyes tried to penetrate the shadows. Then I realized it was entirely possible she couldn't see me, her eyes were almost erased from her face . . . vanishing cream: it looked as if

Sylvia could hardly see at all, perhaps only blurs as indefinite as her features, or rather as the make-up half dissolved on her face. She was wearing a long, sumptuous chemise. Its ample folds obscured her silhouette, blurring her into the blurry curtain. . . . I couldn't make out much, but I did see that she wasn't wearing her arms either; and naturally, looking for something in a dark room without eyes or arms is no easy task. "Sylvia . . . ," I murmured again.

I saw her lean over my clothes as if to peer at them, investigate, perhaps take them away or search them. But she couldn't. Her movements were no more than the desperate gestures of an embryonic, faceless thing; the long body, the elegant silhouette on which the other details could be assembled as adjectives, was the only part alive, unified, unchangeable. How were you supposed to look for something without arms or hands or eyes? But still, that line of infinite elegance, stripped of everything other than its essential grace, expressed a desperate search. An immense compassion welled up in me as I watched this outline of an idea searching for something to complete it and give it access to life: ears, arms . . . ? Everything was so unreal. Which is why I didn't want to turn on the lights. I left the bed lamp on, and stepping into my slippers I crept cautiously toward her so as not to frighten her: from close up, her face was that of a fetus, her features barely insinuated, waiting for the magical invocation of make-up to conjure them into being. I had to help her. The blurred paint over the pathetic protuberances of her eyes was the best-defined part of that face without a mouth, nose, ears or chin. Now very close to her, I spoke as clearly as possible, hoping those embryonic eyes would realize I was a friend.

"Sylvia. What are you looking for?" I asked.

But she didn't hear me. "Do you want me to help you?" I asked.

Still she didn't hear me. Coming even closer, I touched her. She straightened up as if I had given her an electric shock. She stood facing me and wrinkled what was supposed to be her brow in an effort to see me, as if I were very far away, as if she were an Indian raising one of her nonexistent (or lost, or put away, or stolen) hands to shield her eyes and spy me out in the depths of a canyon or on a mountaintop. But she recognized me. It was clear she knew it was me, her friend, and that I was ready to help her. When she recognized me she began to try to talk, though she didn't have a mouth. Her nonexistent cheeks and chin chewed like a child with a great wad of bubble gum. . . . Yes, those were the movements, only the mouth was lacking. Still, I could see she was trying to tell me something, moving her egg-smooth, empty, soft, expressive cheeks. She was pleading with me to help. I said, "I want to help you."

She shrugged to indicate she couldn't hear. I made a gesture with my hands and then with my whole body, asking her to try to show me what she needed. She understood immediately, because she pointed her toe at my blazer. Suddenly, a feeling of pride at having been able to communicate my affection to a creature lacking the necessary cognitive organs sharpened my curiosity. Curiosity and, naturally, compassion: yes, I would have liked to touch her. Perhaps then, when I realized that she had an infinite, painful lack of resources, was the first moment that I felt the impulse to caress her. We were united in an attempt to invent a language proper to this unique situation that could only exist between her and myself, and if she had had a mouth, perhaps I would have thought to kiss it, so defenseless was she beneath her chemise, so stripped of everything. But Sylvia was anxiously pointing her toe at my blazer, and I picked it up. She moved her head, gesturing with everything she had, to make it clear to me, when first I tried to put the blazer on myself and then on her, that that was not what she was after. She wanted me to empty out the pockets. I showed her my wallet, cigarettes, handkerchief, everything, and with movements of her head she indicated they weren't what she was after. She pointed her toe at my pants. I put my hand in the pocket and brought out the booklet of red tissues. She

made me experience the ultimate satisfaction of kissing and perhaps even of loving a woman who is not complete: the power of civilized man, who does not cut out tongues or put on chastity belts—primitive procedures—but who knows how to compel a woman's submission by removing or putting on her mouth, taking her apart by removing her arms, her hair in the form of a wig, her eyes in the form of false eyelashes, eyebrows, blue shadow on the lids, removing, by means of some curious mechanism, her sex itself so she can use it only when he needs her, so that her entire being depends on man's will—singing or not singing "Chattanooga Choo-Choo," naming or not naming Magdalena too often—all this was a truly novel sensation; it was as if my fantasy had been searching for it from the beginning of time and I had at last found it there, that night. Of course now Sylvia could talk, and maybe she would explain things, but for the moment at least, I didn't want to know anything. What I did want was to carry that armless mannequin, her mouth voracious because I wanted it voracious, her body lacking autonomy, over to the bed so that I could make love to a puppet. Whether I gave her the rest of her faculties depended totally on me. As a puppet, she could not look for anything in love, could only be its instrument. But Sylvia was clinging to me with her mouth, drawing me into the lasciviousness of her incomplete body: it was as if her intention was to compromise me so she could later force me into something, or rather ask me to do what she wanted . . . for even in her present embryonic state Sylvia knew that her body, even without arms, that her face, even with nothing but the most rudimentary features, were desirable enough to excite me. We lay down on the bed. After making love, I looked at her inert body, smiling on the sheet. Only her mouth smiled. Were her eyes closed with pleasure? It was difficult to see her in the half-light. In any case, the possibility that she had no eyes, only projections of matter, continued to unsettle me. And I ought to say that the absence of arms was positively an advance, a real improvement in women, since so many times in bed with Magdalena they had seemed superfluous to me; or often, at least, one was enough.

"Sylvia."

"When I wake up in the morning I have the sensation that if I don't make up my eyes I'm not going to be able to see . . . The first thing I do when I wake up, even before bathing or having breakfast, is to put on my eye make-up."

She told me where she kept her make-up in her bedroom, and I went to get it. When I came back, I found her in front of the dressing table in my bedroom. Only then did I realize I was going to have to make her up, because she didn't have any arms.

Surprised, I asked, "What about your arms?"

"I don't know where Ramón hid them. Anyway, don't worry, I don't feel like putting them on today. You make me up."

"But I've never . . ."

"It doesn't matter."

"I'm an abstract painter."

"All the better."

She assured me that my lack of experience as a make-up man wasn't important: my experience in painting, even as an amateur, was enough. She made a broad gesture with her shoulders—if she had had arms, she would have been stretching them to yawn, if she had had eyes she would have squeezed them shut in satisfaction—and when I set the make-up kit on the dressing table to caress her wig, Sylvia leaned back amorously against my body. She never stopped talking, as if to prove her mouth worked.

". . . so happy, just like new . . . I don't know, cheerful: yes, now look, I want very arched eyebrows, yes, use that pencil, open the box, there are the colors. With this blond wig my eyebrows have to be just barely sketched on, almost straw-colored, I'd say. Don't you think so?"

"I must say, I don't understand the first thing about it."

She made a gesture of impatience.

"Well, it's no wonder you're only an amateur painter, if

you don't dare to experiment," she said. "Go to my bedroom and get the latest *Vogue,* it's lying next to my bed. On the cover is the face I want today. There's an article telling how to do it."

When I came back with the *Vogue,* I didn't look at Sylvia's face in the light of the bulbs that framed the dressing-table mirror, only at the female mask gazing at me with empty eyes from the cover of the magazine. I studied it with an attention I had never paid to any face, seeking every detail of color and surface, and began to supplant that delicate paper reality with Sylvia's: projecting a miracle of delicacy, the shades fused or set off from one another like butterfly wings, powders and shades and glosses and tones mingling on the delicate substance of a cheek—any cheek, or forehead, or eyes delicate enough to provide the canvas for a color composition, which was all that mattered—drawing outlines and eyelashes and heightening softness.

"I can't do it."

"Yes you can, Anselmo. I'll tell you how."

"How?"

"First, open the make-up kit . . ."

I spread out on the dressing-table top the infinite, dazzling variety of pots and concoctions, unimaginable after Magdalena's tiny arsenal. I unscrewed their tops, prepared wads of cotton and powder puffs and brushes and pencils, obsessed with the endless resources available to a woman who wants to acquire not only a face, but the face she wants.

"First the eyes: that long, thin brush . . . pick a browner shade . . . Wait, is my face very filthy? Are my eyes smudged?"

"Yes."

"Then wipe me off."

I hadn't felt ill used at the prospect of having to make her up. But when I had to clean her face, I felt a little humiliated, though I didn't want her to know it.

"How?" I asked.

"With vanishing cream."

And following her instructions, step by step I cleaned her face until it was transformed into a perfect egg with a red mouth. After I had given her eyes, I had to retouch them again and again according to her instructions. Eventually my hand managed to transform Sylvia's egg-shaped face into the beautiful mask on the cover of *Vogue*: yet it really *was* Sylvia's face, a soft, subtle, amusing, knowing mask. Time and again, perhaps clumsily, my hand spread some colored, scented concoction over her cheeks and she stopped me (with uncalled-for harshness and impatience, I thought), correcting my shaping of a contour, or my placement of her false eyelashes. I was astounded to discover that this fetus was nothing other than raw matter before Creation, as I gradually caused a real and beautiful human face to emerge: Sylvia's face, although it was the superimposition of the *Vogue* cover. I couldn't help feeling a ferocious attraction toward her again, and kissing her neck I tried to draw her back to the bed. But she slipped away from me, making excuses, saying she didn't want to tire herself, perhaps later. Now she had to do her hair, a different wig to go with the overall tone of the make-up. . . . In face of her resistance I had a fit of temper and threatened to erase her. Terrified, she rose before me, and I stood my ground with a cotton wad full of vanishing cream, ready to wipe away her features like chalk from a blackboard. She threw herself at me, her hot mouth and rich supple lips on mine, searching with her tongue for mine, making me forget my threat. I let the cotton fall to the rug and embraced her. She let herself go, moving against my body, and with her face sunk in my shoulder, near my neck, she began to murmur things that slowly took the shape of recognizable words: ". . . later, love . . . we have all day . . . I'm hungry . . . breakfast. Aren't you hungry? Yes, let's go to the kitchen and have breakfast."

Before releasing her, I offered to look for her arms to eat breakfast with, but she murmured into my neck that she still couldn't remember where Ramón had hidden them last night. I let her go. I was surprised to realize that my habitual morning appetite had begun to predominate over desire: satisfaction could easily be put off for an hour.

The kitchen—also perfect, like the bathroom; another sign, said Ramón, of the good architect—was a space full of clean blue tiles and chromium fixtures and appliances that looked useful but whose functions were completely impenetrable to a man, some hanging like instruments of torture on the wall, others lined up on shelves as in a laboratory. From her chair, Sylvia gave me instructions on how to make coffee and where to find the proper utensils and the toaster (no, she didn't want jam or honey, she had to think of her figure, but if I wanted all that it was behind that louvered door), and after pouring her a huge cup of black coffee, which I fed to her by sips, I made toast and a breakfast that was a little less frugal for myself. While I ate, she remarked on the Roigs' gathering on Saturday night. She seemed a little nervous, as if I were taking too long over breakfast and she was getting bored. I rushed my cup of coffee and, taking her impatience as a compliment to my skillful and generous virility, I stood up. She smiled and stood up too, and we started to leave the kitchen, but she halted before the door. It dawned on me what her problem was, and gallantly I held the door open for her. She smiled graciously and moved on. Like a queen, she waited for me to open each successive door for her, an authoritarian expression growing on her face. In her room she ordered, "Open the curtains."

I did.

"Not so wide."

She didn't thank me. Sitting down at her dressing table, she examined her face closely in the well-lit mirror. "No, no, it's all wrong," she said with disgust. "Every mirror is different and so is all lighting. Now I can see: what you did in your room is terrible, it's all wrong."

"Well, Sylvia, that much technical skill is a little unnecessary under the circumstances, wouldn't you say? I'm not going to make you up again . . ."

"Open the closet. There on the right, yes, there's my pink

djellaba. Please put it on me . . . yes, but first take off my chemise, yes, that's right . . ."

Undressing her and putting on her djellaba, I touched that supple, fresh, perfect body again. It seemed to have been sketched in a single stroke. Truly, arms add nothing at all to the beauty or sensuality of a woman, I thought. In fact, at certain times they are a nuisance: in the end, every self-respecting Venus ought to get rid of her arms; there had to be a reason the goddess lost them, it wasn't simply an accident of history. When I put the pink djellaba over her head, I realized she was right about my make-up job: the color of her cheeks was too harsh, her eyelids too strident, and the shade of her mouth didn't blend with the rest. Sylvia told me—I say "told" because that was her tone of voice now, she didn't "ask"—to go to the library and bring her a pile of *Vogues* from the coffee table. I came back staggering under the weight of the magazines, and stretching out in bed with them, in the clear light of that sunny morning, we looked for another scheme of make-up for her; I turned the pages while she looked and made up her mind. I was getting bored. I realized that if I didn't have her torso and long legs next to me, I couldn't stand the boredom of looking at so many identical women wearing different cosmetics and different dresses in Italian, English, French and American editions.

"Wouldn't you like me to put on your arms?" I said.

"No."

"Why not?"

"I think Ramón took them with him."

That seemed to me impertinent on Ramón's part. "But why did he take them?"

"Men like to leave their women helpless . . . He doesn't want me to go out."

"But what about you?"

She smiled enchantingly at me. Rolling over on her side, where one of her arms would have been, she snuggled close to my body, and I felt the whole long line of her breathing rhythmically with the serene simplicity of a mechanical object, submissive and defenseless because she had no arms and was quickly wrapped up in mine. Between kisses she murmured, "Me? I have you . . ."

I didn't know what she meant by that, but it was enough for me. I held her tight, and was ready to make love again, but she stopped me. "Wouldn't you rather make love to the same woman but with a different face?" she asked.

I laughed. Sylvia had a way of saying things, a tone of voice. . . . She stood up and moved over to the dressing table, waiting, knowing what my answer would be.

"Yes," I said.

"I'm different from women like . . . like Magdalena, let's say, who is always the same . . . Now pick up a cotton wad . . . That's right, dip it in vanishing cream, no, the other jar . . . I can have a thousand faces and give a man—as I give Ramón and now you—the sensation that you're able to make love to many women, to all women, which is what all men want . . . Yes, first erase my eyebrows . . . that's right . . . and then the rouge on my cheeks . . . Softly, gently does it . . . yes, that's right, my love, you do it so well, much better than Ramón, much better . . . now take off my wig . . . don't be shocked that I have so little hair and it's so short and white; I'm almost an albino, that's why I became a model, that's why I wear make-up and a wig and my skin is so white . . . yes . . . draw the curtains a little more, the light hurts my eyes, they're rather weak, you know . . . You must do them very well. Ramón paints them wonderfully for me, very bold; generally I can see very clearly: you'll really have to make an effort if you don't want me to spend the whole day wearing glasses . . . Magdalena told me she wears glasses like yours for reading, but only for reading . . . You do make-up very well, I must tell Magdalena to have you do her. We'll have lunch together when we get back to Barcelona, I'll ring her up . . . Yes, the men at their jobs and the women having lunch together and talking about their own things . . . She'd be a ballsy woman if she only knew her own potential, the things she could do with her looks if she took better care of herself, if she made herself up better, for example . . . now the mouth . . . careful, don't take it off . . . all right, I'll keep quiet while you fix it for me."

Take it off to stop her stupid chattering, to . . . But if I removed it I wouldn't have those lips for my own mouth to sink into . . . I couldn't erase it and force her to stop talking about Magdalena, but she kept babbling about her, like last night, saying they were soulmates, sisters, rarely had she felt such an affinity for another woman . . . she was just smitten with her . . . she was going to suggest some changes, some necessary refinements in her hairdo and wardrobe. And while she talked, I obeyed this armless Venus and changed her make-up, and the mask that developed under my hands was the same but different, another woman but the same one who had made love to me and would do so again. I begged her to, but she said no, she wasn't "ready" yet, she didn't want to, she was tired, she needed a setting, an atmosphere like last night, she wanted me to say things to her, to . . . and finally she became irritated at my persistence. That was enough, she said, she wanted me to leave, take the other car and go back to Barcelona where my wife must be missing me, Magdalena dominated me so completely that I couldn't spend so much as a single unscheduled morning outside the house without her getting upset and setting out to look for me like a little child . . . But under my hands, my kisses, my caresses, Sylvia was giving in, yes, giving in. Her aggressiveness was subsiding; well, yes, if I really wanted it that much, she would make love to me again, just once, although she didn't really want to, she was tired, she didn't have much stamina owing to the strict diet she had to follow to keep her figure . . . yes, she sacrificed herself even in this, since her figure and her elegance were everything to her, the only thing that really mattered, the only tangible, real thing . . . and I remembered from a few hours before the fineness of her legs between mine.

"Draw the curtains," she said.

I pulled them together and climbed into bed with her. In spite of my changes, her mouth was the same deep, ravenous mouth as before, and her supple body in my arms was endowed with knowing, lewd movements that were meant not just for me but to excite her too. At a certain point, she said, "I can't."

"Yes you can, my love . . ."

She let a moment pass. Then she murmured very softly, "Bring me a jar of cream from my dressing table."

In the half-light I picked up the first jar to hand and passed it to her. After using it, she left it on the night table and turned her full attention to making love, exciting me and herself deftly, until I penetrated her and she—more, oh, much more than the first time—enjoyed it and I enjoyed it with her in some ultimate way, as if I had given my very essence in that orgasm. We fell asleep.

I don't know what time it was when I woke up, with the strange sensation that I had behaved like a good little boy and had been given a reward for it. It was odd, I thought, this infinite possibility of transformations that came out of making love to Sylvia, in me as much as in her, as if the two of us were nothing more than interchangeable wrappings around the central fiber of the myriad possibilities of sex. I had to go to the bathroom. I got out of bed quietly. I was naked before the bathroom mirror when, looking at the appropriate portion of my anatomy, I was horrified to see that what had just given me and Sylvia such pleasure had vanished. It simply wasn't there. Silently, I went over to the bed and switched on a lamp. There she was, asleep, naked, luscious, but almost weightless on the sheet, her beautiful artificial cheek resting on her armless shoulder. Then I looked at the night table. There was the white jar. My mind elsewhere, I picked it up and almost unconsciously read its label.

"Elizabeth Arden Vanishing Cream."

Cream to make things vanish, disappear, to erase, cleanse, leave empty, faceless, sexless, weaponless, harmless, defenseless, pleasureless. She had taken away the thing that endowed me with gravity and unity as a person, that allowed me to unite myself to Magdalena. And since that union was what gave shape to my work, my relationships with other people, with my children, Sylvia had dislocated my entire life . . . Vanishing cream . . . Of course: it had been a trap set by Sylvia, that soulless, faceless doll. My vexation at her, the feeling that she had taken away my most powerful weapon to force submission, increased my anger at her, and I looked around for something to attack her with—a lash to mark her white skin, for example—but there was only the jar of vanishing cream on the night table. I grabbed a wad of cotton, covered it with cream and pounced on Sylvia, who woke up screaming—until I erased her mouth. Since she didn't have any arms, she could only kick to defend herself: which was pointless, because in a couple of minutes I had erased her whole face, eyes, nose, brows and forehead, transforming her into a smudge of red, blue, pink, black, her artificial eyelashes stuck every which way on that faceless, wigless egg that capped the body that had swallowed my sex. Revenge. Yes. I couldn't rip off her sex—that would require a surgical operation. (Women are more complicated than men in that respect.) In any case, for Sylvia, erasing her face would be worse punishment. Why not lock her in this room forever as she was: smudged, incomplete, eyeless, earless, speechless? If I could only find the clasps attaching her legs to her body, I could remove those long, slender tubes, and after that her neck and head, cleansing everything, folding it neatly, and putting it all carefully away in a box. . . .

I locked her in her room. I had to get away, abandon that sorceress and return to the world of the living, those marvelous creatures of flesh and blood who have only one face and don't vanish or come apart . . . yes, run away to Magdalena. Ramón could put Sylvia back together again, if he liked. I dressed to leave. But as I was putting on my blazer, I paused. What about that part of mine which Sylvia had caused to vanish? Could I leave without it? How was I to live without it, how would I explain to Magdalena? I buttoned my blazer brusquely. No, impossible. It wasn't true. This sort of fantastic thing didn't happen except in modern novels by tropical writers. It couldn't happen to me, a serious Catalan doctor with a beard and glasses and a certain fondness for painting. A psychiatrist would cure me of this fantasy in a few sessions. This was merely a guilt complex for having cheated on Magdalena: absurd in a civilized man like myself. Masters and Johnson's techniques took care of this kind of marital trauma in a flash. Yes, the thing was to escape, leave that woman locked in, or rather that piece of a woman: I had my own woman, mine, all mine, and I wasn't ready to play Pygmalion to a dim-witted model who in a few years would be a carcass useless to the fashion world because other, younger women would embody the ephemeral fads more successfully than she. Yes, the knowledge that I loved Magdalena, who was made out of flesh and blood, not cloth and paint, and had integrity and presence and was my ally, drove me out of that house and into the remaining car, in which I sped toward the reality of Barcelona.

On the way, I toyed with the names of various psychiatrists whom we, Magdalena and I, could consult together to solve this problem. But after about three miles, I decided that perhaps at first it would be better not to say anything to Magdalena and take care of things on my own. Yes, at first I had better hide it with subterfuges and excuses. I could begin a report on that laboratory experiment, for example, which ought to be done soon anyway; it would require working late at night and getting up early and being continually exhausted—I wouldn't ever have to touch her. That is, not until, thanks to successful psychiatric treatment, my sex reappeared in the place that nature had intended for it.

When I got home, I was astonished by Magdalena's total lack of surprise at my absence. In fact, I was offended. It was almost as if it had given her the chance to do some things my presence didn't permit. In the car, I had fabricated all sorts of excuses, but she asked me no questions. Of course, this was my guilt complex, my expectation of punishment: nothing could have been more natural than my coming back a little late from a weekend spent with Ramón and Sylvia. Magdalena had already warned Mrs. Sanz, my nurse, to cancel my morning appointments. After lunch, she helped me get ready to go to the office. She said that Marta and Roberto had called to remind us that tonight we had tickets to attend a concert of dodecaphonic music. . . . Good, I replied, thinking it would give me a breather: I could arrange things so that we went to bed very late, and since I hadn't been to the hospital that morning, I could use making up the lost time as an excuse to get out of bed early. A day and a night of respite, of peace. Meanwhile—not from the office, but from some bar, so Mrs. Sanz wouldn't overhear—I made an appointment with my colleague, Dr. Monclús, who, I knew, worked veritable miracles not with Freud's antiquated methods but with more up-to-date behaviorism, and yoga techniques . . . a mixture of Masters and Johnson and Jung which seemed intriguing, and would probably work, too. It wasn't that I didn't trust Magdalena and didn't want to make her party to my secret (which didn't strike me as shameful even for a moment): no, I just wanted to protect her, not expose her unnecessarily to humiliation. When the treatment was far enough along and Masters and Johnson—Dr. Monclús, that is—thought the time was ripe, I would bring my wife in.

At my office, Mrs. Sanz gave me a curious look, and told me that Ramón del Solar had just called. She gave me his number, asking if I would like her to dial it. I said no thanks, I'd call him back later, and noticed that Mrs. Sanz's face was identical to Sylvia's—a little older, and with nothing desirable about it—identical, in fact, to all of Sylvia's faces, since all of Sylvia's faces were identical to each other, when you came right down to it. After I had seen several patients, Mrs. Sanz came in to inform me that Ramón del Solar was on the phone again. I told her to take the message, because I was with a patient (which wasn't true). Ramón wanted me to come to lunch the next day, because he had some urgent matters to discuss. I instructed her to tell him it was impossible.

Surprised, Mrs. Sanz asked why. I frowned angrily. What did she mean by questioning me? Did all women want to control me, then, each in her own territory? Did she mean to control my agenda? Now more than ever, she seemed identical to Sylvia, and as dangerous. Yes, that was exactly what Mrs. Sanz was, dangerous. I answered haughtily:

"You've been with me long enough to know that Tuesdays we have lunch at Magdalena's parents'. You're becoming rather forgetful, Mrs. Sanz."

In a dizzying moment of fantasy, I imagined erasing this woman's features and taking her apart like Sylvia when I was fed up with her, putting her away, classifying her piece by piece in the green Kardex that took up one whole corner of her office, taking out pieces of her as they were needed. Maybe this was what she most hoped for: to become the perfect secretary. I would put her together completely only once a year, when she went on vacation with her late husband's sister to Ibiza, to gawk at the hippies.

That night we had an early dinner. I read Jung for a while in front of the fire, in anticipation of my visit to Dr. Monclús. I told Magdalena I was fascinated by Jung, that the perspectives he opened in one's mind were incredible . . . yes, were it not for our date with Marta and Roberto to hear dodecaphonic music, I'd happily stay at home reading Jung in front of the fire.

"Tomorrow we don't have any engagements," Magdalena said. "We can put the children to bed early and climb into bed and read as late as you want."

"Yes," I answered. I put the book down to get dressed.

The next morning Mrs. Sanz called me at the hospital to convey a message from Ramón. "Mr. del Solar says for you to be careful, Doctor."

She wanted a silence for effect after that, but I wouldn't stand for it.

"Any other messages, Mrs. Sanz?" I said curtly.

"No, nothing else."

"That'll be all, then."

"Don't you want to leave some kind of message for Mr. del Solar?"

"No, nothing."

"Not even when you're going to get in touch with him?"

"I'll call him."

Be careful of what? Of whom? To call him up for lunch, which would have been the normal thing to do, raised the dangerous prospect of having to argue and explain, tell him what had happened, and frankly, I didn't know Ramón del Solar well enough. Besides, this was much too frivolous a world, with people ready to gobble up all kinds of gossip, even the vilest, and I didn't dare tell him the shameful thing that had happened to me. Once it passed his lips it would be on all the lips in Barcelona.

That afternoon, between appointments, I went to the bathroom to see if there had been any progress. Although days would pass before my first session with Dr. Monclús, if so much as a button of flesh appeared, it would presage spectacular growth, total recovery . . . maybe I could dispense with Monclús' help altogether. But there was nothing. And every time I went by Mrs. Sanz's desk to go to the bathroom, she lowered her glasses to look over their rims at my back, thinking I didn't notice, and every time I came out of the bathroom and passed her desk again, she had her glasses back in place and didn't look up, concentrating on her papers.

That night when I got home, Magdalena came to the door to greet me and said, "So you don't feel well?"

"How's that?"

"Mrs. Sanz phoned to tell me . . ."

There and then I had a fit of temper such as I had never

had before in my life. What were these stupid women inter-
fering with me for? I would fire Mrs. Sanz first thing in the
morning. This could not go on. I couldn't even go to the
bathroom when I pleased—well, frankly, if a man my age
can't go . . . But as my rage mounted, I realized that the
pretext of being ill was perhaps the best solution of all, because being a doctor I could prolong an ailment at will and
display a great panoply of symptoms to avoid having to make
love to my wife, while at the same time everything would be
affectionate kisses, caresses, hugs . . . Things wouldn't get
out of control, and I'd be left in peace thanks to my afflic-
tion. So before I finished my temper tantrum, which was
being witnessed by my children, who had turned up in their
pajamas to watch the kind of violent scene that as a rule
they could see only on TV, I was silently thanking Mrs. Sanz
for providing me with the perfect excuse of an illness I could
manage at my own discretion, could prolong at will until
something happened, God knows what.

"No, in fact I don't feel well."

"What's the matter with you?"

"I don't know, general debility, loss of appetite, squeamish stomach, loose bowels . . ."

"How strange! You who are always so constipated. Maybe
it was something Sylvia fed you. They say she makes exotic
dishes, she mixes hot spices with preserves, which sounds
revolting, but that's oriental food . . ."

"I ate charcoal-broiled chops and escarole salad."

"Well then?"

"I don't know."

"Do you want to go to bed?"

The truth is, the idea appealed to me, as if not going out
of the house for a few days would save me from the machi-
nations of all kinds of witches. I said yes. She should tell Mrs.
Sanz to cancel my appointments for the next forty-eight
hours or so. Actually, there wasn't anything urgent coming
up, and if something happened she knew who to get in
touch with. Between the sheets, I felt infinite gratitude for

having such a model secretary. I even contemplated giving her a raise so she could go to a decent hotel somewhere besides Ibiza, because Ibiza didn't have hippies anymore and it upset me to think Mrs. Sanz was being cheated out of her money.

In bed, with my hands pleasantly folded over what my grandmother and García Lorca referred to as the place of sin, I spent endless hours keeping watch with my fingers for any tiny protuberance that might signal recovery. I read Jung. When Magdalena left the house, I called Monclús to postpone our appointment for a week. Magdalena, respecting my condition, gave me an affectionate good-night kiss without making any other demands, and attended me at all times with great solicitousness. The children were only allowed into the bedroom once a day, in the late afternoon.

When Ramón del Solar rang up, I had Magdalena say I wasn't feeling at all well, but that when I was on my feet again I would call him to arrange something. He asked if we'd like to spend the weekend with them at his development, but I told her to say no, please excuse me, thanks very much, some other time, I wanted to take advantage of the weekend to rest at home so that I'd be ready to go back to work on Monday. But I could hear the telephone conversation out in the hall continuing. When Magdalena came back in the room, I asked, "What were you up to, talking to Ramón for such a long time?"

"I wasn't talking to Ramón."

"Well who, then?"

"Sylvia."

I sat bolt upright in bed. "You were talking to Sylvia?"

"Yes, what's so odd about that?"

"Nothing." And I slid backward, near death again, until my head touched the pillow and I closed my eyes.

"She's very nice," Magdalena said. "And although she may not seem it, she's very intelligent. She makes the most outrageously funny remarks . . . and incredible things do happen to her."

"Oh yes?"

"Yes. We're getting together in half an hour for coffee and a little chat. She does amuse me so."

She was combing her hair and putting on make-up to go out. My first impulse was to forbid her to see Sylvia: that woman abandoned her child, she's got a dreadful reputation, you can't be seen with her because people will think you behave the same way . . . But no. I kept my mouth shut. To say all that would be to detract from our immoral new morality, to betray the world that our liberated generation was creating for ourselves and our children. I watched in silence as she painted her face; it still looked exactly the way it had before. Ramón's message to "be careful" made me shuffle an infinite number of sinister possibilities: Sylvia was going to tell Magdalena that we had gone to bed together, she had made my sex vanish, she would give Magdalena superhuman powers, she would take Magdalena apart and bring her to me in a suitcase . . . a thousand things ran through my mind at the fear of their meeting. I had been afraid even before the meeting was announced; that first night, during that annoying, monotonous litany of Sylvia's about Magdalena, her so frequently proclaimed "affinity" which had seemed to me ridiculously impossible then and now seemed so much less so . . . No. Magdalena could not and should not keep her date with Sylvia. And yet, one of the understandings of our marriage was our antibourgeois freedom of opinion and lifestyle. We each lived as we liked, so long as we kept our respective ends of the contract. We had a right to our own pastimes, even if it was no more than having coffee with a friend. We even said that in an extreme case, we would understand anything in the other, even infidelity, so long as it didn't become cheap promiscuity or endanger our marriage . . . but a sometime affair, why not? And the place of sin, under my hands, was empty now because . . . Sylvia was to blame for it all and knew everything and was about to get together with Magdalena and divulge everything, everything. Magdalena mustn't go. Perhaps if she vanished, or if I suddenly felt worse . . . but no: that would be beneath me. And besides, there were other considerations: as I drew the sheet higher around my chin, my hand hysterically sought the place that was meant for sin but wasn't ever going to be used for that again, and in my cornered state I decided I ought to allow Magdalena to join Sylvia for coffee, never mind the danger: maybe this meeting would conjure up an emanation, magnetic waves, powers, God knows what, and return what I had lost—in the last analysis, only Sylvia could accomplish that.

I lay there fretting and listening to the rain outside, that chilly onset of autumn promising bad crops, floods, rising prices, lowering skies; it seemed as if that night in the development when the moth had collided with Sylvia's shoulder was the last time the heavens had shown themselves—after that the summer had ended permanently. I couldn't read Jung. No wonder I had never liked him: not scientific enough, pure literature and romanticism, how careless he was. It caused me profound anxiety to think that Dr. Monclús, in many ways, clung to Jungian theory. God only knows how he managed to use Jung to bolster Masters and Johnson. Absurd. Monclús was worthless. I certainly wasn't going to keep my appointment with him, and I closed the book on Jung forever. In the next room, the children and Mrs. Presen were trying to build something; it collapsed amid gales of laughter, and then the three of them fell silent, making way for strange blue electronic voices that extinguished their vitality. Mine too. From my room, without listening to the words, I could tell when the programs changed, what each one of them was—animated cartoons, the news, commercials. . . . Finally Mrs. Presen called to me through the door.

"Come in," I said.

She brought in a bridge table and a tablecloth. "Your wife told me everybody was going to eat here with you in your room, now that you're feeling better, Doctor. She said to set up the bridge table so she and the children could keep you company at dinner time . . ."

Furious, I snapped, "I am not feeling better."

The TV still held the children captive. Mrs. Presen said, "You're not? I made something very light for you, sir."

"Thanks."

"What time is your wife coming home?"

"I haven't any idea."

I knew for sure she would never come back; I was going to have to spend the rest of my life in bed, taking care of boisterous children, packing them off to school, worrying about whether they had enough to eat and something to wear when it was cold, watching their manners and polishing their behavior. But I felt utterly incapable of even talking to this housekeeper whom Magdalena had "borrowed" from Marta while our own girl was paying her annual visit to her parents in Jaén, so when I heard Mrs. Presen coming back toward my room I pretended I was asleep. I actually must have fallen asleep, because later the door opening woke me up. Magdalena came in with Pepe and Luis in tow. As I sat up, she turned on the light.

"Mrs. Presen told me you were asleep," she said. "Do you want to sleep a while longer?"

My curiosity got the better of me. "No, I feel fine."

The children piled onto the bed with their storybooks for me to read aloud. Magdalena stood beside the bed while I began the adventures of Sandokán for what seemed like the millionth time.

"Don't you notice anything?" Magdalena interrupted.

"Anything about what?"

"My face."

"The light's behind you."

She moved her head.

"No, I don't notice anything," I said.

"I don't understand why we women bother to fix ourselves up if men never notice anything. I've spent the whole afternoon with Sylvia and she did this ballsy make-up job for me, completely different, and you tell me you don't notice anything . . . She even plucked my eyebrows differently. See? Come on, children, time for dinner."

"Oh, Mama . . ."

"Come on, Mama, let Daddy finish the story."

"Oh yes, read to us a while longer, Daddy."

" 'Then Captain Yáñez drew his glittering sword, and advancing on the deck . . .' " I went on reading, trying to keep my voice from quavering at the reality of the meeting which had at last taken place between these two women, I didn't know why, nor how, nor by what means, nor for what ends. Magdalena carried the food in and served us, making small talk, but she never brought up the subject of Sylvia and Ramón, or make-up, again. While I ate, the certainty grew that I could erase Magdalena's face with a wad of cotton, even take her apart piece by piece so that when she became intolerably dangerous I could put her away dismantled and folded in a box, and go on living without annoyances. When dinner was over, Magdalena unwrapped a package and set the contents on a tray.

"Eclairs," she announced.

"Eclairs!" The children screamed, clapping their hands. "Eclairs! I want one!"

"I want two, there are six of them!"

I frowned, puzzled. "What made you bring eclairs?"

"Sylvia made them. Didn't you know she's a fabulous pastry cook? She told me, 'When I'm very, very old and can't be a model anymore, by which I mean next year, I'm going to start a pastry shop and get rich and I won't have to go on diets or depend on Ramón or submit to any man, and I'll get gloriously fat.' Very Women's Lib, Sylvia is. Very funny, don't you think?"

"What made you bring them? Who's going to eat them? I've got a stomach complaint, you're watching your figure and won't touch sweets, and I don't know if the children should eat these things after dinner . . . they're so indigestible . . ."

"I'm going to eat one tonight. Look, this one is the longest and thickest . . . tomorrow I'm starting a diet Sylvia recommended, she knows so many things."

The thick, sweet member lay on her plate, oozing cream. I watched Magdalena take it in her fingers: her theory was that you ought to eat pastry with your fingers, in huge bites, to preserve the same taste they had had when you were a child; all other ways of eating them were pure pretentiousness—bring it up to your mouth, and sink your teeth into it, once, twice, three times, until you had engulfed the whole thing.

My hands went to the place of sin. The little button I had joyfully imagined just before I fell asleep had disappeared. I told Magdalena I was feeling much worse, and asked her to remove the bridge table and the rest of the dinner. I was going to take a Mogadon and put myself to sleep right away. I couldn't stand anymore.

The feeling that Sylvia—that woman-adjective, woman-decoration, that collapsible, foldable woman who represented all the comforts of modern life and lacked everything, even individuality and togetherness—had magical powers and was therefore powerful, must have dominated my sleep. I could only remember fragments of my dreams, not capture them whole, and I woke up fearing Sylvia. The first thing I felt on opening my eyes was an uncontrollable urge to see her again. What face was she wearing today? What dress did she have on, she who depended so much on clothes? A scarf knotted a certain way could change her whole appearance, not just physically, but inside, as a person. Might it not be possible to . . . just once more? Examining my emotions, I swiftly reached the conclusion that I desired her, that I definitely wanted to continue my "affair" with her; but more urgent than that, or perhaps what gave strength and shape to that urgency, was the need to erase her face with vanishing cream and throw myself into the delight of painting her and making her up again. This time, she wouldn't get away with copying trite models borrowed from fashion magazines. This time, I was going to take charge of the make-up kit and her vast collection of concoctions, and I was going to *invent* a face for her . . . not just one, but many different ones, tender, audacious, enigmatic, exotic—these were the adjectives that the women's magazines and beauty product ads used—whatever pleased me most at that moment, giving free rein to my creative artistry, whose results had been decidedly poor of late.

At breakfast time I told Magdalena I'd like to "do something" on Saturday night. And I added, as if it were the least important thing in the world, "I don't know, with somebody amusing . . . Ramón and Sylvia, for example."

"They are spending the weekend at the development, with some Americans who are going to buy half a dozen houses, Sylvia said . . ."

"How awful for them."

"I'd like to go out with Sylvia tonight too, but they've already left."

"What a shame."

Then she added, without hearing what I said, "But maybe I can get in touch with her."

I didn't like the way she said "get in touch," intimating not phone calls or telegrams, but sinister extrasensory means.

"No, don't bother them," I said. "Remember the Americans and the half-dozen houses."

She didn't answer, and we dropped the subject. But when I came home from the office that Saturday afternoon, we decided to go out for dinner anyway and then visit a few nightspots. We shuffled around a few names of friends—Marta and Roberto, who would normally have been our most natural companions, had mysteriously disappeared; nobody had answered the phone in their new apartment for the last couple of days—but all the rest seemed dull to both of us, and we dressed halfheartedly. Of course: both of us wanted Sylvia and Sylvia alone to come with us. In this state of affairs, only she could give life to this bourgeois Saturday night. It was certain to be a bore, with every place full of legally constituted couples who had made a date with other couples just as legally constituted to get dressed up and go out together . . . only local people, anonymous, dull, ordinary people; there wouldn't be "anybody" in those crowded places because the people who were "somebody" were all at the shore, in the country, the mountains, the villages, anywhere but getting dressed up to spend Saturday night at the "usual places." Tonight there would be a total blackout of the luminous excitement that can only be provided by "famous people"—even if one does not know them personally.

In spite of everything, we decided to make an effort and go out anyway. I watched Magdalena examining herself in her dressing-table mirror, with a jar of vanishing cream in her hand, ready to erase her face, perhaps completely. Suddenly I had the terrifying feeling that when she cleaned her face with that wad of cotton dipped in cream, the only thing left would be a white, fetal, egg-shaped structure, just like Sylvia's. I stretched out on the bed, flipping the pages of Jung, while Magdalena put herself together. I thought about having to read Hermann Hesse again, at this age, which was what the whole world was doing: the idea prostrated me. I watched Magdalena out of the corner of my eye, my heart pounding with fear and hope, waiting to see what was going to emerge from that mass of cream that she was now removing with another wad of cotton . . . she had even pinned a white towel bib-like around her neck, as if to collect all the particles of the object that was about to disintegrate. But no: I experienced a disappointment that made me despise her, for after all the cream was wiped off, there reappeared her familiar features with their real bone structure, which had not been counterfeited by layered combinations of shades of powder base. There was her large, beautiful nose, the small, familiar flaws in her skin—the tiny red vein near her nostril, the chicken-pox scar between her eyebrows, a few wrinkles

that only gave character to her face, without aging it yet—
all of which I knew by heart, her warm, three-dimensional
mouth, which turned incorrigibly ironic at the corners . . .
unalterable . . . why not admit it, *irreparable*. And yet, in
the warmth of the bedroom, in the intimacy of the pause
before important events that would mark the day and make
it worth remembering, that *irreparable* changed almost instantly into *felicitous*, because Magdalena, unlike Sylvia,
could never be another person, she couldn't have any other
face; hers was fixed, eternal, not a changeable mask; she was
not a doll that once broken could be replaced with another,
once tiresome could be dismantled and put in a box. A rush
of gratitude toward her for being the way she was made me
forget my sad defect. I closed the book and came up behind
Magdalena to hug her as she sat at her table. She leaned her
head backward, resting it against my fly. All her heavy hair
was pulled together in a thick knot at the nape of her neck
to keep it clean while she made up her face. As she rubbed
against me, I thought, thank God for that knot of hair, because she can't have felt a thing, there isn't anything to
feel . . . and retreating a little I leaned over to kiss her
forehead.

"Later . . . ," I said without thinking.

She raised her hand to touch my beard.

"You've been a little . . . I don't know, these days . . ."

"Yes, out of sorts, you know, I didn't feel like doing much
of anything." Then, to protect myself, I added, "I still don't."

"Then we shouldn't go out tonight."

Alarmed, I insisted. "Not at all, yes, yes . . ."

Deciding to stay home, after this scene, would mean
drawing it out, and although drawing it out might not lead
to any conclusion—I could always make an excuse, diarrhea
for example, which I could drop little hints about; the possible suddenness of it was enough to kill anyone's urges to
make love—it would expose me to Magdalena's discovering
my "sin," my defect, my affair with Sylvia, my impotence . . .
no, we had to go out at once.

"You're still plucking your eyebrows," I said.

"Yes, people do, you know."

"I don't like them so light."

"Well then, take this pencil . . ."

"What for?"

"Darken them."

"How? I don't know . . ."

"Any way you want to, you're a painter."

And kneeling beside Magdalena, who closed her eyes, I traced with a firm hand two perfect arcs on top of her eyebrows. I told her not to open her eyes to peek, and with a kind of feverish enthusiasm, I let compulsion guide my hand and inspire me as I began to make her up. I put blue eye shadow on her eyelids, I mixed shades of powder base, powders and rouges on her cheeks, nose, forehead, cheekbones, jaw; I highlighted the eye sockets with smokelike shadows, traced fine lines along the edge of her eyelids, I curled her eyelashes with an instrument I had never before seen among her possessions, I darkened her eyelashes one by one, like Betty Boop's when we were children. She relaxed, eyes shut, not moving her lips, and seized by inspiration, I went on mixing colors, the upper lip a little darker than the lower one, a darker shade of powders on the sides of the face to soften and hide the fact that it was perhaps a little too wide. I went on extemporizing, with the sureness of one who has never done anything in his whole life but apply cosmetics in this surrogate kind of love-making.

"There, you're done," I said at last.

And Magdalena opened her eyes.

"How did you do it?" she exclaimed. She was ecstatic.

"How did I do what?"

"You're absolutely marvelous! I look just like Sylvia."

"No . . . no . . ."

No . . . yes. But that hadn't been my intention, because Sylvia with the thousand faces had to go on being Sylvia, and Magdalena was Magdalena, unique, perpetual. The two of us stared in silence, carefully scrutinizing Magdalena's new face in the mirror. Yes, it was as if she had preserved her own features intact and put Sylvia's mask on top of them, and the two had fused together. It was a game, masquerade and mask . . . and I thought about my childhood, when in summer homes in the hills we would invent costumes, stick our heads inside transparent silk stockings that preserved our individual features while disguising them; on them, we would paint other faces, the bad man's grim scowl, the princess's white, chaste face, the witch's mean beak, the old hag's wrinkles, the patriarch's moustache and beard— but always with our own features preserved under the false, transparent skin of the stockings. Thus with Magdalena now, who wasn't Magdalena but a mutation of the Sylvia-mask, while Sylvia was every possible variation on the egg-shaped Sylvia-mask, and these in turn were every possible variation on the mythological faces that appeared in fashion magazines and newspaper ads, which in turn were infinite variations on a mask created by some make-up artist in collaboration with a manufacturer, whose creation was perhaps based on some face he had seen in his childhood or glimpsed on a journey or in a dream or studied meticulously in a painting created by an artist who was remembering . . . etc. etc. When Magdalena acquired Sylvia's mask by my hands, her face became the magical echo of all those myriads of faces and paintings and masks. Perhaps that was why Sylvia had that power—and when Magdalena acquired her face, she would share those powers . . . yes, in being created by me, now, in the intimacy of our bedroom, where we had enjoyed each other's company for so many years, perhaps Magdalena had acquired the magical powers that would re-store what Sylvia had taken away from me.

At the Bistrot, Paolo waved frantically at us from the other end of the room—at Magdalena, actually. I didn't exist, I was only Magdalena's make-up man. He came over to our table and sat down.

"You *divine* woman! What have you done to yourself? You look like an illustration out of *Black and White* in the

Thirties, before the Civil War, I don't know, like Gaby
Deslys or Cléo de Mérode, something terribly antiquated,
almost faded, as if one could *buy* you at Los Encants . . .
no, at the Marché aux Puces, because I'm here to tell you
that Los Encants is *definitely* not what it used to be and it's
been *ages* since I went there or anyone else did: it's cheaper
to fly a day trip to Paris and back, it would come out to
exactly the same thing. The Roigs? Don't *speak* to me about
the Roigs. I don't ever want to hear about them again . . ."

"But why not?"

"Have you any *idea* what they did last night in my new
flat? You know I redid my whole flat. No? Well, I did, gor-
geous, I just couldn't stand another minute of Bauhaus, you
know, so austere, and all those *cushions*. I said an Act of
Constriction and Examined My Conscience, the way the
Aesculapian Fathers of Tortosa taught me when I was growing up, and I said to myself: Let's see, Pablo Rojo, better
known by your *nom de guerre*, Paolo Rosso: is it really *true*
you adore simplicity all that much? And what am I supposed
to say? I had to confess that no, no, *NO*, my little heart was
with the various Louis of France and that's where it's always
been, so in a single month I redid the whole thing and now
even the sink has cabriole legs; the entire transformation was
accomplished in a mere thirty days. That takes moral courage, you know, I can't stand living a lie once I find it out.
Puritanical, that's what I am *au fond* . . . Well, last night
was my housewarming. *Appalling*. The whole universe was
there, I knew maybe five people in the entire place . . . I
didn't invite *you*, dear, because I thought you were in the
country . . . anyway, I don't know, I forgot, and in the confusion I lost your phone number . . . it could happen to anybody . . . Well, I'll explain later, why are we discussing this
when I simply have to tell you something so you can see *just
what kind of people* our famous Roigs are. Just picture it:
suddenly I spot Ricardo and Raimunda mixing it up in the
corner, which Lord knows happens seven days a week and

anywhere they are, sometimes I think the Tortillería owes its
fame to the scandalous quarrels that pair go in for, and you
know I think their fights are a tonic for any party . . . but
this time, I could see Ricardo was about to smash an adorable little chair of mine over her head, a real Louis Quinze
period piece . . ."

"How awful! What did you do?"

"I ran to save—"

"Poor Raimunda!"

"*No*, not Raimunda. J'ai arraché la chaise Louis Quinze
d'époque à son mari, et je lui ai mis dans les mains une autre
chaise, Louis Quinze aussi, mais pas d'époque . . ."

We laughed and he went on.

". . . now don't you try to tell me the Roigs have personality. *Nobody* has personality these days, I assume it's
not In . . . Except for you, dear, you look straight out of
Beardsley, you know, one of those John the Baptists with all
that hair, you never know whether they're girls or boys . . .
and the miracle is that on you it works, although nobody's
wearing hair these days. Women have to be bald, bald as a
billiard. What I'm trying to tell you is that I'm *sick and tired*
of the lot of them, I've made friends with some fabulous
Rumanian princes who are much more entertaining than the
Roigs and are *absolutely* immoral right down to the uni-
forms and gold braid they never had . . . no, the Roigs are
impossible, the watchword now is to have houses that look
like dentists' offices, or country taverns, with factory furniture and posters on the wall. Well, I for one am not going
to put up with Ricardo and Raimunda destroying my house
everytime I invite them over . . ."

Paolo had had a lot to drink, and little by little his early
brilliance faded into an incoherent protest against the evils
of the world, the Roigs, and people in general, his tongue
slurring his explanation that he was convinced the only place
to live was Paris, yes, Paris, *precisely* because it was passé,
that was the best thing about it, and he decided that next

weekend he was going to move there permanently. Suddenly he emerged from the depths of his drunkenness and stared at Magdalena.

"Do you know who you look absolutely identically like tonight?"

"Who?"

"Sylvia."

"No!"

"I swear it."

"But she's thin . . . She hasn't any hair . . ."

"Identical."

I paid and we left. But opening the door, we bumped into a crowd of people coming in, the Roigs—who shouted to us not to miss coming to their house the following night—the blue-bearded, blue-eyed publisher, and Kaethe with her camera and basset hound and boxer-poet whose book, finally, was not going to be published by the Roigs or anybody else. This encounter took place between the double doors at the entrance to the Bistrot in a tangle of raincoats and flying mufflers, the lot of them dying to get inside because outside there was a wind that promised snow, and myself dying to get out, God knows why, maybe because I was furious that Sylvia and Ramón had said they were going to be out of town for the weekend and instead here they were. . . . Yes, we had to leave without getting involved. But Sylvia beckoned to Magdalena, who went back in with her, and they stood inside talking while I stood outside freezing, waiting for them to stop whispering to each other, and through the foggy windows I could see Paolo hugging and kissing Raimunda and Ricardo, who gave him a pat on the ass, and everybody was kissing one another and Paolo and dragging him along with them toward a long table that was hurriedly set up for them while Paolo kissed Kaethe's basset hound and boxer. Eventually Magdalena emerged.

"What was Sylvia telling you?"

"Nothing."

"What do you mean, nothing?"

"That we'll see each other tomorrow at the Roigs'."

"And she didn't explain why they said they were going out of town this weekend and instead we bump into them and they don't even invent an excuse?"

"She didn't say anything . . . maybe tomorrow."

"I don't know if I feel like going to the Roigs' tomorrow."

"Now, dear, you're in a bad temper."

"I can't stand that awful crowd."

"They're very amusing."

"You're always on their side."

"How cold it is! This wind . . ."

"Nothing I say matters to you."

"Call a cab, dear, I'm turning to stone."

I could see how my strategy should proceed: have a quarrel, so that when we got home we'd go to bed furious at each other, which would give me another night. It wasn't worth it to get drunk, as I had planned. A fight always worked that way, perhaps it would even postpone a confrontation with Magdalena for a few days more, if I could stay in a bad temper until . . . until what? I didn't know anything, except that I was nervous, as guilty as an adulterous husband (which was all the more humiliating because that was exactly what I was, an adulterous husband), and that I hated Magdalena—not Sylvia, Magdalena—because she might find out and maybe even forgive me. Hated her above all because she might know already, Sylvia might have told her. Which was why I had to start a fight with her, not vice versa.

"You're always taking their part because you're a snob. And now you're so chummy with Sylvia . . . Why didn't you marry Monsante, who was making such a fuss over you? He's a musician, he would have given you an entrée into this clique you think is so special. Do you think it's such a pretty spectacle, watching a woman your age making an ass of herself like that time we saw Montserrat Ventura dancing with a black sailor at the Jazz Colón? Remember that? Remember when Paolo played the go-between for you and Ricardo when we'd only barely met the Roigs?"

"How absurd, your bringing all that up now . . ."

"Don't tell me stories. I know what you like. No doubt you did have an affair with Ricardo. I would have understood that, the way I find I have to understand so many things about you . . . Cab! Cab! Run. What say we go dancing at the Jazz Colón and do a little touring around the Chinese Quarter, like hicks after thrills to tell our friends about when we get back to the provinces?"

"You know how I detest all that."

"It's Saturday night, you know, the perfect time for excursions: Barcelona by Night . . ."

"No."

"Where would you like to go then?"

"With you, nowhere, because you're being impossible."

"Want me to tell the driver to take you back to the Bistrot to see if you can pick up a hot date? Kaethe's boxer, for example?"

"Stop being stupid. Let's go home."

I gave our address to the cab driver, and we didn't speak to each other once during the ride. Magdalena got out first, ran inside and went up alone in the elevator. She left the elevator door open at our floor, no doubt on purpose so the elevator wouldn't come back down. Hating and cursing her I panted all the way up the seven flights of stairs. When I got to our bedroom, I intended to take my pajamas to another room and sleep alone. I had a horrible feeling I was never going to recover what Sylvia had taken away from me—"Adultery doesn't pay," said the movies in the days of Kay Francis: Kay Francis—Magdalena reminded you of her when you came right down to it. I found Magdalena in bed asleep, her blinders on and the light at her side of the bed turned off. She was breathing deeply and regularly. On the night table, the little box of Mogadon: I calculated that she had taken two. I also saw a bottle of cognac and a glass: it was obvious she had had a stiff drink. She slept as if drugged or anaesthetized, something she did when she was tired or had the idea for some reason that I didn't love her anymore and our life was a lie or a failure and she didn't want to face that fact or anything else right then. "I'll think about it all tomorrow, at Tara."

Scarlett O'Hara's words were her motto; it roused not only my anger but my fear and disgust, and I would go for days without talking to her when this happened. But now, Scarlett O'Hara had saved me: I could sleep in peace.

The next day, when Mrs. Presen brought breakfast, she explained Magdalena's absence by saying she had gone to the zoo with the children for the morning and at noon she would take them to her mother's for lunch. She, Mrs. Presen, would make me something to eat. An omelette? Some squid? All I had to do was tell her what I wanted . . . Or would I rather go out to eat, to a good restaurant? Of course restaurants on Sunday . . .

"An omelette."

"With three eggs?"

"With three eggs."

That meant I had the whole day to myself; I had mixed feelings about it, since all I could do in my situation was to think without coming to decisions of any kind. I stood up in my slippers and robe and looked out the window: vindictively I noted that the sun held no warmth; she might well catch a cold at the zoo, which would teach her a lesson. What sort of lesson? Well, it didn't matter . . .

What mattered was Sylvia. She was the key to the whole thing. Why had she gone on and on about her "affinity" for Magdalena that night? Why had Ramón suddenly become so odd and aggressive about her attitude and left the two of us alone? Or had Sylvia sent him away so that she could be alone with me and seduce me? No. Sylvia's attention had never once focused on me, not that night or on any other occasion we had met, only on Magdalena. I had suspected certain lesbian tendencies in Sylvia . . . but Magdalena . . .

of course, Sylvia must have realized that things of that sort were impossible with her . . . although everybody, whether they admit it or not, is flattered by homosexual admiration so long as it doesn't go any further and so long as the person isn't, well, just anybody: yes, the phenomenon was much more prevalent among women than among men—You're divine! That dress is absolutely luscious on you. . . . Little kisses, phone calls, mysterious dates at lunchtime, hugs, caresses, everything so natural, but so suspicious when you examined things more closely—and Magdalena and Sylvia could indeed be a case of, well, let's say, mutual admiration, with a certain element of lesbianism mixed in. But no. Somehow the object of that—what to call it? conspiracy? friendship? intrigue?—was undoubtedly me. That date to have coffee together, that tête-à-tête at the Bistrot after our surprise encounter—and wasn't it possible Ramón had really planned to go away with Sylvia that weekend, as they had told us, but she had used her wiles to make him stay in town . . . and had "bumped into" us at a restaurant which, now I remembered, had been Magdalena's suggestion? Yes . . . a conspiracy . . .

But why should I be afraid of her? What if I were to conspire with Ramón? I was certain he would agree . . . he might even have been calling me so often for that very reason. Get together with Ramón against them. A brilliant idea suddenly put me in a good humor: if they had made a date to meet at the Roigs', then Ramón and I would take advantage of their maneuvers to stand together and . . . and what? Fold them? Disarm them? Yes, disarm them. Not in the sense of taking their weapons away, but of taking them apart, as Sylvia could be taken apart. Magdalena too. It was a brilliant idea.

While I took a shower, I happily sang "Chattanooga Choo-Choo," a song that was turning into the national anthem of our friendship with Ramón and Sylvia, as Vinteuil's air had been for Swann. But while I was washing myself, I had to come back to reality: my sex was gone, and in the lather on my pubic hair I couldn't find anything more than a simple sort of pressure-clasp. Dismantled. No, Sylvia was no witch and she hadn't caused my sex to disappear by using magic unguents. Out of simple revenge she had dismantled my sex, detaching it from this little pressure-clasp. While I dried myself, rage began to mount in me: I was a puppet in the hands of these women. I rubbed my skin so hard with the towel that I turned red. Yes, use us, that's what they want to do, that's what their submissive act is all about, and when one of them is submissive or lets herself be seduced, the first thing she does is dismantle your virility, as Sylvia had done that night. Magdalena had better take care, because if Ramón dismantled Sylvia, he might show me the trick, and then she would see what happened to her intimate afternoons with Paolo, her sessions downtown with Sylvia over coffee, her morning-long telephone conversations with Marta, her . . . all those things. Yes, now I was maneuvering into battle position: when Magdalena came home, I would behave as if nothing had happened. I would be sweet, even a bit contrite, so that she wouldn't suspect anything, but there would be no way we could fail to be at the Roigs' that night.

I went to the wardrobe and pulled out my green velvet suit. Yes, it was just home from the cleaners. Perfect. I put it down on the bedroom armchair. Light-green shirt? No, too obvious. White? Beige? I pulled out several to choose among, and some ties to shuffle around in possible combinations. No, I couldn't make up my mind now. Better to do it later. Meanwhile I went back to the living room to read *The Glass Bead Game*, convinced that I wasn't going to need Dr. Monclús now because I was going to beat them at their own game. The truth was, I decided, Dr. Monclús was nothing more than a quack who took advantage of the ignorance of snobs to get rich off them . . . well, nobody was going to take *me* for a fool.

When I heard Magdalena come in later, I cheerfully shouted "Hi!"

She didn't answer. Clearly she didn't want to smooth things over, thinking she could subdue me more easily this way. It didn't matter. Wait awhile. I heard her go into the bedroom and turn on the light.

"What's all this?" she exclaimed.

"What?"

"Your green suit and so many shirts and ties?"

"Aren't we going to the Roigs' tonight?"

"I thought you couldn't stand them."

I put down my book, went to our bedroom and attacking her—so to speak—frontally, I hugged and kissed her, taking care not to press my body against hers.

"The drinks must have gone to my head last night," I said.

"You were very unpleasant."

I humbled myself, which was what she wanted. "I was jealous, Magdalena."

She laughed in my arms, content. "But of whom?"

"I don't know, the whole world, Paolo, Ramón, Ricardo, Raimunda, Sylvia—everybody . . ."

"Of Sylvia! Really . . ."

"All of them, they all adore you, and they only tolerate me because I'm an appendage of yours, nothing more . . . you know that . . ."

This completely disarmed her even as she protested that I knew it wasn't true, that my cleverness, my talent as a painter, my . . . so many things, I shouldn't be such an idiot, and we embraced, she accepting and loving all of me. But during this little comedy, I remained aloof and unwavering in my resolve; I knew that through this woman who was playing my comedy I was going to recover what she and Sylvia had taken away from me. From Ramón I was going to learn the secret of how to dismantle one's lawful spouse—be she legally or illegally "lawful"; in our world a couple's legitimacy depended on more basic things. I would dismantle mine, putting her away whenever I wanted; I could thus use my virility whenever I felt like it, with whichever of the thousands of faces masking miraculously disposable women, or, if worse came to worst, I would put away my virility and not use it at all.

She wanted to cling to me, but I drew back maliciously, saying not now, when we get home. She said, almost pleadingly, "I left Pepe and Luis at Mother's for the night. You know what a treat it is for them to sleep there, and she'll take them to school in the morning . . ."

But I remained implacably innocent. "Did they have a good time today?"

Magdalena's eyes hardened. I was sitting on her dressing-table bench, and now my eyes were hard too, because the next question was, If you left them there for the night, how did you know you'd get to go to the Roigs' no matter what? Yes, don't deny it: you have a date with Sylvia there. But I didn't say a word or ask a single question. From the bathroom Magdalena said, "Would you like me to give you a good head massage, now that we have time? It'll help you get over last night's hangover. After what you drank you must be . . ."

Since I'm crazy about Magdalena's massages, I said yes. I stretched out on the bed and from the bathroom she brought towels, brushes, combs, scissors, razor blades, creams, colognes. She left this battery of equipment on the night table and said, "Now close your eyes, dear, and try to relax . . . breathe deeply . . . that's right . . . let me take your glasses off . . ."

And I could feel the electric discharge of the first light touch of her fingers caressing my forehead and eyes and then her fingertips running over my eyelids, cheeks, moustache, beard, her hands on the nape of my neck, her fingers under my hair then flowing down to the nape of my neck again, around my neck and shoulders, undoing knots and rigid areas, then the swift, dexterous rubbing of my scalp that made my whole head fill with fresh, sparkling blood. Look at all your hair, dear, how lovely, what luck to have so much hair at your age, it's lovely to plunge my hands into your hair, it's wonderful that men are wearing their hair longer these days and you can show yours off, it's a pleasure to give you a massage. Close your eyes, no, don't open them, don't open them again; relax completely, rest, I'm going to massage your eyelids a little, your eyelids. I'm going to trim your whiskers a little, they're very long, snip a little off your beard and hair, especially here around the nape of your neck. Now I'm going to massage your head a little more until you feel your scalp sort of anaesthetized; there now, you see how your hair doesn't hurt when I tug it a little? Relax, relax, don't open your eyes, let my fingers caress your eyelids, I'm going to give you a rinse so that your few gray hairs go silver . . . yes, and cologne too, and I'm going to pluck those long, ugly hairs you have between your eyebrows and clip those black hairs coming out of your ears and nose. Relax, now, don't move. I'm not hurting you, am I? And I'll cut your fingernails too, one by one, first one hand and then the other, my hands are anaesthetizing you with my caresses, you already feel headless and handless, as if I had taken your fingers off joint by joint, and now along with your hair and your eyes that are resting and that you can't open anymore, and your nose and ears, all trimmed, I'm putting you away piece by piece, with your green velvet suit, your shoes, your socks and the rest of your clothes for tonight; and look, now I'm untying and taking off your bathrobe; but of course you can't look; and I'm removing your arms so you can relax them, and now your legs. . . .

Magdalena was careful and orderly and one of her more extraordinary talents was for packing: she folded each piece of her husband so well that everything fit perfectly into one rather small suitcase. Once she had shut it, she left it on top of the bed and began to get dressed, slowly, carefully: her face was almost untouched by make-up; she left bare the slightly savage purity of her emphatic features, just a little red on the lips, nothing more; contemplating herself in the mirror she felt proud of being so *herself*—so un-Cléo de Mérode or Gaby Deslys, so *not* In, so un-Camp, so un-

Andrews Sisters—over and above her nonexistent "face" and elaborate hairdo, wearing nothing more than a simple black wool dress with a low V-neck. She was unmistakably Magdalena, although people like Paolo and Kaethe liked to confuse things. She was satisfied. She looked at her watch and poked around for her black satin purse . . . felt it . . . *it* wasn't inside: a moment of panic, it wasn't there, where could she have left it, that oh-so-important little package that Sylvia had returned to her . . . maybe Anselmo was right and she was disorganized . . . in the wardrobe, the kitchen, the cupboard under the telephone . . . yes: there it was. What if Anselmo had found it! She put on her fur coat, tucked her purse (now all stuffed and warm) under her arm, and picked up the suitcase. In the vestibule, she telephoned Sylvia and said she was on her way. They would meet in twenty minutes at the entrance to the Roigs' building. She hailed a cab and set the suitcase on the seat next to her: it was small and the driver didn't mind. She put a hand on it, affectionately, as if to protect it from the danger of having to travel in the trunk. She could feel her husband's heart beating. She looked at the driver's neck. Yes, he was dismantleable too. She knew exactly how to do it. There comes a time in life when marriages reach a balance, in which all women learn how to dismantle their husbands: take hold of the ears, dismantle and roll the scalp up like a rug. Yes. Sometimes it wasn't even necessary—or so said Sylvia, to whom she owed all this knowledge; and she was going to tell Marta, so she could straighten up that tangled marriage of hers once and for all . . . tomorrow she'd call her to arrange a lunch—you didn't have to put the poor man back together right away, you could keep the pieces in bags, in packages hidden in the back of a wardrobe, or on top with the lights and ornaments for the Christmas tree, where nobody would think of looking . . . and then, when she wanted a perfect man who wasn't exactly like her own, she could take the pieces out and put them together for a while in a different-shaped reality, another whim. How foolish men were, to think that because they "gave the orders," because they "worked," their women had no power. How naïve. Yes, they did go on business trips, of course, but much less often than people thought, because often people thought Anselmo was at a convention in Amsterdam, or Ricardo giving a lecture in London, or Ramón touring the U.S. in search of houses by Frank Lloyd Wright, when it wasn't so. The women would dismantle their men and fold them up so as to have a rest from them . . . they would have lunch and drinks together and go on diets at beauty farms and spend endless hours in boutiques or at the seamstress, and hunt for original buttons to blend with the new Chanel tweed they had bought for the autumn, spending hours and hours together. Were men stupid, or what? Did they think women talked about nothing but buttons and tweeds? Idiotic! Men ought to take more care, for in the cafés where women gather during men's working hours to smoke cigarettes and gossip and pass the morning, what they do is something else, they transmit wisdom from one to the next, just as Magdalena tomorrow would transmit to Marta the wisdom that Sylvia had given her. The women gather in a semblance of ingenuous, mindless gossip to confer, to develop, to perfect their art in that pool of common knowledge.

Now in the taxi, Magdalena was transporting the well-ordered pieces of her husband in a suitcase. When she put him back together again he wouldn't even be aware that she had taken him apart. He would remember the whole trip as if he had been sitting at her side, like other husbands who "travel" and remember unreal business trips to Tokyo or La Coruña, San Francisco or Bilbao, during which they thought they had cheerfully abandoned their wives while in fact they had only spent a few days dismantled. Of course, when he obeyed her and did what he had to do, then she would return what belonged to him, the missing part that men thought was the very center of the universe . . . the little package that Sylvia had given back to her in the confusion of capes, fur coats, and mufflers at the Bistrot door, because after all, Anselmo did belong to her, and if one was going to go to the trouble of keeping a man, it was absurd to have an incomplete one.

Magdalena was very excited at this, her first time. Sylvia was waiting for her in the foyer, sitting on a bench with her own suitcase by her side, to direct Magdalena's first experience and help her in case they were rushed.

"I didn't want to begin before you got here," she said.

"What a divine djellaba, Sylvia!"

"I see you disguised yourself as a chic matron . . ."

"Yes, black with a string of real pearls, etcetera. You have to be original."

"I've always told you you're a ballsy lady; you have real style and personality. You have to have balls to come to the Roigs' wearing nothing but a little black dress and a string of real pearls as if you were my rich aunt. Of course with your beauty, you can get away with it . . ."

"You look marvelous in green."

"I've got to get some green suede shoes to go with this dress."

"I saw some in a new shoe store, on Gracia I think . . ."

"Oh, do let's go. How's tomorrow for you?"

"Tomorrow? I can't. I must get together with Marta."

"Well, the day after, then."

They settled on a time and decided to have lunch together. The green shoes were very important, but it was more important still to trade impressions about that night. As they talked, they opened the suitcases, and piece by piece, without much ado, they put their dolls together.

"Oh, I forgot to tell you . . . ," Sylvia said.

"What?"

"I think the package I gave you—remember?—I think I got them mixed up . . . you've got Ramón's and I have Anselmo's . . ."

Magdalena shrugged. "Does it matter?"

"It seems to matter to them."

"Nonsense! It's much more amusing for Anselmo to have Ramón's for a time—"

"—And for Ramón to have Anselmo's. Yes, how funny! You must admit how convenient it is to be a woman: the fact that men have a removable sex makes infidelity so much easier. That time at the development, remember? when I kept your husband's sex and Ramón left in a huff . . ."

"Why did he leave?"

"Because when he realized that I had recognized you as a woman who understands men, like myself, he got scared and flew into a rage. He came down after me, trying to dominate me in the most stupid way by making love. And I took off his sex and although he took me apart and everything and wiped off my face, I wouldn't give it back to him . . . and when he came back after a few days to put me together again, I gave him your husband's sex . . . very good it is, too, I must say. Ramón's been rather odd since then, I don't know why, so I had to take him apart. Let's see if we can put them back together again correctly this time . . . I think you had better give me back Ramón's . . . I'll lend it to you another day, if you like . . . we'll just settle on a time, nothing could be easier . . ."

"Well, if I remember . . . you know how it is with the children, you've always got your mind on something else, and now it's time to do something about winter clothes . . . Oh, the shoes. This shoe store on Gracia I was telling you about *makes* shoes out of suede or velvet or anything you want . . . divine shoes."

"Isn't it very expensive?"

"Look, the work is so marvelous, it doesn't seem expensive to me . . . The head comes last, isn't that what you told me, it's best to assemble the whole thing before putting on the head? Ah. Ramón's wearing his green velvet suit too. They're going to be twins, so elegant . . ."

"Right. Now, let's put their heads on at the same time."

"Now?"
"Now."

Ramón and I were laughing because Magdalena looked like a widow. Or, as Ramón suggested, "Morticia. Remember Charles Addams?"

Of course Magdalena remembered Charles Addams and Sylvia didn't, but since we'd rung the doorbell it was too late to explain to her who Morticia and Charles Addams were, in the heyday of *The New Yorker*.

Raimunda opened the door, decked out in a pink Romantic dress that was all flounces and gathers. She was hardly recognizable. Her head, minuscule today with her hair pulled back, was buried in the pearly froth of her dress. They all thought one another divine, as were also our matching green velvet suits, and voices calling us over the howls of the music echoed Divine, Divine as they dragged us into the noise. But before we plunged into the crowd, Sylvia and Magdalena handed Raimunda the suitcases they had been carrying. She deposited them in the hall with a smile of complicity.

The center of the gathering today—at least for the time being—was the publisher with blue eyes and a blue beard. Sitting on the floor with his latest blonde's head in his lap, he was shouting abuse at a rather drunk Latin American novelist, whose book he had just brought out with great fanfare as something supremely original, but the critics had received it coolly. The Latin American blamed him, the publisher, for not giving it more advance publicity, for selling him out, for breaking his promises. The flat-chested blonde, who seemed to be made of squeezable sponge rubber, was frowning in concentration over the seriousness of the accusations. But when the publisher suggested that the Latin American's novel wasn't selling because the novel per se was finished as a literary form, the Latin American, who was enormous, picked up the publisher, who was a midget, and the blonde falling off his lap must have bounced like a rubber ball because she disappeared at once, leaving the two furious men each with his hands around the other's throat, while Kaethe clicked again and again at their fists and sweaty, enraged faces.

"The novel form is finished because it suits you to have it finished!" the Latin American was shouting.

The publisher was too drunk to do anything but heap more abuse on him. The Latin American, incoherent with rage and frustration, but at the same time flattered because his violence was polarizing the gathering and thinking that something might come out in the papers tomorrow, screamed: "Yes, it suits you, and you're a whore!"

And he took a swing that landed wide, shattering a pane of glass. The women screamed and his hand started to bleed onto the blonde's prostrate body, and Kaethe's basset hound licked the blood up, to the evident delight of both dog and blonde. It was time to do something. Ramón took the publisher, who was crying and apologetic, into the other room to cheer him up, and several men threw the vulgar Latin American out of the house, where nobody had invited him in the first place. Something had to be done to erase the incident, remove the chill, and Magdalena was pushing me into the center of the light and Sylvia was doing the same to Ramón: something, a skit, something to warm up the atmosphere of the gathering, obliterate the unpleasantness, and change the current.

Ramón and I were left standing alone in the center of the crowd, dressed identically in our green velvet suits, like two chorus boys out of an American revue, the kind who always come on with the girls in the kick-line but nobody ever notices. We didn't doubt for a moment what had to be done. We took each other by the arm, smiled, and the two of us, mature men, began to dance, raising our legs parallel, gesticulating as if doffing our boaters in greeting, and then we began, involuntarily, to sing:

> *Pardon me boy*
> *Is this the Chattanooga Choo-Choo*
> *Right on track twenty-nine?*
> *Please gimme a shine*
> *I can afford to go*
> *To Chattanooga station*
> *I've got my fare,*
> *And just a trifle to spare . . .*

We went on singing and dancing our song, though no-body was paying any attention to us. A slight, slender, acne-faced boy who turned out to be an architect made an entrance like a dictator with his bodyguards, flanked by five enormous, muscular assistants from his studio who hung on his every word. No, nobody was interested in us . . . except for Sylvia and Magdalena. As I sang, I saw their eyes watching us, directing us from a corner while the rest of the crowd, including the publisher, who was as quickly consoled as he was hurt, listened to the opinion of the tiny, pock-marked architect. Magdalena watched me as if she were afraid I might make a mistake, forget the words of this song I had never learned but never forgotten, and that I now, because she was directing me, was singing to please her. In spite of the universal lack of interest in our number, which was taking up the already limited space, the two of them watched vigilantly until we finished:

> *. . . So Chattanooga Choo-Choo*
> *Chattanooga Choo-Choo*
> *Please choo-choo me home.*

The blonde was rolling around on the floor, half asleep, resting her head in the lap of anybody who would have her, until she wound up with the architect, who was giving a lecture on Le Corbusier and the lamentable loss of his sense of monumentality; he looked down at the blonde, who was following his lecture with brows knit in concentration.

"Don't you agree?"

When she realized he was talking to her, she said, "Sorry, I don't understand a word of Spanish," and burst into an hysterical giggle loud enough to stop the conversation and upset all the groups in the room. I was lost in the crowd and had the strange sensation that I was disappearing, fading away. Ramón, my double, had been swallowed up by the tumult, leaving me without a mirror image to prove my own dubious existence. I was standing in a corner trying to look affable, with my hands crossed behind my back, alone and unimportant like the Duke of Edinburgh, when I felt other hands touching mine behind me, and two warm breasts and a stomach pressing against me, and Magdalena's head and profile moving forward over my shoulder next to my face, and her fresh cheek brushing against my bearded one. She kissed me softly.

"All alone?"

I nodded.

"You poor dear!"

"Did I look asinine?" I asked.

"I don't think a soul noticed."

"How could I remember the words to 'Chattanooga Choo-Choo'?"

Magdalena smiled enigmatically, the way they do in the movies. I didn't understand a thing, not even myself; it was as if everything inside me were maladjusted and slack, as if the total lack of attention paid us denied my existence. Why, instead of telling me that nobody had noticed, hadn't she said something to cheer me up, or done something to give me strength? Very softly, Magdalena said, "Come."

She led me to the bathroom and locked the door behind us. There she pounced on me, hugging me and kissing me on the mouth the way we hadn't kissed each other for a long time, her full, warm, open mouth clinging wetly to mine, breathing in unison. During a moment when we stopped to collect ourselves, she murmured into my ear: "You did it just the way I wanted you to."

And like someone awarding a prize, she kissed me again and pressed closer and closer to my body, caressing me with her hands while I caressed her, but now it was my self—my neck, my back, my shoulders—that her hands made me feel, waking all of me up as if from a long, heavy sleep, caressing my eyes so that I could see her clearly, my ears so that I could hear her breathing, my nose so that I could smell her unmistakable, personal odor, which rose from the depths of the Shalimar to my nose and, entering, revived me; she caressed my neck with her fresh fingers, her light hand weighing on my chest, moving down, down, to return something I had forgotten I was missing until I heard the click of the pressure-clasp, and the energy husbanded so long filled me and made me throb under Magdalena's touch, joy, joy, I was whole again, enormous and happy and multiplied in all the mirrors of the Roigs' bathroom, me reflected in the mirrors of the four walls and ceiling and doors and cabinets, making love to a submissive, tender, whole Magdalena who was tired of all the people at this party with whom we had so little in common, yes, we were out of place here, our concerns were different, perhaps more profound than theirs.

"Nevermore . . ." I murmured. I said it automatically, contrite, because now I was certain that Sylvia had told her something about our adventure that night at the development, and I wanted to dispose of my sin quickly and jokingly, like a little boy swearing to his mother that he'll behave himself just to please her and make her proud. Magdalena understood the joke, as she always understood everything I said. "Do you swear?"

And I stammered once again: "Nevermore . . ."

And added after a last kiss: "It's so boring . . . all of them . . ."

We straightened ourselves out in front of the mirrors and decided to leave. It would be better just to slip out quietly, since to judge by the noise, the party had reached its state of maximum effervescence, and nobody would miss us.

"Here, through this door." I led her.

Green Atom Number Five

IT IS A TRUTH universally acknowledged, that there comes a time in the life of a man—and even more so in the life of a married couple—when it becomes imperative to buy the definitive apartment, to install oneself in a permanent way. After a more or less nomadic existence in rented apartments where aesthetic solutions are always a compromise, arranging and furnishing one's own home in a way that reflects exactly one's own taste and personality is one of the great pleasures that middle age can offer. To choose flooring and curtains with the utmost care; to demand perfection in bathrooms and doorknobs; to subtly manipulate, with all the freedom afforded by ample means and good taste, the entire gamut of colors and textures in the living room, bedroom, kitchen—even the corridors—so as to rest the eyes and enhance the beauty of the lady of the house; to exercise discrimination in the arrangement of a lifetime of objects (half a lifetime, really, since the people in question are Roberto Ferrer and Marta Mora, who have just crept over forty); to use only the best things, and put the rest away as presents to fulfill social obligations—all this transforms itself into an obsession, an act of commitment far beyond the superficial, particularly if the couple, as in Roberto and Marta's case, has no children.

Roberto Ferrer dedicated the little spare time his dental practice allowed him to painting: painting of the most elegant sort, in black and white on coarse burlap, always centered on a few atoms of some unusual color. Even though he had had no formal artistic education he had certainly "had a lot of museum," as Paolo often said to him. Paolo had overseen the decoration of the apartment. Roberto felt that a very important part of himself had flowered in the loving demands he had made to ensure that the apartment be impeccable. It had real originality and character, natural enough since he and Marta were not a dull couple; but it wasn't too idiosyncratic—it wasn't, for example, crammed with objects which might be valuable but at the same time would accumulate and rob the apartment of its austerity. Roberto's concern had been to marry the practical with the aesthetic.

Painting consoled Roberto—something his dental practice, which was distinguished enough but perhaps too large, did not. So did his prudent collection of engravings: lithographs, xylographs, etchings . . . above all, examples of the engraver's tool which had captivated him with their spontaneity, that worthy emotion of synthesis. Certain winter afternoons, when he had nothing to do, he amused himself by examining through a loupe the slightly fuzzy line which the immediacy of drypoint produces, comparing this with the chemical precision of the lines in an etching. More and more he became convinced, and he convinced Marta too (luckily for her, once her husband's practice became lucrative, he preferred the civilized hobby of collecting to golf or hunting, which had once loomed as alternatives), that it was a shame so few artists today used the burin. In the end, his own painting, his engravings, all the valuable objects gathered with such discrimination in the new apartment, as well as his interest in the literature on these subjects, came under the category of "pleasure."

In the large new apartment, which had a beautiful terrace-garden, he set aside for himself an empty room with a window facing north. He did not want to put anything in it until he had time: say, when he took his vacation, or when he felt the walls of the new apartment had become friends. Then, he would see how to install his studio. That is, *if* he installed it. He refused to feel pressured by any exterior or interior demand. He wanted to take things slowly, give himself time, so that the urge to paint—when it came over him, if it came over him—would arrive with such vigor that it would determine the precise form the room would take. His relationship to art would become truly erotic, as Marcuse proposes. Could he "realize" himself in painting? Could he, like Gauguin—and supported by Marta, who would praise his attitude—abandon everything and move to a desert island or to an old walled town in the middle of the steppes, a middle-aged hippie dedicating his entire being to the pleasure of painting without considering for what or for whom, nor even what might happen if he did not win a place in the world through his painting? Meanwhile, the room remained empty, waiting for him. It was the greatest of all luxuries. He would not let Paolo touch it, not even to suggest a color for the walls, which were still naked plaster. All this he would decide only when the time came. He also refused to let Marta store things there "for the time being" (women are always storing things "for the time being," a purpose whose imprecision never ceased to irritate him), since even that would be a violation. So, he left the room the way it was, an abstract whitish cube with one door, one window, one light bulb hanging from a coiled wire in the center of the ceiling, no more. Later, he would see.

The Gauguin solution was beckoning to him the Sunday morning Marta went to the Palau with Anselmo Prieto's wife, using his ticket, to hear Dietrich Fischer-Dieskau's *Schöne Müllerin* recital. Or was it *Die Winterreise* this week? Anyway, it was raining, and if he got up—which he had not the slightest intention of doing—and went to the window, he would see how in the street, three stories down, the weather was getting worse. People were turning up their coat collars, their umbrellas already raised defensively against a penetrating, invisible rain. Roberto had stayed in bed to fight one of those disagreeable colds that darken and blur the corners of things but are not exactly debilitating, because the headache dissipates with the first pill. Everybody has his "own" cold, just as he has his own bank account, his own sauna bath, his own superstitions. Roberto's cold generally turned into sinusitis, but this time the latter hadn't troubled to put in an appearance. His cold simply freed him from the puritanical necessity of doing anything at all, even reading, even amusing himself, and allowed his thoughts (or nonthoughts) to wander destinationless and duty-free today: this first Sunday they were truly, definitively installed in the new apartment, right down to the last glass and ashtray. The luxury of this morning alone with nothing to do stirred in him a tide of love toward all his things, from the black cushions in the corner of the tobacco-colored sofa and the Italian table lamps, or rather "sculptures of pure light," to that room awaiting him with the ultimate luxury of its naked plaster. Today he went further than Gauguin: today he felt enough courage to leave his small world intact—a white cube, no more—closed up forever.

Nevertheless, he put on his slippers to go to the window and look down at the street. Now he could make out the minuscule drops that caused people to open their umbrellas. The sky hung so low that it enclosed the street like a dark lid. Like a coffin, he thought. All these people out there are walking in a coffin, that's why they're cold. Inside, though—that is, outside the coffin, where he was—it was warm: the heating system was so well thought out as not to be overwhelming and yet he could walk around in his slippers even with his cold. But did he really have a cold? Could you really call feeling a little stuffy, sniffling from time to time, having a cold? No, the truth was, it wasn't a cold. He merely hadn't felt a compelling desire to hear Fischer-Dieskau that morning. . . . It was the third concert in a series and people were fighting for tickets, but . . . No, whatever he did, it ought to come from a strong inner urge or he oughtn't to do it . . . and if much time went by without his feeling the urge to paint, he could install a small workshop to bind books, for example, something that had always tempted him . . . or a room with a cork floor and ceiling, exclusively designed to listen to music under optimum conditions. . . . Outside it was still raining, chilling the people (but not him) as they hurried by on their way to church, or bad-humoredly carried a small package of French cheese for the ritual Sunday lunch at their in-laws'. Roberto watched them with some irony from the window of his perfect apartment, surrounded by a subtle range of browns and beiges, so elegant and warm, with a note here and there of black or *vert-sec* for contrast.

No. He didn't actually have a cold. Today he didn't have to fool himself, not even with that excuse. What he longed to do at that moment was to *look*, look and touch and perhaps even caress and smell the objects in his new flat . . . strike up a direct, personal, private relationship with them, in a manner of speaking . . . commit adultery with them in his wife's absence and become intimate with the things that (provided the world or he himself didn't change too much) he would be spending the rest of his life with. Because, of course, the Gauguin thing was beautiful but perhaps a trifle passé.

Speaking of Gauguin: there, in the vestibule, leaning against the wall, was Roberto's "Green Atom Number Five." Without a doubt, the best thing he had ever done. Seeing it there, not yet hung, a feeling of revulsion came over him. Not toward the canvas itself—he was perfectly aware of the relative value the canvas had as compared to the "great" Informalists—but toward the only object in the entire apartment which was not completely placed, defined, determined. The night before, he and Marta, nail in hand, had argued about it at length there in the vestibule. He couldn't suppress the feeling that Marta was overprotecting him when she insisted it was absurd of him not to want to hang a single one of his canvases anywhere in the apartment. Absurd not just because "Green Atom Number Five" was a very good painting—perhaps the whites and blacks on the coarse burlap were a little on the Millares side, perhaps the "Atom's" shade of green was too Soulages, but fundamentally it was a good picture, say what you would, refined and sophisticated. But also, and here was where Marta had been most insistent, *because it was hers.* Yes indeed, it was her personal property because he had given it to her, some months before, for their fifteenth wedding anniversary. And she wanted to see it there, in the vestibule, next to the door. Yes, she insisted. "After all, I exist too . . ."

He had thought to give her a piece of jewelry, something truly valuable, an emerald for example, for their anniversary. He had even gone to talk to Roca, to have him show him a few. There was one from Colombia, not very large so the price wasn't too outrageous, lettuce-colored with a few "gardens" inside; it was a beauty. He consulted Marta about it. But she said no, what she wanted was one of his paintings. Specifically, she wanted "Green Atom Number Five," which she had always adored. This gesture had been so typical of Marta: generous, intimate, warm, stimulating, alive. With acts like this she had, during their fifteen years of married life, created that special "ambience of culture" that kept him from feeling reduced to a mere nobody who paved rich old ladies' mouths and sent them exorbitant bills. He could hold himself up as a great and complete human being. What Marta in her wisdom had known to give him more than made up for her inability to have children. Her tenderness, so feminine and complex, was not at all the tenderness of the "sex-object" or the traditional submissive woman; nor, on the other hand, was her love the sexual aggression of a woman who subscribed to Women's Liberation, a movement in which she showed an interest as well-balanced as all her other interests—always tempered by irony.

The night of their anniversary, she prepared dinner. Although they weren't living in the new apartment yet, she served it romantically in the unfinished dining room. The flooring, curtains, and chandelier were still missing; a piece of furniture packed in a box was pushed up against a wall where it did not belong—but in the middle of the room she set a table with their finest linen and in the center a four-armed English silver candelabrum with its fragile candles, *her* anniversary gift to Roberto. While the shadows danced on her beautiful dark face, they savored her exquisite dinner, fragrant with truffles, culminating in a delicious gâteau St.-Honoré, everything highlighted by festive champagne . . . light and fine . . . the prelude to a stupendous anniversary night in the bed they had "improvised" in the new bedroom. That night was its premiere. For Roberto it wasn't the truffles or the champagne or the candlelight that made that night so profoundly . . . so profoundly something, he didn't know what . . . ; what he did know was that it had been enriched not only by sexual satiation but by something else, more . . . well, more profound and complete. Yes, it was something else that had worked the magic: that Marta should ask, in her voice so expert in all the nuances of intimacy, not for the emerald from Roca's, but, as a memento of that night, for "Green Atom Number Five."

There it was now, leaning against the wall next to the front door. Last night they had even got as far as making a hole in the wall, but he won the argument and the picture was never hung. They agreed that the next day they would call the porter to fill in the little hole and hide it with a dab of paint of the same color. They would send the picture over to his good friend Anselmo Prieto's vast messy studio, where it would stay with the rest of his paintings while he decided about installing himself in his empty room. As if she had overheard his thoughts, Marta said:

"What are you sending it to Anselmo's for? Why don't we keep it in your empty room for the time being?"

Marta didn't understand. Clearly there were certain aspects of his freedom which, however sweet and understanding she was, Marta could never grasp, and she always preferred to ignore his explanations of them. And the nail, the plastic plug, the hammer, the drill stayed on the japanned cabinet: it was incredible how this piece of furniture had been transformed by its removal from the heavy bourgeois environment, the indecisively post-Modernist tone of Marta's mother's house, and how moving it into the *dépouillé* look of the new apartment gave it an aesthetic significance that was totally contemporary.

A spotlight had been left focused on the canvas. It wasn't large: twenty-five by thirty inches. And it had to be admitted that not only did it not clash with the japanned cabinet, it really harmonized with it. Yes, and it was light, not only in technique, but in weight: two pounds, four ounces— he remembered it precisely; he had written it down on a slip of paper, since before deciding to baptize it with its present name, he had considered the possibility of calling it "Two-Oh-Four." Again he held it up where it would have hung next to the front door and tried to stand back to see it, but of course he couldn't. Still, it looked very fine in the vestibule. But while his hands held it against the wall he was overwhelmed by the temptation to follow Marta's suggestion of last night and take the canvas to his "studio," or what might or might not be his studio, just to see what would happen. The moment he turned on the light in the empty room and saw "Green Atom Number Five" there, he said, "No, no, it's all wrong, look at those glaring mistakes." It was like an art student looking at his sketch in a mirror carried in his pocket for that very purpose, to reveal the weaknesses in his drawing so he could correct them. "It doesn't belong in this empty room. The room's my mirror. It doesn't belong in this pure cube. It's missing something. Everything. Everything in it is wrong. It belongs in the world of the furniture, not here; in here all weaknesses are exposed, the picture's and mine." He turned off the light and carried the canvas back to the vestibule. This time he resolutely inserted the plastic plug, hammered in the nail, and hung the painting, then stood back to look at it. Perfect. It belonged there, it looked as if it had been assigned that place since forever. Marta would be so happy when she got home! What a surprise it would be to see it at last hanging in its proper place!

Waiting for her, he walked slowly through the rest of the apartment, turning on lights where they were needed, slightly shifting the order of the magazines on the four corners of the Marcel Breuer coffee table so that the covers' colors would harmonize better with the ensemble, half-opening a curtain so that the controlled quantity of light would enhance the richness of the textures. He began to experience in a total way the satisfactions of the environment he had known to create for himself, in which his painting "Green Atom Number Five"—the best and doubtless the last of his series of "Green Atoms"—hanging at last beside the front door, was like the keystone in the arch, the stone that gives it its solidity and resilience. Yes, now, going back to the vestibule and seeing it in place, he realized it was absolutely essential to have *that* picture *there*. Marta was unquestionably right.

What a pity *Die Winterreise* was so long. Or was it *Die Schöne Müllerin*? In any case, Marta was taking a very long time. He was anxious to share his feeling of completion with her, or better, he even dared say, his state of enlightenment evoked by contact with the objects that belonged to him . . . Yes, to have Marta here, to place her protective figure so as to block the odious entrance to the empty room, sealing it up forever, so that his canvas would remain as his definitive work in their definitive apartment. . . . On the one hand it would wipe out the temptation to enter the empty room, and on the other, the other temptation, opposite but equally powerful, to open the front door and run outside and lose himself forever. All he had to do was reach for the doorknob . . .

The doorbell rang. His heart jumped in the happy certainty that it was Marta coming home, ringing the bell instead of using her key because she had forgotten it. That was so typical of her, she couldn't be more scatterbrained. The solitary moment of fullness had passed and now Marta was triumphantly manifesting herself to prolong the moment in a different way. Yes, all he had to do was reach for the doorknob, and let her in. Which he did, exclaiming: "Marta! . . ."

But it wasn't Marta. It was the porter—or maybe the

porter's brother. Roberto didn't know him very well, Marta was the one who had dealings with him. But as far as he could remember, the man looked quite a lot like the porter: tall, gray suit, gray hair, a gray, crumpled face so furrowed, wrinkled, knotted, and marked that one had the feeling an archaeological excavation might be necessary to exhume the poor man buried under all that debris. The porter's brother greeted him courteously, and when Roberto answered, he stepped inside, looking around at everything as if entranced, exclaiming, "What a beautiful apartment!"

He said it with surprise, as if he had never seen it before, as if it were a revelation to him. So, obviously, the man wasn't the porter but the porter's brother. The porter knew the apartment well. Roberto, flattered, smiled. He was so proud of his creation that he could not suppress a cordial invitation:

"Would you like to see it?"

"I'd be delighted," said the porter's brother.

He ushered the man into the living room, pointing out the Tàpies hung not over the fireplace but, avoiding the cliché, to the left, and the collection of lithographs—the most important ones—that formed a *panneau* on the main wall of the dining room. He took him through the bathrooms and the kitchen like a guide showing a tourist around a museum, explaining things, insinuating but not emphasizing their monetary value, inspired by the porter's brother's admiration. Naturally, he passed over the empty room— there was nothing in it to show. But just as they walked past its door he felt a chill produced, no doubt, by his having forgotten to lock the front door. On their return to the vestibule, the porter's brother seemed to have blossomed out of his wrinkles, so great was his admiration; revived, he smiled. Roberto too was smiling as he held the latch to lock the door after his visitor; there was nothing left to say. The porter's brother said goodbye, then just before he crossed the threshold he unhooked the lightweight "Green Atom Number Five" and went out. His gesture was so quick that

Roberto had shut the door before he realized what had happened. He checked, the painting *was* gone, and opened the door again. And there was the man with the painting under his arm, smiling in the knowledge that he and Roberto and the whole world were in agreement that that was what he had come for, to take away the painting. The elevator door opened in front of the porter's brother, lighting his silhouette and casting his shadow in a square of light on the hall floor. Roberto couldn't shout, "Give me back my painting, you thief!"—that might turn out to be an impertinence, and if he caused a scandal at the beginning of his "definitive life" in this "definitive building," his future relationship with his neighbors might be rather ill-omened. Furthermore, the porter's brother seemed so calm, so certain. As he stepped into the elevator, he even called out: "Goodbye! And thanks." And definitive as a guillotine, solid as a strongbox, the elevator door closed behind him. Roberto went out into the hall and stood in front of the elevator. On the panel, each successive number lit up: two, one, mezzanine, ground floor. After that, the light went out. Only then could Roberto react. He raised his fist to bang on the closed door of that implacable box, to demand the return of his painting. A thief had walked right into his house, he would complain to the building's management—stealing a picture like that, to call a spade a spade, and on a Sunday morning . . . a painting of *HIS*, yes his, painted by him . . . valueless, of course, but his. "Well, if it doesn't have any value, what are you complaining about?" the authorities would ask. Besides, he was in his pajamas, he couldn't be seen like this. He lowered his fist without banging, defeated. He felt the cold: obviously, there he was in his pajamas, out in the hall—it was just perfect, now he really had caught a good cold . . . damn it all to hell . . . and tomorrow he had to begin the bridgework for his bank president's wife . . . He went back inside and shut the door. Locked it, just in case. There was the empty wall, a very fine golden beige, and in the center, the absurd solitary nail, stuck to its own shadow, like those inexplicable nails one sometimes sees on the empty walls of a Vermeer. What a hell of a time to think of Vermeer! . . .

But what kind of a time was it? Had it been an assault, a robbery, a crisis, an outrage, a spoliation, an abuse, what? It was impossible to define what had happened. Anyway, the solution was simple enough and it wasn't worth so much fuss: when Marta came home, which would only be a little while longer, he would ask her to get in touch with the porter's brother through the porter, and tell him "it" had all been a misunderstanding, thereby recovering the painting. Offer him compensation in money, perhaps, to smooth over the difficulties of the transaction? But the painting wasn't worth anything! It only had what people call "sentimental value." It was humiliating enough that a picture of his had nothing more than "sentimental value," but, after all . . . And had the man really been the porter's brother? Was he certain the porter even had a brother? He seemed to have heard something of the sort once, but maybe it was a different porter in a different building. And if it wasn't the porter's brother, who was it? And worst of all, if it *was* the porter's brother, why had he come into his apartment, apparently commissioned by someone (assuming the whole thing had been planned), unhooked the painting with such assurance and taken it without bothering to make any kind of explanation? Marta perhaps . . . Marta would solve the whole thing, Marta would know. Doubtless it was something she had arranged . . . maybe a loan to some exhibition of amateur paintings, for example. At the Museum of Abstract Art in Cuenca, perhaps, and in all the confusion of the definitive installation of the apartment, it had slipped her mind to warn him that she had told them to come and get the painting today, at that time . . . Yes, that must be it; he had heard something about a show for first-rate amateurs at the Cuenca Museum, and Marta had simply forgotten to tell him. Naturally, with all the work of moving into the apartment, and Paolo having tantrums when Marta rebelled against his complaints that the color of the towels was just *too* refined . . . and now, suddenly, this gentleman from Cuenca had appeared to collect his painting: yet another surprise, yet another gift from Marta, she always encouraged him in everything. Roberto put on his Italian silk bathrobe, and sat down by the fireplace. After thinking about it for a few minutes, he lit the logs and sat staring at the useless and beautiful fire, remembering the show at Cuenca a couple of years back, where there had been pictures by Tàpies, Millares, Cuixart, Forner, and the goad of his envy, of his desire to emulate them. And now, *he* was going to show at Cuenca too . . . who knows, maybe "Green Atom Number Five" would even be bought for Fernando Zobel's permanent collection . . . of course, he couldn't sell it because it belonged to Marta and he couldn't deprive her of it . . . although maybe in this case she would understand.

But Marta didn't know a thing about it. When she got home and Roberto told her the man had come from the Cuenca Museum, he had to abandon his theory immediately, because Marta had never heard of an amateur show at the Museum of Abstract Art. Everything there was much too professional. Nor had she heard anything about sending a painting of his somewhere . . .

"Really, Roberto, we wouldn't have talked about it just once, we'd have talked about it a thousand times, you know that. And we certainly would have consulted Anselmo."

"Now that you mention it, I think it was one night at Anselmo's that we met a collector who said . . . no, it wasn't a private collector, but the curator of . . ."

"Right, he'd bought a picture from Anselmo."

"You see? Obviously. For an exposition of amateurs at the Museum of Abstract Art in Cuenca."

"It wasn't in Cuenca."

"Well, where was it then?"

"In Palma de Mallorca, I think . . . yes. But it wasn't in the same category as Cuenca."

"Right, it was Palma."

"And it wasn't just a show for amateurs, because, frankly, Anselmo is no mere amateur."

Roberto let a few seconds of cold silence pass, as if a corpse were moving through the room, to give Marta a chance to realize the implications of what she had just said. Then, smoothly, he asked: "And me?"

"You what?"

It pained him to be specific: "Am I a mere amateur?"

She chose her words carefully. "You are a very good amateur."

"But a mere amateur."

Again Marta paused to weigh things. "An amateur. You know that without my having to tell you."

"And my canvases are no better than canvases painted by a mere amateur? . . ."

"Roberto . . ."

". . . a rich dentist who doesn't care for sports, so he spends his free time painting little nothings?" _____

"Roberto . . . please . . ."

". . . by a lowly Philistine who wants to fool himself that he isn't a lowly Philistine, that he too can aspire to the rarefied regions inhabited by the chosen spirits of *real* artists like Anselmo?"

Marta shut her eyes, covered her ears, and shouted "Roberto!"

He had been pacing back and forth in front of the fireplace; now he halted brusquely in front of Marta, inquisitorial, furious:

"Then why in hell did you ask me to give you 'Green Atom Number Five' for our wedding anniversary?"

She stood up and very slowly, like a cat, moved toward him:

"Roberto, listen to me. Those days were so bad, so depressing, remember how you get when you begin to repeat and repeat that nothing has any meaning, that all we ever do is buy things with the money you make from paving the mouths of a herd of rich old cows . . . that you cannot have your life reduced to the satisfaction of being able to send them bills that get higher and higher . . ."

He drew away from her. "Aha! Then your admiration for 'Green Atom Number Five' is a therapeutic one, like gargling with Amosan? . . ."

"Don't say that . . ."

Roberto drew even farther away from her, sitting on the other side of the Marcel Breuer glass table in front of the fireplace.

"Thanks for your charity, Marta."

"But why don't you want to understand? It isn't that I don't like your painting. How can you think that? I love it! But we have to strike a balance somehow . . ."

"That's charity. Thanks." He hesitated a moment before adding, "I understand. Sometimes I've been . . . charitable with you too . . . That's why I don't mind."

As he said this, he looked pointedly at Marta's barren womb, penetrating it as he did the empty room, which now they would never decide to fill with anything. Marta felt the force of that look that pierced her afflicted anatomy with the guilt of fifteen years of pretending it didn't matter at all, that other things were what mattered. She covered her face with her hands, and waited, as she had at other times, for Roberto to come over and embrace her, console her, tell her it was all right, rock her like a little baby because she was a little baby, nothing more, a poor little girl who because she was a little girl couldn't have any little girls of her own, and kiss her like a little girl. . . . But this time Roberto didn't come over: across the cold platform of the Bauhaus table, with its severe accents of a single African sculpture erect in the center and the four piles of magazines under glass paperweights—("If you're going to put out those ghastly Victorian paperweights, at least pretend you're using them as paperweights, otherwise they're terrible," Paolo had said.)—his eyes still contrived to wound her. Marta's hands slipped from her face, traveled the length of her body, and came to rest protectively on her womb. She ran out of the room. Roberto sat down and lit a cigarette. Hearing Marta open and close the front door, he waited a moment. Then he stood up, throwing his cigarette into the fireplace, and said in a low voice:

"Marta?"

Then louder, "Marta?"

He began to look for her everywhere, room by room, repeating "Marta, Marta" in a low voice, knowing he wouldn't find her because she had gone.

Gone?

"Gone" was very different from "gone out." And, of course, she had only gone out . . . after all, at our age and in our position, people don't leave, they just go out . . . Maybe his look had been too hostile, his revenge a little sudden . . . but it wasn't as if she hadn't asked for it. He went into his empty room, turned on the light because the Venetian blinds were lowered, shut the door and sat on the brand-new, shiny, clean parquet floor. Nothing in the whole room: his own space. And *so what*, what if she *had* left and not just gone out? Then he would have the supreme comfort of living without witnesses, of having to account to no one for any monstrosities the mirror might reveal, and he could remain—figuratively speaking, of course—in this empty room without ever having to decide what to do with it. Or even go into it.

He made himself a plate of ham and eggs to appease his hunger, and afterward a cup of coffee. He sipped it, sitting by the dead fire. Never mind what Paolo said, that chimney didn't draw properly; it was a bit of a bore, but it didn't matter that much, since the radiators worked splendidly. What bothered him was the uncomfortable sensation that now nothing in the entire apartment pleased him. The proportions of the table in the center weren't right. The kind of upholstery they had used in the tobacco-colored sofa had a disagreeable slippery quality. The Empire cornucopia, simple as it was, contradicted the significance of everything in the living room. And the same was true of the bedroom. And the vestibule, kitchen, and bath. Finally he shut himself into his empty room again with a slam. Here everything went together perfectly. He sat down on the floor, his back to the wall. His cold had gotten worse. His eyes, especially his eyelids, were throbbing, which produced an intolerable giddiness, and he slipped little by little down onto the shiny parquet floor. It had arrived: "his" sinusitis, violent and vengeful now, making him dizzy.

Marta had gone out. She knew what to give him when he felt like this. Gone out, not *left*. Women didn't leave after a scene, throwing fifteen years of married life in the garbage pail. They simply *went out*, and used the opportunity to buy butter or ham. Afterward they came back with a long face, as in Antonioni's films, as if they had been walking in the rain. Until you comforted them: an embrace, a kiss, wasted words of another reconciliation, breathing that quickened and deepened, hands caressing, the bedroom, the bed that erased everything, then peace, and sleep that erased even more thoroughly.

"Roberto?"

Suddenly the door became a rectangle framing Marta's silhouette. Calling to him. Gone out. She turned on the light. Roberto had been asleep for God knows how long, stretched out on the cold parquet floor with "his" sinusitis. . . .

"I fell asleep."

Marta knelt beside him to help him up, gently support-ing him so he could stand: no, today it wouldn't be necessary to perform the opera of reconciliation.

"But why here?"

"What time is it?"

"Midnight. I called all afternoon and all night, I wanted to talk to you . . . but nobody answered the phone, so I thought you'd gone out to . . ."

Gone out, thought Roberto, not left. We can't leave. Only go out, now and again.

"Here, let me feel you . . . You've got a fever."

"Where have you been?"

"At Paolo's."

"Ah, your personal sob sister."

"Well, he did let me cry. It's nice to have a gay friend to tell your problems to . . ."

"And complain about how perverse husbands are . . ."

"Bad, bad, bad . . . You should have heard the awful things I said about you."

"And he agreed."

"Naturally. Why else would I have cried on his shoulder? And he suggested alternatives . . . lovers . . . friends who would admire me in spite of everything . . ."

"And he's going to spread the word that you're available now?"

They both laughed.

"Come on, let me turn down the covers. Lie down. I'll take your temperature . . . now your pills: that's it, with a little Vichy water . . . Here's a handkerchief with cologne to freshen your forehead."

Yes, it was "his" sinusitis. But this time the fever lasted for a couple of days, and he had an absolutely killing headache. Marta nursed him, but she was uneasy. He tried to hide it from her, but he was depressed, probably a side-effect of the illness that would go away soon. What had happened between them on Sunday wasn't important and besides, they had both forgotten it. While Roberto was in bed, Marta called the porter and asked if he had seen a man on Sunday leave with a painting at such-and-such an hour—No, madam —if he had a brother who looked something like this man— No, madam—and without pressing the matter she asked him to remove the nail and plastic filler from the vestibule wall, plug the hole with a little plaster, and the next day, when the plaster hardened, to cover the small spot with the right paint (there was a little left in the can). That way, when Roberto got out of bed in a couple of days, there wouldn't be a trace of "Green Atom Number Five" or all the discontent it had produced. Evidently, Marta explained to herself, it had been a misunderstanding, somebody got the wrong apartment, wrong building, wrong block. Best to forget the whole thing. Another pointless confrontation of that kind with Roberto, frankly, at their age . . . these scenes didn't accomplish anything. What's unchangeable is best left alone, as she had said to Paolo that Sunday, in his *echt* Bauhaus apartment with cushions all over the floor, drinking orange pekoe tea, watching the rain and telling each other their life stories and problems, as they had done before and—Marta expected—would often do again.

But Marta didn't want Roberto even to think about getting up to go back to work without seeing Anselmo first.

"Woman, I've had sinusitis since I was four years old, ever since the Civil War . . ."

"Never mind."

"And I know how to take care of it. I don't want Anselmo."

Actually, what he didn't want was to hear the doorbell ring. Ever again. Mrs. Presen had her own key because she generally came in the morning before they were awake— and he refused to have any stranger inside the apartment. Marta made some noncommittal answer to avoid one of those silences that had to be filled, and moving the silver candelabrum to one side of the desk, she picked up the telephone and dialed Anselmo's number, over Roberto's protests. After hanging up, she told him that his friend and physician would be there within the hour.

Anselmo was related to Marta. He was a tall, robust man, hairy as a bearskin now that he was letting his hair grow and wore a beard that covered most of his face; what was left was hidden by a pair of glasses with large lenses, so that according to Marta, he had turned his face into pure Dada: spectacles, gray eyes and a frame of hair. In the vestibule, opening the door for him, Marta explained that Roberto wasn't really sick, just a little nervous—no, not nervous, Anselmo, he's been a little neurasthenic, as they used to say, I don't really know why—and she asked him to examine him but above all to keep him company for a little while.

"You do have time, don't you, Anselmo?"

"Sure. Sick people are always careful to wait for the doctor to visit them before they die, that way they can blame it on him."

"Well then. Stay with him for a while. And . . . listen . . ."

She intercepted him again before opening the bedroom door.

"Don't bring up the subject of painting."

"Why?"

"I'll tell you later."

Anselmo examined his patient, said there was nothing wrong with him, not to be so goddam delicate, and why had they dragged him over when Roberto knew perfectly well how to take care of his eternal sinusitis. He demanded a cigarette, lit it, and stretched out at the foot of the double bed, admiring the way the bedroom had turned out, with its antique Catalan commode, the desk that Marta and Roberto both used for urgent business, topped with its telephone and the silver candelabrum, and last the inviting presence of the moss-green chaise longue: "I like bedrooms with chaises longues and dining rooms with a sofa and a coffee table," Paolo had decreed, and thus their dining room had a sofa and coffee table, and their bedroom a chaise longue, "for some night when you quarrel," the decorator insinuated.

Roberto agreed. "Yes, the whole apartment turned out very well."

"I haven't seen it. We have to organize a housewarming."

"We're not up to a housewarming."

Anselmo was about to ask why not, but stopped himself when he remembered Marta's warnings. He felt uncomfortable: although the subjects they could talk about were infinite, the most "natural" was painting, and with the discomfort of knowing this habitual door to communication to be locked, he feared there would be dead silence within ten minutes.

Roberto said, "Would you like to see it?"

"What?"

"The apartment."

This was an opportunity to avoid silence. "Of course."

"Call Marta: she'll show it to you."

"She said she was off to the hairdresser's so as to be decent for tomorrow . . . Remember we're going to *Boris* . . ."

"Oh. Well then, I'll show it to you."

"Don't you have a fever?"

"No, a couple of days ago I was up a few degrees. I've still got some pain, but not much . . ."

He knotted the belt of his silk bathrobe, stepped into his slippers, and grinned when he discovered that he didn't feel any pain at all now when he stood up. He opened the bedroom door so that Anselmo could begin the tour from the vestibule. Anselmo liked everything, particularly the japanned cabinet. He approved of the Empire cornucopia, which took a great weight off Roberto's mind because he had never been sure of it and he had faith in Anselmo's taste. He praised the black idol—Roberto knew perfectly well that it wasn't museum quality, but on the other hand it wasn't one of those bits of trash they sell to tourists on all the cruise boats that stop at Dakar. He admired the color scheme, the transparency of the curtains, everything. Roberto lingered over things because Anselmo showed a lively, civilized interest in them. Although their tastes were very different—Anselmo's fondness for bric-a-brac and his love of Modernism were unacceptable to Roberto, whose taste lay somewhere between Paolo's Bauhaus *dépouillement* and Anselmo's effusive, anecdotal indiscriminateness—it couldn't be denied that Anselmo had imagination and an "eye." Passing the door to the empty room, Roberto was so immersed in explanations that he almost opened it, but stopped himself just in time. He said: "A closet."

"Rather a large closet."

"Yes, too large . . ."

And hurried on to keep Anselmo from opening the door.

In the bedroom, with its night light lit and the rest of the room in semidarkness, warm, protected—outside, it rained and rained—he talked a while longer with Anselmo, until the doctor said he had better rest well if he wanted to go to work in the morning, and to *Boris* that same night . . . he was leaving. Roberto thanked him for his concern, saying that one of the great pleasures of middle age was the loyalty of old friends. He and Marta, Anselmo and Magdalena, were "married friends" who shared, if not everything, then certainly a great deal: the Ferrers were the godparents of the Prietos' latest child, they went together to the movies, to dinner, to the theater, to the Palau. . . . They always had a lot to say to each other, they were always on the same wavelength. Anselmo's placidity complemented Roberto's slightly acerbic irony. Together, Marta and Magdalena went shopping, attended lectures, lunched downtown, and did those mysterious things that women do together while their husbands are working. They went to Los Encants, they caviled at each other as good friends do. They went on diets together to lose weight and compare results, and they fought each other for Paolo's favors. Anselmo gulped down what was left of his whisky and looked around uncertainly for a place to set the glass, finally depositing it on the desk. Saying goodbye, he told Roberto he would ring him early the next morning to find out how he felt. Then he went out, closing the bedroom door and the front door behind him, and Roberto was alone again.

Soon Marta came home and turned on the lights. She made him a light dinner, then got into bed: he read *Los Xuetas en Mallorca* and she read Forster's *Maurice*, and after she made him take one last pill just in case, they turned out the lights and fell asleep.

Next day Roberto woke up with a clear head and no discomfort of any kind, precise and sharp as a knife, eager to work, looking forward to seeing *Boris* that night and even to dressing up in black tie, which he ordinarily detested. When he came home at noon he kissed Marta. He asked her to wear her green sequined dress that night. Oh, she'd planned to wear the black one and Mrs. Presen had it ready for her, but she would go to the bedroom immediately to have a look at the green dress so that Mrs. Presen could take care of it before leaving after she'd washed the lunch dishes.

Roberto was in the dining room, raising the last bite of salad to his lips, when he heard Marta's distraught voice calling him from the bedroom: "Roberto!"

He dropped his fork and ran. He saw her standing speechless next to the desk.

"For God's sake, Marta, what's the matter?"

"The candelabrum . . ."

Roberto didn't understand.

"The candelabrum: it's not here."

"What do you mean, not here?"

"It's gone."

He told her it couldn't be, they would have noticed it before. Who could have taken it? Things don't just *disappear* like that. She was a little absent-minded and careless, not to say disorganized—look at the state of your green dress, a Pertegaz, cost a fortune, and it's the one I like you best in. Surely she must have moved it somewhere when she was straightening up the house that morning.

"I didn't straighten up anything today. Mrs. Presen did."

"Well then, ask her."

Marta didn't budge.

"Aren't you going to ask her?"

Marta bit her lip.

"She might have taken it to the kitchen to polish. Ask her."

"I don't dare."

"Why not?"

"She might be offended, you know what those people are like."

"Don't be silly."

"I'm *not* going to ask her. I don't dare. I have too much respect for that poor woman; there she is at the age of sixty, having to go around doing housework for other people to feed her family and her husband, who they say is a useless drunkard. I don't want her even to suspect I could be insinuating she might have stolen it. No."

"But I'm not saying she stole it, I'm only saying she might have taken it to the kitchen to polish it."

"It wasn't in the kitchen."

"Look, Marta, face the fact that you're terrified that the woman will get angry and leave you, and since it's so hard to get a good cleaning woman these days . . ."

"Don't be an idiot."

"If you're going to scream at me and call me an idiot over a cleaning woman that . . . whom we've barely had a month . . ."

"Can't poor people have feelings too?"

"We hardly know her . . ."

"You make me sick. Insinuating these things about a poor woman . . . You and your apartment, you and your fine period English candelabrum!"

"What do I care about the goddam candlestick!"

At that moment Mrs. Presen appeared, umbrella in hand. She was thin, with tired eyes, wisps of hair escaping from beneath the flowered plastic rainhat with its two blue ribbons tied under her chin. She carried a minuscule bag. The candelabrum could not possibly fit in any nook or cranny of her exiguous person or clothing.

"Will there be anything else, ma'am?"

"No, I don't think so . . ."

"I cleared the table, washed the dishes and left the finger bowls and fruit. The coffee is in the kitchen. Forgive me if I'm in a bit of a rush today—"

"But you're already fifteen minutes over your morning, Mrs. Presen. Don't worry, I'll clean up what's left . . ."

"It's just that I have to go take care of my widowed sister in Viladecans. She's sick in bed with phlebitis, and I have to do her housecleaning because her daughter works at a hotel on the Costa Brava during the summer, and since she wants to get ahead, she's learning French in the wintertime and today's her lesson and she has to leave my poor sister all afternoon. So you don't mind, do you, ma'am, if I didn't wash everything today . . ."

Roberto, placated, said: "Don't worry, Mrs. Presen. You'd better hurry if you want to catch your train . . ."

"Bus. You have to take the bus to get to Viladecans. My niece has a boyfriend with a Fiat Six-Hundred and when they get to my poor sister's house, they'll bring me home in the Six-Hundred. If only you could see what a good girl my niece is, and my niece's boyfriend too. He's . . ."

"See you Monday, Mrs. Presen."

"Yes. See you Monday, sir. See you Monday, ma'am."

"See you Monday, Mrs. Presen. I hope your sister's well. Don't get wet now . . ."

"I won't . . . thank you. Goodbye."

They let her shut the door, and stood there in the vestibule, where "Green Atom Number Five" wasn't (something the two of them knew but preferred to forget), waiting until they heard the little bell that announced the elevator's arrival on the third floor. The bang of the door informed them that poor Mrs. Presen had begun her journey to the nether regions.

"You see?"

"What, Marta?"

"She didn't steal it."

"But I never said she stole it. The only thing I said was that you ought to ask her about it. You were the one who added all the rest."

"But she didn't steal it."

"No, she didn't steal it."

"You say it like someone acknowledging defeat."

Roberto let a moment of silence pass to see if Marta would realize why it really was a defeat, a defeat much more horrible than if they had found the candelabrum hidden under Mrs. Presen's raincoat. But he didn't want to prolong the silence.

"Anselmo," he said.

"Are you crazy?"

"He's the only outside person who's been in the house, apart from Mrs. Presen."

"Call him and ask him, then."

"Are *you* crazy?"

"Aha! You see? Now it's you who's being squeamish. What makes you so afraid of accusing Anselmo, if you really think he's the one who stole it?"

"Are you telling me that you want me to call Anselmo Prieto and ask him if by any chance he stole the silver candelabrum on my desk when he came to see me?"

"Well, where else could it have gone?"

Roberto was about to open his mouth to answer when he realized it already was open and he couldn't answer because he couldn't offer any alternatives. Could Anselmo have stuck it without thinking into his medical kit? Absurd. Nowadays doctors used hard, thin, flat bags; nothing fits in them . . . And furthermore, how could they have been intimate friends all these years without him noticing that Anselmo was a kleptomaniac? Was he so absent-minded that he had thought it belonged to him, that he had confused it with one of his own, that pair they used a little tritely on their dining-room table? Nonsense. One absurd hypothesis followed another in his mind, dizzyingly, one erasing the next, all useless, all impossible, and still he closed his eyes and ears and tried to explain Anselmo's behavior. Finally he rebelled against the supposition he had at first implicitly accepted: that it actually had been Anselmo. He followed Marta into the bedroom without listening to what she was saying and announced: "It wasn't Anselmo."

She turned to face him: "You had no qualms whatever about asking me to confront Mrs. Presen and accuse her of theft, and now you want to stop me from asking your friend . . ."

It wasn't that, it wasn't that. Marta didn't understand anything. She didn't understand the fear, she didn't want to give into it, sink into it, associate two events and have the synthesis surround them with fear. Which was why, with her green sequined dress hanging over her arm, she was dialing Anselmo's number. Roberto couldn't take it. He left the bedroom. He opened the door to his empty room, went inside, shut the door, and flicked the light switch. The light didn't go on.

"Shit. The bulb's burnt out."

He went into the vestibule. He heard the harsh, anguished sound of Marta talking to Anselmo, and while he put on his raincoat and reached for his hat and umbrella, he heard her hang up the receiver. When she came out of the bedroom, she said to him:

"Anselmo's coming over at seven."

"You have it out with him, then."

And he slammed the door behind him.

He rang for the elevator, and it opened at once, as if it had been waiting impatiently to go down. Roberto pressed the ground-floor button: two, one, mezzanine. As the mezzanine light came on he felt an irresistible certainty, and when he got to the ground floor, even before the door opened, he pressed three again, his floor—his beautiful, elegant, civilized floor where everything had been perfect before "Green Atom Number Five," and now the candelabrum, and maybe even the light bulb, had disappeared. Someone had stolen it and that was why he had to go back to his apartment, to prove it—mezzanine, one, two . . . four, five, six, seven. Roberto pressed three again, knowing what was going to happen, what might go on happening forever. Six, five, four . . . two, one, mezzanine. He would never find his floor again. It had disappeared. Along with Marta. Along with all of his things. This time he let the door open on the ground floor and went out. The porter was standing on the sidewalk under the marquee, leaning against a marble pillar while he played with a ballpoint pen, making it work with a clicking noise that irritated Roberto. Didn't he have anything better to do? Roberto barely said hello to him and went out without hearing the porter tell him to take care not to get wet, seeing he had been ill. Roberto had to take a walk: he didn't go downstairs to get his car. What obsessed him was the possibility of going over the edge, something Marta refused to see but he didn't. This prevented him from going too far away from his house; he was afraid of getting lost, and so instead of driving his car God knows where . . . in this infernal weather it was impossible to go anywhere or think about anything, this wind, this damp, this fine rain, this ineffectualness of raincoats, mufflers, gloves . . . It would be better to walk around the block a few times. His fear was turning to certainty: if he crossed a street instead of going round on the same sidewalk until he came to his door, he would never find his house again. But in spite of his precautions, he recognized fewer and fewer of the shops and building fronts. . . . Of course, he wasn't used to his new neighborhood yet. After all, whenever he left the house it was from the underground garage, in his car. . . . But here was the boutique with its neckties hanging from a Thonet rocking chair painted red; there was the pharmacy, but not his house, not his house. It had disappeared. His fears were confirmed. He couldn't go home, he was going to get lost in the city, in the storm, far from all telephones and known addresses, in streets tangled up in the night, multiplied to infinity in the lights refracted by the rain.

After a spell of not recognizing anything, stores or buildings, billboards or trees, when he was about to start running God knows where, it dawned on him that he was getting wet. And at that same instant, the porter was there beside him with an umbrella to shield him, and led him back to his building.

"You oughtn't to get wet, sir."

"Thanks."

When the porter opened the large glass door for him, Roberto turned to thank him again for his kindness, but stopped at the sight of the red door to the elevator. He would have to go up . . . but where? Would he be able to find his floor, all by himself, without help? He hadn't even been able to find his own building without the porter. Would he float from floor to floor in the elevator, skipping from two to four, now that three didn't exist, the lights lighting up and the bell ringing at every floor that wasn't his own, assaulting his ears for all eternity?

No. He could not let this happen. Taking advantage of the porter, who was following him closely, keeping an eye on him, he tottered a little. The porter responded to the stimulus: "Don't you feel well, sir?"

"No."

"Shall I accompany you to your floor, sir?"

Exactly. How well-trained these service people were! The porter went into the elevator with Roberto and pressed the red button labeled three: mezzanine, one, two . . . and then, miraculously, three! The door opened as usual, obeying the porter because, after all, in addition to being a doorman, at times he had to serve as an elevator boy, and he knew his job. He helped Roberto out gently, as if leaving the car were an operation of the utmost difficulty. Roberto leaned on him all the way to his apartment door while he took out his key. When he had the key in his hand, again he said, "Thanks."

He perceived from the porter's face that he had disillusioned, even wounded him. Doubtless he had been expecting a scene with telephone calls and ambulances, which he could afterward describe to his wife at the dinner table as the high point of his day, over their chickpeas and wine. But no, Roberto said to himself, you can't worry about whether or not you've hurt a porter's feelings. "Watch out," he warned, "the elevator may leave."

He watched the porter retreat. Just before the door closed, swallowing the man who had found him in the storm, Roberto put the key in the lock and said, "Good night. And thanks again."

He opened the door and went inside. Hearing him come in, Marta hurried to meet him, no doubt expecting a scene of reconciliation, of dialogue, even tenderness, perhaps. But he wasn't in the mood for any nonsense now. There were much greater terrors to quell. Without explaining or saying hello, barely glancing at her, he went straight to the empty room, and she followed without a word. The green sequined dress she was readying for the evening to please him was hanging over her arm—if Marta thought *he* was going to *Boris* that night, and with Anselmo and Magdalena, she was *very* mistaken—and she had a needle with green thread in her hand. Roberto opened the door to the empty room. He pressed the light switch. The light didn't go on. Behind his shoulder Marta murmured, "The bulb's burned out."

"No."

"What do you mean, no?"

"Bring me the flashlight from the upper left-hand drawer in the desk."

"But why?"

"Go on, I tell you!"

His voice was troubled, irritated, peremptory. She couldn't see his face, only his shoulders, the wet raincoat, the turned-up collar, his hat in one hand, the other flicking the light hysterically. With a kind of everyday boldness that seemed to Roberto completely inappropriate at that moment, Marta hung the green dress over his outstretched arm (the one whose hand was flicking the light switch), and went to the bedroom to look for the flashlight. When she came back she saw that Roberto hadn't budged; everything was the same, shoulders, raincoat, hat, arm draped with the green gauze dress fluttering hysterically as he tried to force the switch to work even though he was convinced that it couldn't. Without turning around, he said, "Give me the flashlight."

He held out his hand mechanically, like a surgeon asking his nurse to pass him a pair of forceps. He turned on the flashlight. Marta, over Roberto's shoulder, watched the ray of light penetrating the darkness. The ray slowly moved up the naked walls. Moving, vibrating, the ray searched: it halted right in the center of the ceiling, on the short wire that curled up on itself and ended in a gilded socket and a bulb. Except the bulb wasn't there. Roberto, as if flabbergasted, switched off the flashlight and remained mute, staring into the vast darkness of the empty room. After a moment, he said:

"You see?"

Marta, behind him, asked softly: "Who could have removed it?"

Roberto turned to look at her, hating her for penetrating the fear with him and accepting it, and when Marta tried to relieve him of the green sequined dress, he yanked it away from her, tearing it. Some sequins scattered across the floor.

"Roberto . . ."

The doorbell rang. As if it were bringing the answer to all the questions that they didn't even know how to begin phrasing in their minds, they both ran to the vestibule, Roberto with the green dress vomiting sequins in one hand, his hat in the other, and Marta behind him with the threaded needle in one hand and the flashlight in the other. Thus they opened the door.

Four placid, unanimous, perfectly coordinated smiles offered a world of security to the terrified eyes of Marta Mora and Roberto Ferrer. Farthest away were two clearly identical tall, thin women in raincoats, hair cropped very short, so well-washed that their pores and veins were meticulously sketched on the everyday ugliness of their faces. But Roberto registered the fact that the one on the left, though she might look like a provincial notary's clerk, had a certain mistaken notion of what was sexy: from her earlobes hung gold-plated gypsylike earrings that contradicted the puritanical austerity of the rest of her attire. In front of them were two men, much shorter, and fat as armchairs, also perfectly matched, except that the one below the woman without the earrings was bald, and in the middle of his bald head he had a fat mole like a beetle that might have crawled up there to install itself on his polished pristinity. Simultaneously the four of them chanted, "Good afternoon."

These four polite voices in unison produced the effect of an organ, and Roberto, who had a very fine ear, at once perceived that the registers of the four voices were different, like those of a group well trained to sing as a church quartet. Their "Good afternoon" was the note hummed before launching into harmony. Something gave him a certain respect for these four grotesques, and as he responded with a "Good afternoon" which he was unable to charge with any warmth, he stepped back with his hand still on the latch, opening the door wider. He stepped back because the man without the beetle on his cranium exhaled that unpleasant mouth odor that, as a dentist, he recognized as the result of slow digestion. The quartet, as if accepting a tacit invitation, stepped into the vestibule.

Horrified, Roberto watched Marta close the door behind them. Four umbrellas gushed onto the carpet. Sequins crackled underfoot. And there they stood, differently aligned: short man, tall woman; another short man, another tall woman. All four carried old-fashioned brown leather portfolios, packed so full that they looked like the bellies of pregnant bitches full of puppies. They smiled their unanimous smiles. The beetle seemed to have climbed higher on the bald man's head, and the earrings belonging to the lay nun, whose eyes rendered everything urgent, tinkled lightly. This woman, tilting her head slightly to peer through the half-open living-room door, whispered:

"What a beautiful apartment."

High soprano, said Roberto to himself. The owners of the house thanked her for the compliment. The beetle man, a baritone, said:

"Might we speak with you for a moment?"

Marta and Roberto wanted to know what it was about. In answer, all four characters, voices in harmony, organized a kind of fugue of questions, gentle, polite, heavenly, like a village choir.

"Have you opened your heart to the word of Jesus?"

"Don't you feel the moment has come to repent of your sins?"

"Have you taken care of your immortal soul?"

"Why don't you let the Lord touch you?"

"Immortal soul" was the light soprano with the dangling earrings, who apparently asked her question without concentrating fully on its mystical content. With the tip of her shoe she had opened the living-room door, and had managed to wedge half of her body inside, her hungry, curious eyes rifling that civilized room, with its beautiful colors licked by the glow from the fireplace. Marta saw. She saw how the woman inserted herself inch by inch—while their voices continued to produce the fugue of mystical questions on salvation and the immortal soul. At last her entire body stood inside the living room, and now, inch by inch, the others too, as if they were little wooden ducks she was towing on a string, slowly followed her in.

The tenor who smelled of mouth asked, "Do you allow the word of God to guide each of your steps?"

And the contralto who looked like Ana Pauker: "Do you bear in your breast the thorn of repentance?"

Roberto stood there with his hat in one hand and, in the other, the torn dress, which had begun uncontrollably to vomit green glass beads onto the floor. His only wish was to get these scarecrows out of his house so he could sweep up and save not his soul (which he didn't care about) but the floor. He opened his arms and shrugged, saying, "Look, I don't know . . . frankly . . ."

But even as he said it, the man with the beetle on his head took a step forward and, with intense humility and an apostolic expression, implored more than asked: "Could we not talk quietly with you for a few minutes? It's obvious you're simple people, perhaps you have suffered a great deal, you are good parents who seek refuge against the inclemencies of contemporary life, which is as polluted as the air we breathe . . ."

In the face of such humility, in the face of such an original conception of the two of them, Marta and Roberto, whose mindless good manners made them incapable of denying hospitality to anyone who might request it, could not refrain from saying: "Would you like to step into the living room for a minute?"

The file of little wooden ducks followed the woman with the gypsy earrings and distributed themselves around the living room, sitting on the tobacco-colored sofa, the Le Corbusier armchairs, the pouf, then around the glass coffee table in front of the burning fire. Marta offered them something to drink. The man who smelled of slow digestion answered for all of them, offended:

"We *never* drink alcohol. It is one of the surest paths to perdition, moral as well as physical. Our bodies, just as much as our souls, belong to God."

Marta, chastened, sat down again. "I'm so sorry, I didn't mean . . ."

The light soprano was looking at everything. She twisted her head to try to "understand"—Understand! said Roberto to himself—the Tàpies to the left of the fireplace, and stretched her neck to give her stringy hair a futile primping in the reflection of the cornucopia. Then her gaze passed around the corners of the glass table and over the magazines flattened by the four Victorian paperweights to collide with the African idol, so obviously erect. The lady with the earrings elbowed the Ana Pauker lady—the grayer of the two, the one with the most beatific, ineffaceable smile of all —and pointed with her chin at the idol, which by African-idol standards was not so very outstanding. Ana Pauker's apparently indelible smile disappeared, and her face turned scarlet. At her companion's blush, the gypsy-earring lady's smile also disappeared; before that, she hadn't seemed to have encountered any definitive offense to her modesty. But Ana Pauker's indignation transmitted itself immediately, and the two ladies sat side by side on the tobacco-colored sofa, rigid and serious and red, their faces turned toward the fireplace to avoid the inhabitant of the glass table. Across from them, in an armchair set somewhat apart, sat Roberto with his hat on, because he didn't know what to do with it or anything else, as he clung to the green dress as if to keep it from shedding more green glass beads on the living-room floor. He seemed flattened, erased. Seeing him, Marta took over the task of keeping up their end of the conversation. The two men, the one with bad breath and the one with the beetle crawling up his pate in a hopeless quest for the summit, spoke of cleansing oneself from sin by means of repentance and pain, by the word of Jesus. They began to open their pregnant portfolios, giving birth to books which they offered to Marta. She, without looking at the books, gently rejected them, trying not to hurt their feelings. . . . I'm not interested, I'm not interested in anything you're saying, I'm sorry . . . Meanwhile, the beetle-man made a sign to the two women and, in obedience to the order, they also began to open their portfolios and drag out books. The earring-lady, smiling now, held out a volume to Roberto. Faced at last with a frontal attack, he reacted. Rising from his chair and brandishing the dress that still spewed its inexhaustible stream of sequins, he shouted:

"Enough! Enough! Marta, get them out of here! I can't stand these people! They don't even have the rudiments of sensitivity to realize what kind of people we are. They don't have any business here . . . Enough . . . I can't take anymore . . ."

"All right, Roberto, they're leaving. "

Roberto let himself fall back into the big armchair beside the fire, and the visitors, bearers of the word of God, but terrified, stopped smiling and humbly began to repack their portfolios with the books with which they proposed to spread the truth. Then each of them took one of the glass paperweights and stuck it inside his portfolio with the same naturalness and coordination there would have been if they had taken them out with their books. Marta and Roberto watched them do it. They knew perfectly well what they were doing: taking the paperweights. But seeing them hastily close their portfolios and stand up, so flustered, so meek, so ingenuous, so well-intentioned, they were speechless. All they could do was escort them across the floor that crackled with little green glass beads, let the impossible happen, follow them to the door treading on the sequins themselves, hastily say goodbye, let them go, and close the door behind them.

Marta came almost running back to Roberto, who had let himself fall corpselike into the armchair beside the fireplace. She took off his hat, but when she tried to disengage him from the green dress, he stood up as if someone had pressed a button. Yanking the dress back from Marta, which only widened the tear, he strewed the entire living room with green beads by throwing it into the fireplace.

"Are you aware that those people have stolen four paperweights right under our very eyes?" he shouted.

"Yes . . ."

"And you're just standing there?"

" . . . "

"Are you aware that they're stripping us?"

"Who are?"

"The light bulb . . . the candelabrum . . . I don't know . . ."

"They can't all be the same people."

"Don't be an idiot."

"Frankly, I'm not in the mood to put up with your insults. Is this the only way you can react? Why did you throw my green dress in the fire?"

"Do you really want to know?"

"Yes!"

"Because I FELT LIKE IT."

The last phrase was shouted with all the strength Roberto had in his lungs. But Marta moved over beside him and threw his hat, which she had been holding all this time, into the fireplace.

"I'm going," she said.

"To Paolo's?"

"That's my business."

"Then go."

But as she went toward the door, the hundreds, the thousands of sequins, pearls, and glass beads crunched under her feet, shattering to powder on the beige floor, which was permanently damaged. When she realized what she was doing, Marta stopped.

"Good God, look what's happening to the floor!"

"What are we going to do?"

"Try not to step on . . ."

"Look, over here there are less . . ."

"Go get a broom."

"No, the vacuum cleaner."

"They were supposed to deliver it more than a week ago, but they didn't. You know how casual those household appliance people are. They think you . . ."

Roberto shook a few sequins off the sofa, as if he didn't have strength to do anything more than sit down again. But he didn't get to sit down because Marta said:

"Don't sit down, we're going."

"Where?"

"We're not going to stay here without doing anything."

"No."

And as she handed another hat to Roberto, put on her raincoat and picked up her umbrella, she muttered:

"What cynicism . . . thieves . . . right before our very eyes, as if they had the *right* to take them . . . send them to prison . . . we must call the police . . . frankly . . ."

"They must be downstairs by now."

But it wasn't a case for the police, Roberto was sure of that. Women always take care of everything with the telephone—the police, the household appliances—and yet, they had to get help, they had to believe they would be able to find the culprits, because otherwise one might begin to think; and indignation, protest, anger were preferable to thinking. They left, trying to step on as few sequins as possible, but even out in the hall the ones that had stuck to the soles of their shoes kept on crunching.

On the street, it had ceased raining for some time and in the cloudless sky greenish galaxies shone mockingly, millions of tiny stars strewn around the heavens. Somehow, Marta thought, this is all Roberto's fault, and although she could not organize all the pieces of her hostility toward him into any coherent form, she could perceive the odious silhouette of her rancor: yes, there was her husband, looking like a hunting dog on the trail of the thieves, sniffing the sidewalks near their building, the known streets, the everyday stores that were closing now. She let herself be dragged along by this Roberto who couldn't stand to have anyone violate the sanctity of his apartment, who was in love with his objects, imprisoned by them, dependent on them. In a word, contemptible. He hadn't even had the strength to react at the moment when, right before his eyes, four absurd characters had stolen his adored Victorian glass paperweights. Oh yes, Roberto was so sensitive. But strength? Where was his strength? There was a good reason for his being a second-rate painter even among amateurs, third-rate even, barely in good taste or decorative—white, black, brown, beige, gray: all trite, and when you came right down to it, "Green Atom Number Five" was a dreadful painting. It was lucky it had disappeared from the vestibule, because to tell the truth, it spoiled the whole apartment.

"They've disappeared," Roberto mumbled.

The words exploded in Marta's consciousness as fear. But she said nothing.

"Disappeared. Everything disappeared."

"But Roberto, you know what robberies are like these days. Yesterday, in the paper . . ."

With an irritated movement that the people passing them in the street couldn't fail to notice, he let go of his wife's arm. Household appliances, police, phone calls . . . now the newspaper. Women! Stupid, the lot of them. Including Marta. The fact that the household appliance people don't come allows them to avoid the truth behind the fact. One day he would confront her with the whole truth: the empty room waiting for him. For now he confronted her with at least part of it: this affair had nothing whatever to do with police or household appliances. Things disappeared. They weren't robberies. Or rather they were robberies that were not robberies. Yes, things disappeared even though the agents might be four Seventh-Day Adventists, Mrs. Presen, Anselmo, the nonexistent brother—yes, nonexistent—of the porter . . . but Marta ought to face up once and for all to the fact that they were not robberies. They were something else.

Marta walked a little apart from Roberto, almost on the curb, doubtless conscious of what he was feeling toward her, because that was something all women have, antennae of astounding sensitivity that detect each tiny change in what men feel toward them . . . but that's all they're good for. In everything else, they are idiots, incorrigible idiots.

"We're not going to accomplish anything by looking for them," he said.

"You shouldn't lose hope like that, Roberto."

"We're getting farther away from the house." Saying that, Roberto stopped on the sidewalk, frozen. Moving over to his wife and gently taking her arm, he murmured:

"Wait."

"What?"

"Look."

"What?"

"Over there on the corner, in front . . ."

At the curb they saw a shabby truck parked, with a sign saying SWALLOW TRANSPORT painted on the side. The rear gate was open, serving as a ramp for the loaders. And at that very moment, two men on the ramp, with great care and effort, were loading the large vertical japanned cabinet that adorned the vestibule in the apartment belonging to Marta Mora and Roberto Ferrer, and which had once been Marta's mother's: a stupendous piece which the previous

generation had not known how to appreciate. They watched
—sadly, powerlessly—as the men loaded it. Then they
watched them come back down the ramp, close the rear
gate, and climb into the cab. The truck's motor started up.

"Come on . . . let's go . . . before they get away!" said
Marta.

"What do you mean to do?"

"Ask them . . ."

"What?"

"My mother's japanned cabinet . . ."

"Your mother's?"

"Well, ours. They're taking it. Run!"

"You run!"

"My mother's": she, the little girl who didn't want to
have children so she wouldn't have to stop being a child,
threw herself howling into the stream of cars while Swallow
Transport moved off. She, Marta, ran along the avenue
shouting, "Stop! Stop!"

The lights glinted off the wet street, yellow, red, blinding. She ran between the cars shouting "Stop, stop," as if they
were driving away with her soul.

"Marta!"

A passing car grazed her and knocked her down. A vortex
of cars eddied about her, people crowded around, fascinated
by the accident that had happened under the cold sky and
the prismatic lights, whistles summoning, people running to
the telephone while the body was borne to the sidewalk.
"Nothing. It's nothing," they assured Roberto. She's only
fainted, and her little finger is bleeding. It was the lady's
fault, she ran across the traffic in the middle of the block, so
legally there was nothing to be done. It was her fault; she's
coming round now. She groans. Her little finger must be
giving her pain, says Roberto. What if there's internal
damage? Get her to the hospital, to San Pablo Hospital. Yes,
right away, there won't be any internal damage. To the
emergency ward. But at the emergency ward they discovered that Marta Mora had suffered nothing more than

slight bruises, and really the only thing was . . . well, it wasn't serious, it was just a nuisance, it was that the last joint of the left little finger had been smashed. It would be necessary to operate immediately, not a serious operation at all, really, but it was essential to amputate the last joint of her little finger.

Afterwards, Roberto commented: "This will be horrible for my poor wife."

The doctor raised his eyebrows; this was hardly a common remark for a husband to make about a wife who had suffered a street accident.

"I'm sure the manicurist will give me a discount for nine fingers instead of the usual ten . . ."

Neither Roberto nor the doctor had realized that Marta, although groggy, had come out of the anaesthesia. They looked at her in surprise. Roberto kissed her and she kissed him back, complaining that it hurt quite a lot. The doctor said that the pain would disappear and there would be no complications of any kind. Roberto arranged for a room with two beds at the hospital, one for her and the other for himself, because he intended to keep her company night and day. Although the injury was inconsequential, she ought to remain in the hospital a few days for observation, and he wanted to stay with her. At the patient's bedside, Roberto asked the doctor, who was taking her pulse on the other side:

"What did you do with the joint you cut off?"

Astonished, the doctor looked at him: "You're a dentist, you ought to know what we do with these things . . . They're taken away . . ."

Roberto slept as heavily as Marta under sedation. The next day he woke up early. He phoned a colleague to take care of his emergency work for a couple of days, and asked his secretary to cancel his appointments. His intention was to stay close to Marta every moment, not to go back to the apartment, to send out for everything, even the clothes he would need. When the doctor left, she said:

"They removed part of me."

"Just a little piece."

"Let's go."

"Where?"

"To the apart . . ."

"What if . . . ?"

They spent the day talking in broken phrases, watching through the wide window of her hospital room as it rained on the trees, stripped and hard as steel, on the landscape of the hospital buildings, on the stunted cars, shiny as beetles near the entrance. The second day, the doctor announced that Marta could go home that afternoon. When he left the room, she looked at Roberto with tear-filled eyes, saying:

"What if it isn't there?"

Roberto moved his head slightly, signifying he didn't know precisely what. Her fear that she wouldn't find her mother's japanned cabinet in the vestibule was nothing compared with his own, much greater fear. When she said she was too weak to leave that day, Roberto felt the relief of a benign, merciful deferment: but that night, thinking about the day to come, neither of them slept. They listened to the hysterical sirens of the ambulances that penetrated the night with their terror, bringing or removing unknown sick people, victims of unknown accidents or unknown illnesses, from unknown places in the immense, harsh city which also could not sleep or rest. The next day, when the doctor told them they had to leave because the hospital was very short of rooms and Marta was perfectly all right, Roberto protested that his wife was too weak, she had hardly slept all night. The doctor said, "Do you have your car here?"

"No . . ."

Even if they did have it, would they find the house? Might not the number have disappeared? Might not *they* have taken it, along with everything else, and he and Marta would keep going round and round in the car through the city streets looking for a street number where once they had installed their definitive apartment, which now no longer existed? Searching and searching for it, going around the block to the point of exhaustion, of old age, side by side in the front seat of the car, decaying while time passed and the city grew and changed, perhaps even dying without finding the number? Marta must have been feeling the same thing because she said to the doctor:

"It's odd . . . I'm so exhausted that I don't think I could stand on my own two feet for a minute . . . I couldn't walk . . ."

The doctor provided the solution that both were looking for:

"Well, then, an ambulance. An ambulance will take you."

Giving the street and number, delegating the responsibility for finding the address to the driver: that was peace. They could even protest if he was slow to find it in that neighborhood of new, short streets. Roberto climbed into the ambulance with Marta. He took her hand. The ambulance started off—siren wailing, violent, aggressive, insistent, moving through red lights, leaving expressions of commiseration on the faces of passers-by, police deceived by the false emergency—but carrying Marta and Roberto safely protected inside; and the main part of that protection was the driver's duty to find the address he had been given.

At last the ambulance came to a halt. The orderly covered Marta's face with the sheet and he and another orderly lowered her from the ambulance. Behind them, out of the ambulance window, Roberto saw the porter run solicitously out of the building. He and his wife made a great to-do around the patient, turning on useless lights, helping, participating, escorting the orderlies as they walked up the stairs to the third floor. The porter said to Roberto:

"You go up in the elevator, Don Roberto."

Roberto said he preferred to follow them up. They should go ahead of him with the porter leading the way. He gave him the apartment key. They opened the door and went as far as the bedroom without uncovering Marta's face. In the vestibule, Roberto desperately wanted to have his face covered in place of Marta's, for then he would not have had to see what he now saw . . . or rather, didn't see: yes, they had taken the japanned cabinet.

The extraneous people left, closing the door and leaving the two of them alone in the new apartment. New, yes, but lacking the candelabrum, the japanned cabinet, the paper-weights, and the last joint of Marta's little finger . . . lacking so many things. Marta lay in bed with her eyes closed. Although he knew she wasn't asleep, Roberto tiptoed over to the desk and reached into the upper left-hand drawer for the flashlight to go to the empty room and see if it actually was still empty. The flashlight wasn't there. Marta had hidden it. Or misplaced it. Marta was so careless, and in an avalanche of rancor there rushed into his mind the detritus of all the things that had been ruined owing to Marta's care-lessness, her thoughtlessness, since she never thought about anything except herself despite all the outward show that he meant everything to her. Hateful, hateful and cowardly, pretending she was asleep in bed so as not to have to face the responsibility (disagreeable, to be sure) of verifying with her own eyes that during her absence some things, maybe many, had disappeared. He thought to shout this at her. But what did Marta matter? He closed his mouth. Why talk? Accept. Don't mention the affair again. Live as if none of this had happened and was only part of the natural course of things and wasn't worth the effort of trying to change it. But one thing ought to be made clear: if anyone was to blame for everything that was happening, it was Marta, not he. Yes, to take an example: Marta could very easily get out of bed and keep him company. Her duty—since she hadn't been able to give him children—was precisely not to leave him alone. But she was, above all, a "child" and stayed in bed when she wasn't even sick because she knew he was keeping watch. Not to talk, not to lose sleep over it. Accept, no more. Turn one's back on events and maybe that way, by ignoring them, avert them.

Roberto said softly, "Marta."

"M m m m m m m m . . ."

"How do you feel?"

"Okay, it seems."

"Are you going to spend the day in bed?"

"I don't know . . ."

But how to spend one's entire day—one's entire life—not knowing, not touching oneself or anything, not seeing, just the two of them in this apartment that was wide open for people to come in and take things?

"Where's the flashlight, Marta?"

"Where it always is."

It wasn't there. She wanted to keep him from going to the empty room, now that he needed to lock himself up in there forever. Marta had removed it to hide it. When he threw this in her face, she opened her enormous eyes, sunk in her ravaged face, and sat up in bed.

"No, I did *not* take it. Don't blame me for everything. You're not perfect, Roberto. These things aren't my fault, they're yours; you're an egotistical bastard like all men, yes, you are. Take the japanned cabinet, for instance: it belonged to my mother, and so when you saw two men putting it on a truck you didn't budge, and you let me go after it. And *I* got run over . . . and it was *my* little finger. Yes, you took it away from me, it's your fault, you egotistical bastard. Now if the japanned cabinet had been *your* parents', imagine how you'd have run and screamed, just imagine . . ."

"Calm down."

"I don't feel like calming down."

The telephone rang and Marta fell back into the pillows, sobbing. It was Anselmo. He was somewhat upset. They had disappeared for days without a word, and on Friday had left them with the tickets to *Boris*. But actually they hadn't missed anything, it was a *Boris* like any other *Boris*, nothing to write home about. Marta sat up among the pillows. She whispered:

"Tell Anselmo to bring Magdalena over this evening for drinks."

Roberto conveyed the invitation, and when he hung up

he said they'd accepted. Marta asked him to call Mrs. Presen to come and cope.

At the scent of tragedy, Mrs. Presen dropped whatever she was doing and came running, teary-eyed and unselfish, to do the few chores in the house. She prepared a light lunch, served it, and left a roast for dinner, some cheese cut up in cubes, potato chips, and olives in bowls so that ma'am wouldn't have to lift a finger when her guests came in the evening. When she said goodbye to Marta, who had put on a comfortable gown to wander around the house in, Mrs. Presen was carrying a package wrapped in newspaper under her arm. Mrs. Presen saw Marta eyeing the package, which was not small, and in answer to the question which Marta had not dared to ask, she explained:

"I'm taking the Waring blender, ma'am. If you only knew how much I've been needing one! They say you can make mayonnaise with one egg, a little salt and some oil, and it turns out much better than store-bought, and you don't have to stand there beating it with a fork till your arm falls off. I'm not young anymore, you know. Well, I'm glad nothing's wrong with you, ma'am, and you're in such good spirits. Tomorrow's Sunday, so I won't be in. Goodbye, now . . ."

Marta felt there was something final about Mrs. Presen's goodbye. And something contemptuous, which she had never noticed before. Was it perhaps because she let her take the Waring blender without protest, not raising her voice or rebelling? Did she feel so much contempt for her that she preferred not to come back and work for her again?

When Roberto heard the door close behind Mrs. Presen he appeared in the vestibule.

"What did she take?"

"The Waring blender."

"The new one?"

"I suppose so. I didn't see it. But I can't imagine why she'd take the old one when the new one was right there in front of her."

"Of course."

Roberto lit a cigarette. As he did so, Marta could read all the suppositions passing through her husband's troubled eyes: Mrs. Presen had stolen the candelabrum; she and her miserable family were the ones who were taking one thing after another . . . for example, now that he thought about it, the Seventh-Day Adventist who looked like Ana Pauker also looked extraordinarily like Mrs. Presen; she could be her daughter or that niece who worked on the Costa Brava and was learning French; the other Seventh-Day Adventists could be wives or husbands, uncles, nephews; the Swallow Transport men were some other relatives, the man who ran over Marta's little finger might be the niece's boyfriend with the Fiat 600—and all of them could be related to the porter, who, if you looked into it, would probably turn out to have not just one brother but half a dozen plus respective children and sons- and daughters-in-law, all poverty-stricken, all related to the likewise poverty-stricken family of Mrs. Presen; yes, yes, that was why the porter had kept quiet about the comings and goings of the culprits. Poor people have a lot of family loyalty, everybody knows that, and on Sundays they get together and eat lots of fried food seasoned with garlic and onions on tables stained with olive oil, lots of snotty-nosed kids crying, and they set off on reconnoitering expeditions in Fiat 600s, crammed to the roof . . . yes, yes . . . and it was during those terrible boisterous family gatherings, at those Sunday dinners with roasts drowning in grease, that they made these plans to have things disappear. . . .

No, they weren't robberies. And it wasn't them. That night, when Anselmo and Magdalena came—they who were related neither to the porter nor to Mrs. Presen—they took something too. Anselmo took a Saura lithograph. Magdalena took a cream to keep freckles from coming out on your hands. Anselmo simply said: "I like this Saura very much," and took it down off the wall. Magdalena simply said: "I need a cream like this and it's impossible to get it anywhere but in Andorra, so I'm taking it."

Marta and Roberto didn't say a word. And the next day

they didn't go out; it was Sunday. Monday Roberto called his secretary to cancel all appointments of any kind, indefinitely. Mrs. Presen, as predicted, did not appear. If she *had* appeared, they wouldn't have let her in. They weren't going to let anybody in. By phone, Paolo announced he was coming over next Sunday, saying he wanted to check whether the African idol was as good as he thought or better: probably better. . . . An intimate friend of his had just arrived from Brussels, a very well-known dealer in that class of objects—they had probably seen his ads in *L'Oeil*—and would they let him come round and give a little kiss to poor Marta and pick up the idol to have his friend appraise it. . . . No, they wouldn't: they didn't feel well. Nothing, it was nothing, he shouldn't get alarmed, they were just a bit out of sorts, that's all, they'd call him next week to dine together and have a long chat. But during the week the gas went off and they didn't call anybody to fix it, not even the porter, who was so willing to do odd jobs like that and understood those things so well. When the porter came up, it was to pass them bread, meat, wine, fruit, cheese, things to eat, through a crack in the door. The garbage was rotting. The plates were piling up unwashed in the poisonous dishwasher, and the smell of dirty dishes was pervading the new apartment, which by now was messy and not so new. Open magazines were scattered around on armchairs. Crushed green sequins stuck to the soles of their slippers, squeaky and abrasive and getting ground-in everywhere. The bed was never made. Clothes were strewn on the floor. But they didn't call anybody to do the work. Except for food, they wouldn't even open the door: it could be dangerous.

To think that the new apartment had never really been finished! They had never hung "Green Atom Number Five." Or rather, it had been hanging for a while that first morning before the first time something was taken . . . the painting, in fact. But it had been such a short time and he hadn't shared it with Marta, and its taste had dissipated in his mind as if it had never existed: the keystone in the arch had not been in place long enough to prevent the whole thing from collapsing. Only the empty room remained untouched, solider than all the rest. And while Marta busied herself in the apartment with the trifling feminine chores with which now she no longer even attempted to simulate order, Roberto shut himself up inside the empty room, inside that perfect space, memorizing it as if he feared they would come to take away its proportions and purity too; he tried to internalize it, leaving his mind blank so that its angles, its closed window, its shiny parquet, its light fixture in the center of the ceiling would take possession of his entire being and belong to him. . . . Day after day he sat on the floor; day after day he kept watch.

Of course, after fifteen years of married life they didn't really have things that belonged to *him* as opposed to things that belonged to *her*. That was the problem: in their long years of cohabitation, they had confused their boundaries in the name of so much consideration and so many positive feelings that now neither of them had anything of their own. Never emptying the ash trays or getting dressed, Marta sat smoking beside the fireplace, in which she never managed to get a decent fire burning, remembering the thousand ways Roberto had frustrated her, without ever leaving her anything really her own. Even "Green Atom Number Five": she was convinced that there had been a conspiracy between her husband and Anselmo to get rid of his "masterpiece," which, when you came right down to it, embarrassed him. That was why she hadn't wanted the emerald from Roca's: it was something so expensive, so magnificent, that it would never really have been hers: rather it would have been a part of the patrimony. Buying it was no more than a way to keep another several thousand pesetas in the bank, and it wouldn't really be hers; indeed *nothing* was really hers; even her little affair with Paolo was soured by Roberto's endless sarcasm which kept her from enjoying the make-believe. And with an audacity that she would never have given him credit for, he had even managed, somehow, to dispossess her of the last joint of her little finger. What was left, to be frank, was an ugly little stump: it was as if, under Roberto's pressure, she had begun definitively to disappear.

Roberto, locked inside his empty room, didn't know what his wife was up to in the rest of the apartment, and didn't care; the important thing was that she should not encroach on him, she should not trespass on his space the way she had always trespassed on everything else of his. Sometimes he sensed her going through the house at night with a flash-light in her hand: it was as if she would wake up in the middle of the night and make the rounds, to see if other things had disappeared without her noticing. . . . Or was she racking her brains to find something that still belonged to him, something she had not participated in, to steal it or destroy it and thereby achieve a fixed line separating her from him, and him—he who needed it so much—from her? They barely spoke to each other. What interchange could there be if they could only interchange the same things? But they hovered round each other, keeping watch with dry, cold hearts, and now they didn't want or need or remember anybody except themselves. They told people they were going on a cruise to escape the worst of winter, while in fact they were obsessively engaged in searching for something—another little finger—to take possession of in the other: but it *had* to belong definitively to the other.

One afternoon, alone and cold, Roberto was rummaging through their desk when he found an odd slip of yellowed paper, its edges wrinkled and fuzzy. GREEN ATOM NUMBER FIVE, it said, and gave an address: Pound-Ounces—the street —number 204. He shouted for Marta to come. Together, they examined the paper. They didn't recognize the hand-writing, although it somewhat resembled Roberto's. Neither of them could remember why the paper should be there, or what it meant. Roberto's fists clenched. After days of not speaking to her, he felt he held the skein of the whole prob-lem in his hand and said: "It might be worth it to go and see."

He watched her with riveted eyes to catch her reaction, and she understood and reacted immediately. Her face cleared and set determinedly when he insisted:

"The painting belongs to you."

"Yes. *My* painting . . ."

With the prospect of recovering something—the hope of rebuilding the entire edifice of civilization and form they had lost—a complicity immediately established itself between the two of them: a détente, one of so many in their relationship, but the first in a long time. Together, the two of them went into the bathroom, combed their hair, got dressed, and then, because it was rather cold, they both put on all-weather coats. For an instant, in the vestibule, they dreamed of what it would look like when they came home, when they had recovered everything they had lost—a dream of the peace and rest provided by the language of loved objects which serve as bridges to communication, as masks that protect against the hostile nakedness in which they had been living for so many days. But as he opened the door, Roberto held it half ajar for a few seconds, and the fresh air that came through the crack, up from the stairwell into the hall, made him hesitate. Looking at Marta, who took his arm as if imploring him not to go out, he saw that at last she too was beginning to recognize the existence of a fear beyond the control of the police, newspapers, even little men from the household appliance company. This irritated him. Brusquely he freed his arm and snapped:

"Don't be silly."

Was she feeling it too, then? Was she capable of being afraid that one day (like today) a middle-aged couple (like them) could go out for a short walk and on their return be unable to find their house? . . . That it might disappear? Weren't Marta's fears more immediate: Waring blender, paperweights, candelabrum? . . . No, the terror *he* felt, that soon they might strip him of . . . of North, South, East, West—*that* she couldn't feel. And he resolutely went down in the elevator. Now it didn't matter whether they went down or not; he knew that if they went out, they were risking everything, but he reassured himself a little shakily that his terror of not finding the apartment on their return was absurd, because if the ambulance driver could find it so easily, so could the driver of the taxi in which they would return, loaded down with paintings, paperweights, candelabra, Waring blenders, light bulbs, smiling at having all their problems solved because it hadn't been anything more than a very Labiche comedy of errors. This slip of paper with an address was somebody's fatal mistake. Maybe some rather unintelligent flunky had left it on the desk by mistake. Yes, it was going to be possible to reconstruct everything from the beginning, thanks to this yellowing slip of paper which he had balled up inside his pocket, and on which were written a number and the name of a street, so miserable a street that even he, who prided himself on his knowledge of the city, had never once heard it mentioned.

But he stopped on the corner and wouldn't let his wife call a cab, because he still couldn't make the decision. Wait, he said, wait. Another hypothesis had occurred to him. What if the gang of criminals, instead of lying in wait for opportunities to break into the apartment and remove the few beautiful, undamaged objects they had left, had decided to induce them to *leave the apartment* so that they would finally become lost in the city, with no possibility of finding their house again? Then, instead of stripping it bit by bit, they could install themselves in the middle of all those beautiful things (which in spite of everything were still beautiful) and fill up the apartment with their filthy shawls, their "custom-made" credenzas with shiny imitation-wood formica surfaces, their stridently colored religious pictures, their painted plaster ornaments, their children, their broken plastic toys, their relatives, their endless Sunday dinners, their television sets, their transistor radios, their monstrous sandwiches . . . horrible. But very likely.

But it was too late to turn back. And yet Roberto couldn't bring himself to hail any of the taxis going past in the stream of traffic that poured dizzyingly through the streets at rush hour. And they could not go back, because by now they certainly would not find the house again. Roberto nostalgically imagined the peace of all these people going home to houses which they knew exactly where to find—and there, waiting for them, would be their children, husbands, parents, wives who held no surprises from day to day . . . yes, going home to apartments perhaps not so perfect as Roberto Ferrer and Marta Mora's had not-quite-but-almost-been, but nevertheless brimming with security. And now they had to go to Pound-Ounces 204. What was the use of dwelling on it? Roberto raised a hand to call a cab. Marta said:

"No . . . not that one . . ."

"Why not?"

"Let him go."

"It's hard to find a cab at this hour."

"Another will come along."

It wasn't the things in their apartment that he minded their taking. It was the empty room, the space that nobody had ever decorated, or found beautiful, or understood. And on the corner, waiting for another taxi, he felt it didn't make any difference which taxi it was. Any of them would be taking them into exile.

Roberto realized that Marta had shied away from the first taxi because she thought she had spotted it waiting—no, not "waiting," lying in wait, just as all things now seemed not merely to exist but to lie in ambush—at the curb, and as soon as they had raised a hand to hail a taxi, this man, doubtless following orders from the gang, had pulled over to pick them up and carry them off. They hadn't seen the cabby's face or license plate; there was nothing to prevent him from driving around the block and coming back for them as if he were a different cab. Everything was futile. Well then. Now that they were mixed up in the thing, they might as well go on, for they certainly couldn't go back. Roberto raised his hand. A cab coasted over to the curb and stopped in front of them. They opened the door and got in. The taxi moved on:

"Where to, folks?"

"Do you remember the address, Roberto?"

"No, wait, I have it written down on this paper in my pocket . . . I can't quite make out what it says. You can't either, Marta? Here, you read it, driver . . ."

He passed the slip of paper to the cabby, who turned on the light and read: "Pound-Ounces Two-Oh-Four."

"That's it, Pound-Ounces Two-Oh-Four."

"Whereabouts is that?"

"I haven't the faintest idea."

The cabby pulled over to the curb, turned on the light, and leafed through his street book, saying:

"It seems to me it's over in Pedralbes. Pound-Ounces . . ." He turned the pages. "What a queer name!"

Finally he found "P-O's" on the map and said, "Here it is. It's in Clot."

He made a U-turn, and got into the stream of traffic headed toward France, which little by little thinned out until he, too, turned off the expressway, entering a network of side streets, almost all with high, blind, deaf, windowless walls. Going by the signs, they must be warehouses. Homes with people and family life hardly existed in this neighborhood, only broad old brick walls, lit up from time to time by a security light that spread like a spot of grease. The workers went home before dark, leaving the streets deserted, dirty, the sidewalks sometimes blocked by a mound of wood-shavings to be baled or a wooden crate or cardboard box waiting for the municipal sanitation removal the next morning; but nowhere were there garbage cans heaped with the rich, nourishing remains of everyday life. After an abrupt left turn, the cabby said:

"I'm sorry, mister, but the streets here are narrow and all one-way. Where you want to go is an alley only one block long, and to get there we have to back up and turn around, and do a loop of about seven or eight blocks . . ."

He turned his friendly face toward them apologetically. "All right," Roberto and Marta stuttered.

But as the cabby resumed his function, Roberto looked at Marta. Yes, they had both seen his face: the gray, furrowed, deflated features of the porter's brother who had taken "Green Atom Number Five." The two of them were in his power, he could do what he wanted with them. Maybe P-O Street was not in Clot. Maybe he had brought them to this place because the rest of the gang was waiting here, in the night, among the unending rows of closed warehouses, where no one lives and there is no one to hear the screams of a person calling for help. . . . The density of population that vitalizes the downtown area made itself fearfully scarce here at night, and what was left was only these enormous spaces crammed full of innumerable lifeless objects. In these alleyways, during the daytime, trucks loaded and unloaded, but by nightfall the area was deserted, high walls and large doors defining warehouses full of hundreds of thousands of objects, all alike and perfectly ordered and classified before being ejected into life. And what if—the thought flashed through Roberto's mind—what if among all these warehouses there was one that was brand-new—an enormous, perfectly empty space? No. All of them were full of shoes and books and rolls of felt and metallic cloth and paper, ensconced in spaces custom-built for storage. Marta was asking the cabby:

"Excuse me, but aren't you the brother of the porter at . . . ?"

"Brother? I don't have any brothers, both of them died in the Battle of the Ebro, in 1938. I only have a sister; she's married to a Manchego. Bad people, the Manchegos. Drunken sots."

Roberto and Marta, to fortify themselves, held each other's hand in the back seat.

"I thought I recognized you . . . Didn't they once send you to pick up a painting? . . ."

"What was the painting of?"

Marta and Roberto looked at each other, their suspicions confirmed: if he wanted to know what the painting looked like, then by implication he was admitting he had once gone to pick up a painting. That was enough . . . or, on the contrary, it might mean that the end of the game was nearing, and he was voluntarily revealing his complicity in the crime.

"Abstract."

"What's abstract?"

"Not abstract, Roberto, Informalist, it's different."

"But it had Formal elements. The green atoms were highly regularized rhombuses. Let's say like Vasarely."

While the cabby moved them deeper and deeper into the alleyways, Marta and Roberto immersed themselves in a vertiginous spiral of explanations and defenses of abstract art, pointing out to the cabby that on the international level, after Picasso and Miró, only the great Spanish Informalists . . .

"Here it is . . . We're there."

The cabby's voice sounded peremptory. But even after the car stopped and he got out to open the door for them, they went on arguing about Spanish Informalism, comparing it with the School of Paris . . . no, they were *not* comparable, no, they didn't want to get out of the taxi, they wanted to wait, if only a few seconds. . . . The cabby, with the car door open, leaned over to ask them:

"So this valuable painting was stolen?"

Roberto said, "Yes, very valuable."

Tartly, with the denouement in view, Marta said: "You know perfectly well that 'Green Atom Number Five' has nothing but sentimental value—if you can call our feelings toward that painting sentimental . . ."

Roberto preferred not to hear her and continued to address the driver as he helped his wife get out. Now he was explaining not to delay but to confront, or to defend himself, or even to attack:

"Yes, they stole it. One afternoon they came into the house and stole it. You have to take care these days."

The cabby shut the car door. Silently, with the collars of their all-weather coats turned up and their hands pushed down into their pockets, the three of them stood there at the entrance to the deserted alleyway. A single street lamp lighted vast expanses of peeling wall. At the end of the alley they saw an imposing cast-iron gate, half open. The cabby—who was an excellent actor—pretended to look down both sides at the numbers on the doors, all penetrated by the smell of solvent or leather: on one side of the street was number 202, on the other side, 206. The half-open gate barely visible at the end of the alleyway therefore had to be the number 204 on the paper. The cabby said:

"I'm going to come with you to look for this painting that's so . . . so . . ."

Roberto jumped in to keep him from finishing his stupid sentence. "Yes, do come with us, that way you can help us find our way out of this labyrinth afterwards . . . the painting is rather large and it would be good of you to help us carry it; we haven't seen a living soul on these streets, never mind a cab, so it's better if you come too. Of course we'll pay you . . ."

"That's all right. Thanks."

They came to the gate at the end of the alley and looked inside. Nobody in sight. Nor any thing, although it was clear that something must be stored in the uneven rows of outbuildings, but there was no odor or window, so it was impossible to guess what filled these warehouses so jealously sealed with metal curtains and padlocks. What if there was an empty one? The long canyons between the walls were partially revealed by a feeble light of unknown origin, and by the reflection of light from distant parts of the city that glanced off metal roofs and shards of glass in the depths of darkness.

As if he were the owner of all these large, disordered spaces, the porter's brother led them confidently onward. But now, in the night, the terror, the isolation, the silence, those spaces ordered themselves in a way that was completely unfamiliar to Roberto. He couldn't keep himself from admiring their beauty . . . another kind of beauty, but still beauty. Then, despite the rancor that separated him from his wife (thanks to that mean remark about his painting—so uncalled for), Roberto took her arm on the pretext of helping her down a winding staircase, but didn't let her go. Feeling the warmth of Marta's arm as it penetrated the cold of the gabardine and warmed his own, he also felt that maybe things hadn't changed so much after all, that entering this labyrinth of warehouses was not quite, but almost, like returning to their new apartment.

From time to time a thin light fitfully sketched their route through the outbuildings. They stepped successively on earth, pavement, flagstones, cobblestones, wood, mud. Now that their eyes had got used to the dark, everything was not in fact formless. Masses and shapes suggested themselves: shades of black, the grays of loading docks and vaults with stairs and railings and arches, of passageways invented by some unknown Spanish Piranesi, all solid and cold—yet beautiful, said Roberto to himself—but he immediately banished the remembrance of Piranesi from his mind, so as not to destroy the purity of his conviction that he could find something new here. They went up a tottering circular staircase behind the porter's brother, who in spite of the darkness seemed to know exactly where he was leading them. They passed through a door and descended to another level by means of a ramp. Marta and Roberto were by now too confused to think about anything other than the complexities and obstacles of the path, and grew tenser by the moment as Marta misinterpreted an exclamation of "This way" or "Watch out!" or Roberto hesitated too long after a "We're going down now" from the porter's brother. They followed him willy-nilly because he seemed to know what he was doing and anything was better than getting locked in this place. At last the cabby announced decisively: "Now turn right."

Roberto separated himself from Marta; squaring off in

front of the man who was leading them, he asked: "Where do you think you're taking us?"

Surprised by Roberto's audacity, the porter's brother halted. They were standing between two long, low warehouses made of ancient-looking brick, an endless corridor filled with disemboweled boxes, a fork lift, a pile of bricks, and there at the end, in the glare of a bald light bulb, the impenetrable face of another tall building that meant more alleyways, more full-bellied warehouses, more voids. The porter's brother said: "On the gate it said P-O's Two-Oh-Four."

"Well, what are you looking for, then?"

"Somebody . . ."

This "somebody" was dangerous. They must act quickly. Through the small dark void that separated them, Marta said: "That isn't the address we gave you."

"Now that you mention it, I don't think it is either," echoed Roberto.

"I'm sure it is, lady. I . . ."

They had offended the cabby in his professional capacities. He might call "somebody." He might get aggressive, now that he was on his own turf. "Don't lie," said Roberto, "the address was different."

"Certainly it was, Roberto; furthermore, the handwriting the address was written in on that piece of paper was terrible, you could barely read it, so it's possible that . . ."

The cabby was dangerous. He was going to attack. A moment longer and he *would* attack. In a falsely sad voice, he began his last line in this comedy:

"But for God's sake, lady! How can you say that? Why don't you check it yourself?"

"Look at the paper!"

"You've got it, Marta."

"No, you gave it to him."

"It was you. I remember very clearly."

They looked at each other with hatred, dying to lock horns in a furious marital quarrel over minutiae, accusations hurled back and forth in rancor, each throwing the past in the other's face. But the time for this was not yet ripe. First they had to take care of the porter's brother to keep him from destroying them. Roberto said:

"We gave the piece of paper to you."

"To me?"

"Yes. To you. Don't play the fool."

"Why should I play the fool?"

"I don't know why you've brought us here to Clot, to get us lost . . ."

"Jesus, Mister . . ."

Marta and Roberto cornered him against the brick wall.

"P-O's Street is in Pedralbes, or so I seem to remember. This is a hijacking, that's what it is . . ."

"Mister, you yourselves . . ."

The man was about to scream. They had to hurry if they wanted to keep him from calling out to the people who might be hiding unseen in the shadows.

"You give us back that piece of paper!"

"Get him, Roberto! He's going to escape!"

Roberto, shoving him against the wall, cut off his flight. Marta grabbed one of his arms with all of her strength. The porter's brother made no effort to run away or resist.

"Where have you hidden our piece of paper?"

The man didn't answer. Roberto slapped his face. Now, now, scare him, make him more afraid than we are. The man closed his eyes, his face fell in profile against the wall while Roberto's and Marta's hands rifled his pockets, violating, tearing; whenever the man tried to move, Roberto or Marta would punch him or slap his face, which was now covered with tears. Yes, he was crying. Marta and Roberto were in command of the situation. The porter's brother was so terrified that he couldn't even raise his voice sufficiently to call his accomplices. Hurry, hurry, they might come . . . "It's not here. Look in his pants pocket, Marta. He has to have it."

"Look."

Roberto showed his wife what appeared to be a gold

ballpoint pen. Exactly like one that had been stolen from him, he couldn't remember by whom. No, it wasn't *like* his, it *was* his: the ballpoint pen, at last, reassured them they were on the right track to the rest of the stolen goods. Yes. Stolen. Why imagine that it was anything but a series of thefts? The cabby and all the others had fleeced them bare . . . well, now it was *their* turn to fleece him of everything he had on him. The couple's convulsive fingers stripped him of his torn coat, his tattered shirt, their claws intent on the stripping, as if they were occupied for the very first time in their true calling. Pockets were emptied, everything thrown on the ground while they shouted at the porter's brother to tell them what he wanted from them, why he had brought them there. . . . They let his fat wallet drop to the ground— money, photos, bills paid and unpaid, handkerchiefs, key chain, a pack of cigarettes, lighter, a child's marble—every- thing in a pile on the ground next to his torn clothing, every- thing examined more and more minutely as they discovered more and more things in the cabby's pockets, until at last they forgot the cabby altogether. Letting out a cry, he ran off between the buildings and disappeared in the darkness, never looking back.

Roberto and Marta, sitting on a crate, divided the posses- sions of the porter's brother; this for you, this for me. Al- though it made no difference what went to which of them, they kept on feeling the things in the dark, trying to guess what they were, and dividing them up, hiding them so that the other wouldn't know that he or she had kept something back, until Marta thought Roberto had hidden the paper with the address on it.

"Where's that paper?" she snapped.

"What paper?"

"The one that says where we are."

"You can't believe I didn't see you hide it."

"No, *you* hid it."

"No, *you* did."

"You don't believe me?"

"No."

"I don't believe you either."

"You're turning into such a deceitful old bitch."

"You've been a lying bastard all your life."

"Give me that paper!"

"You stuck it in your pocket. I saw you!"

"No, *you* did."

They began to search each other's clothing and pockets, almost amiably at first, then with greedy haste, until finally their hatred made them lose all control, and they were ripping off bits of garments—Roberto's tie, Marta's pocket— punching each other, shouting everything they had never shouted at each other before. Now that they had stripped the cabby of all he owned, they had to continue. They knew that their powers of despoliation had not yet atrophied and each turned onto the attack. First they shouted all the truths, obscenities, and rancors that had been stored away because they were civilized beings: parasite, failure, amateur, asshole, idiot, whore, faggot, barren cunt, impotent bastard. Then they ceased being personal and began hurling generic insults which were more accurate for the emotional force they discharged than the defects they pointed to. They clawed each other until they bled, they ripped off more clothing, they beat each other with sticks they found to hand on the ground. Bruised, in rags, their hands convulsively grabbing at each other's garments, each other's limbs, each other's fears, each hated the other with a hatred that swelled until it annihilated all else: this is mine, no it's mine, it's not yours, it's mine, give it to me, you've lived off my labors your entire life, you kissed my mother's ass until finally she gave us her japanned cabinet . . . give me that . . . and that . . . No . . . look how I'm bleeding . . . I'm sweating, I can't even see . . . give me back my little finger which I lost because of you, you stole it from me . . . gimme . . . ouch . . . shit, leave me alone, you dirty bitch, get out of here . . . no, *you* get out.

The feeble light at the end of the alleyway died, wiping

out the details of both setting and event, and Marta and Roberto, now completely naked, stood face to face in an enormous emptiness of ground, immense angles, gigantic dimensions that might contain a door or a window or a single electric wire with a light fixture. The rest was space and more space in which the couple's puny howls were lost. Everything ached, inside and out, the corrosive truths leaving scars that would never be forgotten, their bruised and battered bodies trembling with fear and cold, gaping at each other through eyelashes sticky with blood and sweat, naked. Death wasn't so terrible. It was the nakedness that each saw and feared in the other: Roberto's obscene stomach over his whitish thin legs; she no different, her breasts withered, cellulite devouring her already flaccid hips.

Seeing each other like that, naked in the darkness, they stopped fighting and drew breath. Each took a step backward, slowly, terror-stricken at what they saw, crouching, lacking memory of past or thought of future, possessing only this narrow present of violence in the midst of empty space, slowly drawing away from each other, united only by their iron glances, moving backward, crouching and pale, like two animals that separate in the moment before pouncing on each other to destroy or to possess, or turn their backs and flee, howling with fear, into the vast, empty space surrounding them.

Gaspard
de la Nuit

1

SYLVIA CORDAY dropped the mirror and tweezers she was plucking her eyebrows with onto the red felt cushions of her immense sofa, and picked up the latest issue of Italian *Vogue* to study Valentino's fall collection; this year it was simply sensational. Ramón hadn't phoned yet to arrange what they were going to do today—Sunday—and when they would see each other. Everything more or less depended on how Sylvia was going to handle her brand-new role of mother. Mauricio had arrived out of the blue, after a phone call from the boy's father in Madrid saying he was sending their son to her for the summer because he would be making frequent trips abroad and Granny, who deserved a rest, had booked passage on a cruise organized by her Bridge Club friends. This arrival threatened to fix Sylvia and Ramón's life in an artificial and unaccustomed routine. Up till now it had been so agreeably free. If this had been one of those few Sundays they spent in Barcelona during the warm season, Ramón would have slept in Sylvia's apartment and spent this lazy morning reading newspapers, magazines, letters, talking on the phone, the two of them sunbathing nude on the penthouse's large terrace, and having a leisurely breakfast of black coffee and toast. Last night, it was true, they had gone to bed late after Ramón's ex-partner's wedding. Or rather, Jaime Romeu's *daughter's* wedding. There, after something more than the usual number of whiskies required to keep him afloat in such a terribly conventional milieu—golf, private schools, S'Agaró, the Floating Dike— Ramón had begun to sing "L'Internationale." This created a delightful panic, but it was already getting late, so there

were no consequences more serious than a frown from a
stuffed shirt who looked at his Patek Philippe then got up,
and a woman who sent for her mink after somebody whispered in her ear what it was that was being sung by poor
Rosario del Solar's son.

Ramón had been perfectly right to split professionally
with Jaime Romeu. As the years passed, it became increas-
ingly obvious that they hadn't been born to be partners, in
spite of their friendship dating back to days with the Jesuits.
Now, after Ramón's little number at the reception, it was
unlikely that what was left of a nominal friendship would
last longer than a few months. Sylvia was just as happy. That
particular world no longer understood Ramón or his archi-
tecture . . . and so what? she thought. Her passport to these
circles consisted more in blood relationships rarely acknowledged than her fame as a fashion model. Jaime Romeu was
the exact equivalent of Sylvia's husband in Madrid: an opu-
lent decadent who was closer to the village than to the international set. And poor little Mauricio had had to grow up in
that environment. But what else could she do? Sylvia and
her husband had been separated since Mauricio was ten:
her then-lover and the "desertion of domicile" of which she
had been so vindictively accused to remove Mauricio from
her custody were less important to women of her political
stripe than the assertion of personal freedom that consisted
in refusing to have another child, and taking the Pill without her husband's knowledge in order to protect her figure.
Most women had no more imagination than to give birth
with the astounding fecundity of pre-Conciliar rabbits. And
why shouldn't she protect her figure against the wind and
the tides of nature? It was just at that time that her spectacular career as a model was accelerating and she realized
that only through her work would she at last find her inde-
pendence, her dignity as a person. Upon their separation,
she turned down the extremely comfortable living allowance
offered her by Mauricio Sr. to give up her career. The scenes

over all this were ghastly, straight out of Benavente, incredibly old-fashioned. At that time nobody understood anything and they all said she was crazy. But she wasn't about to "sacrifice herself" for the sake of unborn children, not even for the sake of Mauricio Jr., as the chorus of scandalized women urged her to do. She knew she would only wind up hating him. So leaving Mauricio in his father's charge hadn't seemed such a horrible thing to her. At least he would have a strong father-figure to identify with or rebel against. Then too she couldn't offer a Ramón to her son, because Ramón did not yet exist. Nor did the present Sylvia Corday exist, and she, it had to be admitted, was not the most suitable woman to provide a home for a sixteen-year-old boy, since her profession required frequent trips, overnight absences without warning, general neglect of domestic activities, seeing a crowd of flamboyant people—everything, in a word, that one would disapprove of in a mother. Her image, modeling luxurious clothes on the pages of fashion magazines, was a multiple refraction of different, beautiful masks, all sharing as their common denominator the vague face that was, without doubt, one of the best-known of her generation. Her way of life was the only thing Sylvia was in a position to offer her son in lieu of the "warmth of a home." She had seen Mauricio intermittently and only briefly over the last five years, and nothing could force her to sacrifice for his sake a career that was just about to make her an international celebrity.

Four days ago, Mauricio had landed at the airport to spend what could be a terrifying three months with her, loaded down with one tennis racquet and a tiny suitcase. Sylvia thought it incredible that he didn't have more to wear. She asked Mauricio about it.

"No. I don't have anything else."

"Granny doesn't take care of you?"

"Yes, Granny takes care of everything."

"Well then? With your father's fortune and his taste in

clothes, you ought to have the most spectacular wardrobe . . ."

"I never thought of asking him."

"Why not?"

"I don't know."

He answered in sentences as colorless as the clothes he wore. Momentarily appearing in the role of mother before she had had time to formulate a plan whereby these duties would not be neglected but would not enslave her either professionally or as a woman, Sylvia began to hang up her son's clothes in the closet. This she did with some disappointment—they were so bland, so lacking in imagination, all alike: light-blue shirts with short or long sleeves, all from Galerías Preciados, the big Madrid department store, khaki pants, some commonplace jerseys, a badly cut, conventional blazer . . . in other words, nothing that revealed any taste, a desire to conquer or to affirm himself. It didn't matter. In the end, maybe it was better that Mauricio Sr. hadn't tried to enlighten his son in this respect because at least this way the boy wasn't conditioned to conventional good clothes, and she would have the chance to expose him to a more contemporary concept of dress as a manifestation of imagination and creativity. In Barcelona it was easy to find the most contemporary things for sixteen-year-olds. And in Cadaqués, where Ramón had invited them to spend a month in his beach house—that was what she had told the boy, in case his morals were as conventional as his clothing—he would look absolutely ridiculous in these clothes . . . yes, yes, at least as Sylvia Corday's son he would look ridiculous . . . And his hair was too short. There was time before they went to Cadaqués—for the moment they would only be going there on weekends—to convince him not to trim his hair for any reason whatever. She inspected him, imagining him with his blue-black hair longer: handsome, yes, very handsome, as she'd had to explain to him while he blushed. He would have to learn to dress in a way that did something for him, to attract girls.

"Do you like girls?" she asked.

"No."

After a pause, perhaps too daringly: "What about boys?" Mauricio didn't bat an eye. "No."

Sylvia couldn't stop. "I wouldn't mind, you know. I'm very open-minded."

"No."

"What do you like, then? Movies? Swimming?"

"No."

"Well, what?"

"Well . . . I don't know . . . walking . . ."

"Ah!"

Sylvia lit a cigarette. She blew a smoke ring and exhaled. She offered a cigarette to Mauricio.

"No, thanks," he said. "I don't smoke."

Topics of conversation were obviously going to be very limited between the two of them. It was clear that Granny, under whose tutelage he had spent the last few years, had forbidden him—doubtless along with a lot of other things— to smoke. Repressed. It was so unhealthy. Even his clothes were repressed. Forbidding him to smoke! At an age when boys from other homes were already experimenting with pot and acid! Well, tomorrow she would take him to the boutiques, buy him tight jeans, fantastic belts, Moroccan shirts, mysterious amulets to wear on his beautiful adolescent chest. If he went around in the insipid clothes he had brought with him, he would cut himself off from all the infinite possibilities of relationships, which would be a shame at his age, in a world so much freer than Granny's in Madrid. What she hoped for most was that he would develop, miraculously, a good father-son relationship with Ramón. Nobody could deny that Ramón was charming, open-minded, funny, full of odd bits of information about rocks and plants and animals and books and famous people he knew personally, who doubtless would impress Mauricio . . . And then there was his small yacht . . . A boy of sixteen just had to be thrilled with the idea of learning to sail a pretty yacht . . . Sylvia, encouraged by this thought, said to Mauricio:

"Aren't you excited at the idea of spending a month at the beach?"

Mauricio didn't answer.

"Don't you just adore the sea?"

"No."

"How can you not like it?"

"It's not that I don't like it."

"Well?"

"It's all the same to me."

"You'll like Cadaqués."

"Why?"

Sylvia thought it over. "It's different."

"But that could be worse."

Sylvia didn't know what to say. After this conversation she had been a little edgy. But last night she had really enjoyed herself at the Romeus': it was like raiding enemy territory that was unfamiliar . . . well, at least forgotten. She dumped *Vogue* on the sofa—reading it was getting on her nerves—and again took up the tweezers and mirror. How could *Vogue* demand something so compromising as pulling out *all* your eyebrows? It was a horrible decision to make. In a few months, when eyebrows weren't being worn so thin, letting them grow out again would be a real bore. It was eleven o'clock, and still Mauricio hadn't put in an appearance or asked for his breakfast. Mrs. Presen had told her that the boy only liked a cup of coffee with milk and toast, and one day when she went in to clean after the boy had gone out, she found the tray untouched and cold. No wonder he was so thin! But it was just that thinness, Sylvia was forced to admit, combined with his pale complexion and thick, dark eyebrows meeting over his nose, that made him so beautiful. And he had inherited it not from her but from his father, who, if he could claim any quality as a man, had been handsome in a trite sort of way, along the lines of the types who turn up their raincoat collars and look tragic, à la Yves Montand or Albert Camus; but then *his* looks had captivated the romantic little Sylvia fresh out of the convent.

An hour had passed since she heard Mauricio turn on the shower.

She was dreading the odious mother-son comedy that was expected of her . . . but Mauricio didn't come out. This business of waiting was getting a little tiresome. She rang, and Mrs. Presen appeared at once.

"Has the boy had his breakfast?"

"I brought it to him. I don't know whether he ate it . . ."

"Well, go pick up the tray. It's Sunday and you have to leave early. See what Mauricio is doing and then tell me."

She heard the hypocritical old witch knock gently, and the boy say "Come in." There was a brief conversation between the two of them which Sylvia overheard because Mrs. Presen had conveniently left the door open.

"You only ate one piece of toast, Mr. Mauricio?"

"Yes."

"You don't eat very much."

"Not much."

"Don't get sick now, Mr. Mauricio."

"I won't . . ."

"I'll tell your mother. What kind of food do you like?"

"Everything . . . it's all the same to me."

Mrs. Presen, wearing an accusing expression, reappeared in the living room with the tray.

"Look at this, miss. He doesn't eat."

"Not much . . ."

"You ought to give him cod liver oil. It's very good. I give it to my grandchildren, and you should see how beautiful they are."

The idea that Mauricio, with his pallor and long legs, might ever look like Mrs. Presen's pink-cheeked grandchildren, who probably took after their grandmother and were built like little tanks and had hands like underbaked dough, horrified Sylvia. She asked what Mauricio was up to.

"Nothing."

"What do you mean, nothing?"

"He's dressed already. He was standing next to the closet as if he was going to open it and tidy up his things . . . you have to admit, miss, he's very well brought up and he keeps his things very tidy . . . He takes good care of them too. Yesterday I caught him sewing a button on his shirt, as if he lived all alone by himself, and I had to take it away from him . . ."

"That's his grandmother's discipline. So he'll know how to get along by himself if he has to, she says. What nonsense! . . ."

"And he was whistling."

Sylvia set the tweezers and mirror on the coffee table. Whistling. It wasn't something you normally said about somebody, or noticed them doing. Nevertheless Mauricio did it. Yes: now that Mrs. Presen mentioned it, she *had* noticed Mauricio whistling. Several times. Mrs. Presen seemed determined to keep the conversation going, so Sylvia asked her, "And what was he whistling?"

"Well, miss, I don't know. My hearing is so bad and Don Anselmo hasn't been able to fix it . . . anyway, I'm not as young as I used to be and I don't know what young people like these days . . ."

Sylvia, regretting having given in to the desire to gossip with Mrs. Presen, cut her off. "Thank you, that'll be all."

Having deposited this tiny detail in her consciousness, the witch departed. So Mauricio was whistling. But Mauricio had always whistled—even, Sylvia seemed to remember, on past visits; somewhere along the line she had apparently accepted the fact that when her son was alone, he always moved in a musical cloak of his own whistling. Odd. But at least this quirk of his was something from which she could begin to put together a picture of her son and give shape to his blurry substance. It wasn't that Mauricio was more or less timid than any other sixteen-year-old boy. It couldn't be that he was harboring a grudge against her, either. It was something else. He had always whistled. Even now, he was spending this glorious, early summer Sunday morning locked in his room, whistling. Maybe it meant he liked music. What kind of music didn't matter. Just knowing he liked music was like finding the end of the yarn in the skein, and maybe by pulling little by little, more and more things would come out until at last she would have enough information to build a satisfactory picture of what her son really was.

Being so experienced in domestic intrigue, the witch, Mrs. Presen, had left the doors to Mauricio's room and the living room open: this was one of the worst faults of Magdalena's famous Mrs. Presen (whom Magdalena had "lent" to her for Mauricio's visit), this business of leaving all the doors open. Sylvia got up to close the one to the living room. But halfway there, she stopped herself and sank into the scarlet cushions of the sofa, with its back to the thin curtains and the great glass doors opening on the sun-drenched vegetation of the terrace. She went completely rigid. Yes. Mauricio was whistling. It was clear he didn't know the door to his room was open, because otherwise he wouldn't be whistling . . . at least not the way he was whistling . . .

What *was* the way he was whistling? If only Ramón were listening! He was better at analyzing and defining what she felt than she was. Furthermore, he knew something about music, just as he knew something about all forms of civilized activity. But hearing Mauricio whistle, Sylvia felt she was hearing his confession, and she wasn't about to be one of those mothers who pry into their children's secrets. But wasn't all her worrying what Ramón disdainfully called "literature"? Wasn't that what her sudden sensation of surprise was, "literature"? Surprise at the simple fact that her adolescent son was whistling for a while, alone in his room, while he organized the clothes in his closet?

Sylvia listened, her mind blank, for five minutes. No, she decided. It wasn't "literature." She had been listening to him with a feeling of surprise that contained an element of fear. She would have felt the same thing witnessing some

religious act which, regardless of her own volition, impli-
cated her. And yet, so terribly distant . . . and aloof . . . and
. . . This was absurd! But how could Mauricio whistle like
that? She listened again. It was what he had always whistled:
something very simple, not simple the way a popular song
is simple; rather, musical phrases, notes with a lot of silence
in between, ordering themselves in such a way that the
silences were just as important as the sounds themselves,
uniting inexplicably in a combination of impregnable delicacy and desolation, of transparent coldness . . . Sylvia felt
a shiver stab through her. Was that what her son was whistling, then? No, it wasn't that simple. It was the opposite of
simple, and that was what was so alarming about it . . . it
was something so final, so sophisticated, and for that reason
so . . . so sad? so solitary? so terrifying? She had hoped that
what she kept hearing her son whistle, without paying any
attention to it, was something else. She didn't exactly know
what. Maybe she had hoped he would be humming dis-
connected, easy phrases from some hit tune, or jazz, or pop,
or at least something classical that Ramón would surely be
able to recognize, even if she couldn't . . . In other words,
something ordinary. But not *this*.

Sylvia listened again. Mauricio's whistling went on. He
arranged spaces and notes in some extremely complicated
way, gentle sonorities which seemed, in their slowness and
elegance, to spring from and exhaust all the possibilities of
the keyboard and all the terrors of a mysterious void. What
Sylvia was listening to had an utterly pure, exasperatingly
anguishing form, not because it was tragic, but because it
was so . . . so . . . how to say it? Obviously she had a stereo
in her apartment with records she hadn't listened to for
months: unimportant things, things people hum in the street,
movie soundtracks, jazz concerts everybody had been to, a
record autographed by Guillermina Motta when they were
introduced, nothing more pretentious than that. What
Mauricio was whistling was not only different . . . it was,
well, almost its exact opposite because of its . . . well, maybe

this *was* "literature," but even so: because of its solitude. It was as if, lightly stroking the well-spaced notes, he were locking himself inside the exacting perfection of a long piece which he had already been whistling for fifteen minutes, as if he wanted to use that perfection, so refined, so cold, to trace a circle around himself . . . to protect himself? To drive other people away? Why?

Sylvia, apprehensive, went on listening to the allusive chains of complex sounds that Mauricio was somehow producing with his docile whistling: it was as if the very difficulty of whistling what he was whistling transported him by means of some magical spell, some sudden plunge, into a concentrated, fluctuating rhythm, into water, a bell, something that moved and pulsed and was dark and subterranean, all having a fragility, a sadness, an elegance, that pierced Sylvia with the certainty that her son, who was whistling something she didn't understand and few people would appreciate, was unutterably lonely. Sylvia couldn't get it out of her mind: the circle Mauricio's music was tracing would conquer and devour her.

The sun crept forward on the arm of the red felt sofa, grazed the white djellaba she was wearing, then crawled onward like a secretive beetle, keeping pace with the suddenly fluid, suddenly angular musical phrases that Mauricio was whistling, until his whistling drew to a close; after a thousand musical stratagems the shining beetle crept up her face and stung her eyes just as Mauricio ceased. On waking, Sylvia could at last define what she felt: she recoiled absolutely from that music. I don't understand it. Somehow it's farther away from me and closer to me than anything else on earth. What's wrong with this weird son who has landed in my arms with his load of teenage problems? Plus the weight of this . . . inadmissible . . . incomprehensible . . . The speck of sun, which she hadn't reacted to except to shut her eyes, moved on past, but she kept her eyes closed, her mind a blank, empty, for God knows how long.

When she opened her eyes again she saw Mauricio, with his light-blue English-teacher's shirt and his khaki-colored pants, hovering in front of her, smiling down at her from a height. As she glanced up, the boy asked, "Did you fall asleep?"

Sylvia had the disturbing sensation that Mauricio had been there, watching her, for some time, that he controlled her. She couldn't concede her son any power until she knew what this power was. So she answered, "No."

"But you had your eyes closed."

Trapped, Sylvia didn't want to admit defeat. "Yes. Just resting awhile before putting on my face. All beauty treatments recommend complete relaxation before putting on make-up . . ."

Mauricio said, "And did you relax?"

Sylvia didn't want her arm twisted. "No, but after all . . ."

Mauricio smiled his strange triangular, archaic smile, meaning he emphasized the smile he was already smiling a trifle more. Then, as if everyday family life could begin only now, and their earlier exchange belonged to another level of relationship, he unleashed his whole smile as one releases a bird and said, "Good morning."

"Good morning, child."

She took up her hand mirror and, opening her make-up kit, began to apply cleansing creams, as if to wipe away any importance their words might have had:

"Great day today. What do you want to do?"

He answered without hesitating: "I'm going out for a walk."

Sylvia, stunned by the novelty of the program, was going to ask him where and how, but restrained herself. She had imagined her maternal duties to be something very complicated, including the preparation of a big Sunday dinner, taking him to the movies, introducing him to her friends' sons, driving him to the tennis courts, the swimming pool, the beach . . . that is, the typical, nerve-racking slavery of the classical mother she was not and never wanted to be, the image of everything she had fought against her whole life. And here was Mauricio simplifying the job by telling her he was going out for a walk. How did one go for a walk? she wondered with surprise. She realized she didn't even know how, or where, on a Sunday morning in a city like Barcelona at the beginning of summer, you did anything so simple-minded as going for a walk.

"Where are you going?"

"I don't know."

"Don't you need a map or something?"

"I shouldn't think so."

"I thought maybe we might go to . . ."

"No, thanks, I'd rather go for a walk."

"I'd like to talk to you," Sylvia stammered. "Ask you . . ."

Mauricio continued to smile, the smile trapped again in that stylization of a teenage face. But it wasn't a smile, Sylvia thought, because it never changed or went away.

"Let's talk tonight," Mauricio said. "Right now, I'd rather go out . . ."

"Tonight? You mean you're not coming home for lunch?"

Then, as if to correct the incipient maternal anxieties that were beginning to blossom and had to be put aside, she tried to make Mauricio feel free and not think that she meant to pressure him with rigid schedules for meals and other conventional rituals.

"Don't come if you don't want to. It's all the same to me. I'm going to spend the day here resting. Ramón will be coming over later on. You come home when you feel like it and do whatever you want, come and eat in the afternoon, or have dinner, whatever suits you; don't bother to phone me or anything . . ."

"I don't have to phone, then?"

"No. What for? I'm going to be here all day. In this house, you have all the freedom you want, this isn't Granny's. Mondays I'm never here. I have a lot of hard work to do, so don't bother ringing up then if you aren't coming. Mrs. Presen will always leave you something ready just in case, and you can cope, you're already grown up. That's what modern life's about, Mauricio, not Granny's rigid schedule. After all, she has three Andalusian girls working for her."

Mauricio's smile became more pronounced, more triangular, but made no identification with happiness.

"Thanks," he said.

And he left the living room, barely giving Sylvia a chance to say goodbye.

She wanted to call to him, what for she didn't know, but Mauricio had already slammed the apartment door behind him, leaving something terribly incomplete in Sylvia. What was it? Did she want Mauricio to be more *affectionate* with her, even though she told Ramón she realized she had no right to demand it from him, her life being what it was . . . apart from the fact that she wasn't interested in that sort of thing? Notwithstanding her doctrines of personal liberty, as demonstrated by her life, deep down did she really want hugs, kisses, caresses of the Virgin-and-Child variety? Was that why she felt frustrated . . . yes, so disgustingly frustrated? It was as if she had been wanting Mauricio to ask her to take him to the Tibidabo to ride the merry-go-round and buy him whistles and candy and balloons. No, she didn't have to dramatize. That wasn't what she wanted. But she would have liked, she suddenly and vehemently decided, she would have liked some explanation that defined in words this disturbing skill of his in whistling an unknown music which enclosed him in a circle so strange, so complete, so incomprehensible, so complex . . . and yes, why not say it, so terribly mature that it was as if Mauricio knew everything and was capable of coping with anything. Underneath his teenager's shyness there lay such confidence that Sylvia could not worry, as other mothers did when their children went out without saying where they were going, that something might "happen to him." What she feared, or at least what upset her, was something very different. She pulled the telephone to her and called Ramón.

"Ramón?" She cut off greetings and preambles. "Listen:

Mauricio. He's so, so peculiar . . . He was whistling this morning. Yes, I know there's nothing wrong with that. But . . . I mean . . . whistling, alone in his room *all morning?* You're not going to try and tell me that's not odd. No, I don't know what it was. It wasn't one of those popular songs you hear other kids whistling. That's what's so . . . I don't know, that's the terrible thing. It was something completely different, more like, well, something religious . . . magical. No, don't be silly, it wasn't Bach or Vivaldi, nothing like that . . . more Chinese, it strikes me. Of course I don't know what Chinese religious music sounds like! But it struck me that way, because it's so different . . . and I had the impression that it was something a little . . . I don't know how to say it . . . maybe decadent, even cruel. Very odd for a boy brought up like Mauricio. I couldn't ask him. And the worst thing is, now I don't dare ask him. I don't know why. He scares me a little. It's as if he were whistling something tremendously intimate and secret . . . With all that repression in my mother-in-law's household, you can imagine how repressed *he* must be, poor boy! Just look at his clothes. He says he doesn't like the beach and the country doesn't interest him. I offered him a motor scooter and he didn't want it . . . you know, one of those adorable little Vespas . . . Any other boy would have jumped at it. He doesn't want anything. If I only knew what he was whistling this morning, it would be a clue! If only you could hear it . . . Yes I know you don't know much about music and all you like is baroque and the same things everybody else likes, and not much of that either . . . I know you don't take it seriously . . . I know you're not a cave man and you have to like those things as well as jazz and pop . . . but I don't think you know what *this* is. It must be something *very* strange . . ."

Sylvia listened for a long while to what Ramón was suggesting. Then she said:

"He doesn't want to go to the country. He went out for a walk. You tell me, Ramón: how do you spend a Sunday morning walking around Barcelona? I'll be damned if 'going

for a walk' to the kid means walking down to Las Ramblas
to buy postcards or something. It just can't be. What he was
whistling was too sophisticated. Refined . . . that's it, too
refined. The awful thing is that it's so refined he might not
like anything except whatever it is he's whistling. He didn't
bring any books or magazines when he came. Only his tennis
racquet, and he left that at the airport. I asked him why he
brought it and he told me Granny forced him to play tennis
because it was healthy, but he didn't like it . . . and of
course the first thing he did, poor child, either intentionally
or by accident, was to lose his racquet. You go to the
country. . . . Why don't you ask Roberto and Marta? Yes,
I know they've been a bit weird since she lost her little
finger in that awful accident . . . no I don't know what I'd
do if I lost my little finger. Well, then, go by yourself if you
want, but you'll be bored . . . luckily you have so much work
to do there . . . What about me? What am I going to do
with this son of mine? Wait until he decides to come home?
Spend the day here by myself? I'll die."

She listened carefully and after a long while said:

"What a marvelous idea! That's perfect. I'll call Paolo
and ask him to spend the afternoon. Fags never have anything to do on Sunday. And if Mauricio comes home . . .
Paolo knows everything there is to know about music. If
Mauricio whistles something, Paolo is sure to know what it
is right off . . . Yes, yes, I know it doesn't really matter what
it is . . . but if you could hear how weird . . . But I'd like
to know what it is just to be able to talk to him a little, or
at least Paolo or you could talk to him . . . and get some
tickets to a concert or something. Yes, of course the idea of
sitting there in a chair in the dark bores me to distraction.
But what do you want me to do? I can't stand music, but
he *is* my son and I have to do something to force him out of
that dreary box they've squashed him into, those boring
people in Madrid . . . Yes, share something with him. After
all, he's only going to spend three months with me . . . Yes,

I know I told you I thought it was an awfully long time . . .
But it strikes me that if I can figure out what he's whistling,
maybe it won't seem so . . ."

2

MAURICIO was an untiring walker. His long legs allowed
him to devour great distances in a short time, moving slowly,
apparently not paying attention to anything, without any
set direction, his hands thrust down to the very bottom of
his pants pockets. But he never moved without direction:
everything in him had form and obeyed a plan even though
he didn't know what that form or plan was; some part of his
existence always made him walk toward it. The form was
attracting him from a definite point. Thus, he walked for
hours through the streets, barely whistling, not pursing his
lips, so as to keep passers-by from finding out that he was
the whistler, repeating the long, slow musical phrases until
their complexity wiped out everything inside his head; concentrating on the problems of the music, his imagination
stayed fresh and his impulses free.

Walking along Vía Augusta, he came to Balmes. He
briefly considered turning up this avenue, but he realized
that even though it was Sunday, the cars were moving very
fast, and the people didn't have time for anything except
reaching their precise destinations. Furthermore, the street
was too straight: it cut brusquely through the winding slope
of Vía Augusta. When the light turned green, he crossed.
A couple crossing toward him arm in arm looked at him,
and he went on down Vía Augusta because it had the kind
of trees he was fond of, like the ones they had uprooted to
widen the street he lived on in Madrid. He avoided the
cloudy eyes of a tired man carrying a briefcase, an office

worker whose turn it was to take yet another hateful Sunday shift. A young priest attempted to penetrate him with a glance as they crossed paths, but penetrate him professionally, and Mauricio veiled his eyes. A gray-haired lady, of good family, almost but not quite smiled at him. More looks, all banal, from a group of little girls dressed in cheerful Sunday clothes, their arms bare; he could smile at them because their kind of smile made no promises and Mauricio could remain hidden under the thickness of his black eyebrows. He did not give himself to this Sunday crowd that was headed toward the festive goal of a drink, or walked parallel to him and passed him, or in crossing his path ignored him as he did them.

The young woman who had waited beside him for the light on the corner of Balmes had at last decided to turn down Vía Augusta. Or was it she? Mauricio stopped to look at some lamps in a window and saw that yes, it was, as she crossed in front of the wide mirror: now passing him, pushing the baby carriage, she had caught up with him step by step, this young lady dressed in white slacks and a dark jersey, the long heavy locks of her hair held back behind the ears by a pair of sunglasses, à la Jackie Kennedy. She didn't look at him, nor he at her. But Mauricio was eager to follow her, watching everything she did, trying to keep her from finding out that her path that morning was determining his: she checked the glasses on her head, handed a rattle to the baby, unenthusiastically greeted somebody going by in a red Fiat 850, and pressed her lips together to spread her lipstick more evenly over them. Mauricio let her get ahead of him, and then, barely whistling, trying to keep her unaware of his company, only grazing the borders of consciousness of that unknown person pushing a baby carriage, he passed her again. He could—he felt tempted to—imagine all sorts of things about her, but he rejected this possibility because he wanted to keep the space empty to put something else there, or nothing; to preserve himself, again he began whistling the slow, complex phrases that drove everything else out of his imagination.

The important thing was to keep the woman pushing the baby carriage from realizing he was hovering around her. Sometimes Mauricio could keep these semirelationships he struck up in the street going for a long time, letting his consciousness absorb the other person, stripping them for a few instants of something ineffable but real, never letting them guess he was absorbing it. Mauricio felt that today was especially propitious, with carefree people floating on the surface of this early summer morning, in this city sparkling with colored balloons and children in their Sunday clothes. Whistling among the leisurely strollers, he continued to follow the lady pushing the baby carriage; from time to time the baby let out a gurgle . . . he followed her two steps behind, she on the side of the shop windows, he along the curb: but she had no idea that Mauricio, surreptitiously, from a point outside her consciousness, had forced her into the rhythm of "Ondine." It was satisfying to watch how, by her movements or by a little laugh directed at her child, she obeyed a tremolo or an arpeggio, how her expressions adjusted to the changing but still coherent chromatic scale —satisfying above all because Mauricio wasn't exactly whistling "Ondine," just repeating its notes inside his head; and when she drifted away a little or stopped at a corner to consider the possibility of turning down a street where Mauricio didn't want to go, and didn't want her to go, he let the phrases escape through half-opened lips like modulations of breath that didn't quite achieve sound. Yes, now the lady with the baby carriage had decided to plunge down a narrow street where the sun never shone, and he wasn't going to let her do it. He raised the level of his whistling. Now it was audible music, an entire keyboard that he manipulated with his mouth, halting the woman and proving to her that she wasn't free, that she was dependent on other powers; and from the frontier of her consciousness,

Mauricio at last plunged into her, whistling pure liquid in the first notes, one hand and the pedal synthesizing the great expanse of water, the other hand insinuating a feminine presence with more clearly defined contours, calling to her, commanding her. The woman was on the verge of following him to the very depths of shared concentration . . . but then he whistled too loud. Suddenly, she glanced at him. For a second, Mauricio saw terror in that look. She had at last realized that they had been walking very close together for the last five or six blocks, and the realization drove her down another narrow street, leaving Mauricio standing on the corner, his hands in his pockets, trying to reach her with the last chords whistled at the top of his lungs.

As the lady with the baby carriage disappeared, Mauricio's music was absorbed by the medley of anecdotal events that populate the surface of a day, and he was left silent and alone. He crossed the street and followed Vía Augusta to Diagonal, going down to Gracia without encountering the thread that would allow him to begin the music again. Had she taken it with her on disappearing? No. Obviously she wasn't the person he was searching for without really searching, looking at faces, barely whistling along streets, inserting the rhythm of his own steps into the steps of others.

People were entering or leaving church. A lady with a hat. Another with a tight blouse. Everybody dressed up for Sunday: they wore what Granny contemptuously called "hairdresser hairdos." Nobody had eyes or ears. They were all too complete, there were no chinks to penetrate . . . nothing could revive the music today. But still, his steps moved on eagerly, his eyes looking for somebody to intrude on. Nothing. Nobody. Which was normal, because when he looked was always when he found least. Things had to happen in a natural, complex way, like the music that gave him his power. But what was he to do when everywhere he looked there were "hairdresser hairdos" and the well-pressed pants of men who still hadn't decided what to do with their Sunday? Everybody wanted entertainment with a name: movies, soccer, sex, motorcycling, outings . . . that was what those impenetrable looks demanded, those inviting smiles that couldn't invite him into anything because he didn't know how to define them or even want to. The only thing he knew now was that he didn't like that plaza with its obelisk. Or that ugly triumphal arch. Crossing an esplanade called Salón, he came to the tall iron gates to a park.

There, the crowds were enormous, paying cabdrivers, scolding children, getting into taxis, parking their 600s, buying ice cream, commenting on what they had just seen or were about to see according to the arrow-shaped signs: Zoo, Museum, Botanical Gardens, Exit, Rest Rooms . . . so many things to choose from, all with a name. The crowd was thicker and more excited at the exit, the children brandishing pennants, eating fruit or chufa, chocolate ice cream melting all over their new clothes, the set of the hairdressers' hairdos already rather rumpled.

Mauricio sat down on a bench under the linden trees at the entrance to the zoo. But he didn't look at the people. A blue machine with a platform and a stereoscopic viewer monopolized his attention. He couldn't take his eyes off it. The people put coins in it, went up to the platform, and looked inside the viewer . . . ooh . . . ah . . . how beautiful . . . afterward they descended to tell their companions about the wonders they had seen. Then the machine would stand unoccupied for a while. There were others exactly like it, but it was this machine that attracted Mauricio's attention. He was about to stand up and head for it, find out why it summoned him . . . but somebody had already taken it: ooh . . . ah . . . how beautiful . . . At last it was abandoned. Mauricio put in a coin and climbed onto the platform. Very excited, he put his eyes to the viewer. Columbus's Caravelle. Guell Park. The Liceo. La Rambla de las Flores. Vallvidrera, its woods, its swamp, a refreshing sense of light and shade and branches, of untouched solitude. He wasn't able to see much of Vallvidrera because a child with ice-cream-stained hands pulled at his pants leg and said:

"Let me look."

Obediently Mauricio got down and let the little boy climb onto the platform to see what Mauricio hadn't yet seen of Vallvidrera. The child's mother, who was talking to a group of relatives, suddenly noticed what her son had done. She came over and gave him a slap, yanking him down off the platform. "Bad boy, Jordi!" she said. "We'll never bring you to the zoo again!"

"See if I care!"

Mauricio sided with Jordi. Sunday was a drag if you had to go out as a member of that vilest of categories, the tribe: parents and brothers and sisters and grandmothers and uncles and aunts from Sardanyola, cousins and in-laws all eager to go and pollute themselves with wine and sausages and omelettes. Jordi went on his way with a piece of Vall-vidrera in his eyes, and Mauricio headed for the other end of the park, looking for less traveled paths, to recover what he had seen in the slides. The oleanders looked glorious in the fields. The trees weren't as beautiful as the ones in Retiro Park in Madrid, but they were artificially arranged in a way that pleased him. Fewer people came down this path, lined with banana trees, and the benches followed each other with the regularity of bells ringing, one . . . two . . . three . . . four . . . the slow steps of the music, the sad tolling that repeats the order of the gallows . . . another bench, and another, his steps following the inexorable rhythm. He chose a bench and sat down; the tunnel of trees and benches was deserted . . . but not completely, because there in the distance, at the beginning of the tunnel, a man's silhouette gradually took shape. He, like Mauricio, was advancing slowly, and, his hands in his pockets, he too took up the rhythm of the gibbet's bells which Mauricio had relinquished when he sat down. In Mauricio's mind, the whole of "Le Gibet" spread itself out, so that the man in his brown suit might make his way into it. His steps existed solely to mark the phrases on the musical staff that Mauricio's imagination was offering him. His brown suit was a good one, Mauricio thought, neither too fashionable nor too old-fashioned, and not Sunday-new: an ordinary suit worn by an ordinary man. He was about thirty years old. Smoking a cigarette, he passed in front of Mauricio without looking at him, and sat down on a bench in the facing row, a little farther on. He seemed to be concentrating on the light that filtered down through the leaves of the banana trees. His eyes focused momentarily, indifferently, on a girl passing by, or on a family laughing among themselves. When he finished his cigarette he flicked it away. Mauricio was afraid he would get up and leave just as he was beginning "Le Gibet" again from the beginning. He wanted the man in the brown suit to climb the scaffold with him. The bell was tolling for this man with his fine, pale face, as he stamped out his cigarette. Mauricio, observing (without looking) how expertly he did it, thought he was too motionless. As if he were already hanging from the gallows, brutally hampered by the noose. Too bad. He couldn't share in the macabre ceremony because he had already been hanging a long time before he chanced to graze Mauricio's consciousness—if indeed he had grazed it. Mauricio's breath, its intensity, modulated as it passed through his half-open lips and shaped itself into sound, enveloped the man in the brown suit but didn't change him. At the end of his long, brown arm, extended along the back of the bench, his hand hung, wilted, white: strangled. His long legs stretched out comfortably. Could this movement be a response to the still-silent music? He raised the pitch: now it was not just breath, his whistling rose gradually, giving shape to the impeccable, cold music.

The bench on which the man in the brown suit was sitting was not exactly in front of Mauricio, but a little to the left. But the boy realized that on hearing his whistling the man had turned his head in Mauricio's direction, not to look directly at him, as if he knew that he was the person whistling, but as if another person, farther off, were making the sounds, or as if the music were coming from the branches, from the air, one more element of the park's artificial nature. The important thing was, he did not look at Mauricio. The man didn't want to start a personal relationship. He wanted to remain closed, secret. Mauricio whistled louder: the condemned man was advancing step by step, in time with the bells, toward the gallows. But the man in the brown suit still didn't look at Mauricio because he knew that if he did, he would destroy everything and would never achieve the orgasm of death. Mauricio had surrounded him and was leading him to the gibbet. Now they must advance physically. He stood up, whistling the precise, well-spaced notes, and without looking at him or being looked at he passed wide in front of the man in the brown suit whose hand was already hanging from the gallows.

Behind him, Mauricio sensed the man in the brown suit had stood up and was following him, the way he wanted it, slowly, enslaved by the rhythm of the death knell that Mauricio's lips were sketching, advancing toward the end of the tunnel of trees, not far now, to where an arrow stuck in the grass pointed to a walkway in the dazzling sunlight. The man in brown followed on, then, breaking the somber pace, he hurried to catch up with the boy. Without looking, he strode past. Should he hasten the tempo of the phrasing to keep the man in brown from escaping? . . . Your troubles will soon be over. Steps leading up to the gallows platform. The tolling follows. The knot sways gently against the sky. Your troubles will soon be over, but you have to go through with it . . . yes, whistling with all his might, he wasn't going to let this man escape. Now it was the man in brown who approached Mauricio as he came to the end of the tunnel. He stood there with his hands in his pockets, next to the arrow that said REST ROOMS. And Mauricio, whistling, caught up with him. The man in brown, unsmiling, a look of attention in the sad mask of his face, stared deep into Mauricio's eyes, and then, with a glance, pointed to the arrow that said REST ROOMS and walked down that path.

The condemned man was never executed. The music froze on Mauricio's lips as he ran as fast as his legs could carry him to get out of the park and escape, to keep the condemned man who would never be executed from following him. He ran not because he was afraid or disgusted at what the condemned man wanted, at what so many mute, condemned men had begged of him with their eyes in parks or on streets . . . No: he was running away because it always shattered everything when this happened. The man in the brown suit, by revealing that his "absorption" in the music was a mere trick, had reawakened Mauricio's childlike vulnerability. Now he was nothing but a child running away from a man with an insinuating mask and a wilted hand, away from the counterfeiter who had made him believe he was powerful. The man in brown had physical and psychological traits independent of those invested in him by Mauricio's music. Mauricio had wanted him to be a blank page . . . but this insolent invitation from his abject eyes had left Mauricio with the noose empty in his hands; the rope wasn't terrifying, it was only good for jumping, or for securing Ramón's boat the way his mother wanted. And as if beset by the childish fear instilled in him by Granny's phrase "Be careful of perverts"—though not because of it— he ran to the area in the park where people buy ice cream, laugh, take taxis, make remarks about the zoo, and eat paper cones full of chufa. Mauricio headed for a cab, got in, and gave the address of his mother's apartment in Ganduxer.

He collapsed in the back seat, panting. His mother had said if he didn't want to turn up for lunch he didn't have to. He had planned a marvelous long day rambling around the unfamiliar city, a day full of glances, strangers' steps that he could appropriate and use to lose himself in . . . now it was ruined: the frightened boy running home to Mama. Ruined! It was so little, what he asked of people: only to let him be them for a few minutes, to let his music fill them completely without their being aware of it. Nothing more. They wouldn't notice the change. Only much later, maybe—days, weeks, months, years later—one of these people with whom he had been able to join himself through his music would remember a boy in a light-blue shirt and khaki pants once glimpsed in a plaza or on a street corner, whistling something they didn't know the name of, but which now, in a sudden flash of memory so long afterward, squeezed their hearts with its ferocious presence, fastening itself to their very heartbeats. Today, as other times, he had tried to unburden himself on the lady with the Jackie Kennedy sunglasses and the man in brown, but they had rejected it, leaving him holding the noose, the slack rope without the tension produced by the hanged man's weight. Two more people among the many failures he would forget. But one doesn't forget or fail without pain. And with every person he forgot, Mauricio grew and grew without maturing, and the load they made him carry became more intolerably heavy. Where could he unburden himself of it? When? The cab came to a halt and the driver said, "Is this it?"

Mauricio looked out the window. "This is it."

He paid and got out. He went up in the elevator and unlocked the door with the key his mother had given him (Sylvia's "Now that you're a man and have all the freedom you want," when she gave him the key, was no more than a sophisticated version of Granny's "If you can't come home to eat, at least telephone"). As he opened the door, he heard two voices, one unfamiliar, one his mother's, talking in the living room. He shut the door as quietly as he could and slipped into his room, closing the door behind him. But another moment and the door opened.

"Hi, handsome!" Sylvia said.

"Hi."

"Where have you been?"

Feeling himself assaulted without provocation by his mother's kiss and her question, he lied. "In Vallvidrera."

Sylvia laughed. "How ghastly!"

"Why?"

"I don't know."

"Well then?"

"It strikes me that it ought to be ghastly."

"It's not."

"We didn't expect you for lunch. But I'm glad you came. Paolo's here."

"Oh."

"Comb your hair and freshen up a bit, you're a mess. We'll wait for you in the living room. Are you hungry?"

"No."

Then Sylvia, instead of leaving the room, glided over to her son and kissed him again, gently, inserting her long, perfumed fingers into his mass of black hair.

"Mauricio," she pleaded, "don't shut yourself up so much. I want you to feel free in this house . . . with me."

"Yes."

"Well, why don't you admit you're hungry, then? After spending an entire morning wandering around Vallvidrera! What did you have to eat?"

"A paper cone full of chufa."

Sylvia laughed as she was leaving. "Come on, handsome. We'll wait for you in the living room."

A wave of perfume drifted from her thin white djellaba. Rape. That was what his mother did to him. Strangers on the street, whom he didn't know but at times almost knew, frustrated him by turning him into a vulnerable little boy, yet they didn't violate him. But his mother did. His father did. His grandmother did. His schoolmates, teachers, everybody whose relationship to him had a name, or who had some right to him, all of them violated him. . . . When he went for a walk, it was only to graze people's consciousness with a mere glance, with his whistling. To erase his mother's violation, like someone cutting a flawed strip out of a film and splicing the other two pieces together to mend the sequence, Mauricio went on whistling exactly where he had left off at the moment of the man-in-brown's insolent look at the exit from the tunnel of trees . . . fifteen . . . twelve . . . ten measures, then the finale: the rope now tense with the weight of the corpse, the dead man's tongue hanging out, wilted, like the man in brown's hand. Mauricio washed his own hands, combed his hair, cleaned his face, and went into the living room wearing his mask of a well-bred boy. Sylvia called out:

"Come here, Mauricio. Come closer."

She was sitting in the usual place on the enormous red sofa with its back to the leafy, flowery terrace behind the transparent white curtains. Next to her was a person observing him who, Mauricio decided, was wearing Crypto-Sunday Clothes: an oh-so-simple shirt with unpretentious checks, an ordinary pair of trousers, loafers without socks; he was sitting not facing front but to one side, with one leg tucked underneath him and the other dangling, hanging barefoot because he had let his loafer fall onto the carpet. Now his mother was introducing them and telling them pleasant things about each other which he didn't listen to because everybody was intent on violating everybody else, making statements and explanations that killed everything before a real relationship could be established.

"Would you like something to drink before eating?" Sylvia asked.

"No, thanks."

"Then sit here, you big hunk of man."

And she slapped one of the fat red cushions next to her, putting herself between Paolo and her son. She hugged Mauricio playfully, explaining to Paolo how much she loved him and how glad she was to have him staying with her for such a long time now that he was a man. She's playing the adorable mother, Mauricio thought, loading me down with costumes and masks. Anyway, he had to put up with them, these superficial definitions that came from outside and didn't have anything to do with him. If they were loading him down with disguises, they were really doing it to protect themselves. It was better to smile his archaic smile, triangular and frozen: an expression that was meaningless and could be interpreted however they wanted.

"You whistle extraordinarily well," Paolo was saying to him.

Mauricio had to make a conscious effort to keep from blushing. They had heard him whistling the last part of the hanged man after his mother had gone out, leaving his door open. This was scientific, organized rape. He shrugged, emphasizing the triangular smile again.

"You know," Paolo went on, "you have to have a very fine ear and real musical sophistication to be able to whistle Ravel the way you do. Did you know that Ravel sometimes wrote those simple-sounding harmonies on five parallel staves? They're very difficult to play. I don't understand how you can do it . . . and so perfectly . . ."

Mauricio emphasized his enigmatic smile even more until it changed into a pained grimace. What importance did it have, anyway, what Paolo was saying? He, Mauricio, was immune to his violations. Yes, and even to his mother's, although sometimes he thought he might not be; but for a different reason, because she didn't know or understand anything and was nothing but another version of Granny.

"Were you whistling *Gaspard de la Nuit?*" Paolo asked outright.

"Yes."

Sylvia interrupted. "But why Ravel, Mauricio?"

The best solution was to play the fool. "He had the same name as me," said Mauricio.

Sylvia looked at Paolo hopelessly before continuing. "I don't know anybody who's interested in Ravel. Boys your age are generally interested in rock . . . or jazz, or something. And Ravel . . . well, of course we're all interested in good music . . . the baroque composers, Beethoven's quartets . . . we know all that's very interesting, but the truth is I hardly have time for . . . You like the baroque composers, don't you, Paolo?"

Paolo frowned. "Very much."

"What about Ravel?"

"Well, I don't know . . . He's a great composer, of course. But one hardly pays any attention to him these days. You don't hear very much of him anymore. Do you like him, Mauricio?"

"Yes."

"Why?"

This was interrogation, like the priests at school, systematic violation: the guilty man, before being sentenced to hang, would be subjected to questioning but still would not be able to escape his hanging. In the depths of his consciousness Mauricio heard the steady knell of the implacable bell, and answered:

"I don't know . . . he's so elegant . . . . refined . . ."

Paolo and Sylvia smiled at the same time. Mauricio looked at them questioningly. But he didn't say anything, and they continued to interrogate him before passing sentence. Sylvia began, followed by Paolo, without even waiting for answers.

Sylvia: "But Mauricio, tell me, aren't there tremendous problems in the world today, terrible passions and injustices, that won't let us cling to the elegant . . . the refined?"

Paolo: "I thought all those words, like *elegant* and *refined*, were anathema to your generation; you're all after such different things . . ."

Sylvia: "We are, too, Paolo. Surely you recognize that. People like ourselves don't follow the beaten path, we're profoundly committed to the problems of today. It isn't just the kids . . ."

Paolo: "Yes, but . . ."

And abruptly breaking the rhythm of the conversation, Paolo turned to Mauricio.

"It's odd that a boy like you . . . There are so many odd things. For example . . ."

And then again, over the dining room table where the

three of them had already begun to eat shrimp cocktails, Paolo started off:

"I don't know which critic said that all his life Ravel was trying to 'tame the savage beast of romanticism.' Do you think he tamed it, Mauricio?"

Mauricio shrugged and answered indifferently, "I don't know about those things."

Disillusioned, Paolo turned to Sylvia.

"Did you know that Ravel would disappear for long periods of time and nobody ever knew where he went or what he did? Ravel's whole life is mysterious. Maybe he wasn't able to tame the savage beast of his own romanticism. It's odd that this boy has started me thinking about Ravel again. I'd almost forgotten him. The last time I heard Casadesus . . ."

Mauricio smiled a little more openly and said: "Casadesus . . . yes. He plays it very well. They were friends."

Sylvia looked at her son with surprise. She didn't understand how she could have given birth to a creature that talked about such things. "How do you know?"

"I like the way he plays Ravel."

His mother picked up the interrogation again.

"How do you know so much about music?"

Mauricio had made a mistake; he retreated, feeling trapped. But they could only deal with the names of things, so it didn't matter. "I don't know anything about music. I just have a reasonably good memory."

"Probably absolute pitch too," Paolo added. "This boy ought to study music, Sylvia. Drop all this nonsense about getting a college degree and develop the talents he has."

"Yes, he could have a stupendous career."

After thinking it over, Sylvia turned to her son. "Did your father buy you a stereo in Madrid?"

"No."

"Typical! How stingy. He's getting worse with age."

"It wasn't Papa. It was Granny who didn't like it."

"Did you go to concerts, then?"

"Sometimes. In the balcony. When I had the money."

"Wouldn't your father give you money?"

"No. I don't think he wanted me to like it . . ."

"I hope you realize, Paolo, just what a hell of conventionality my husband's family is. Mauricio, tell me: what is it that your father didn't want you to like? Ravel?"

"No, music. All of it. I'm going to be an engineer, he says . . ."

"What nonsense! So what did you do?"

Mauricio laughed a little, blushing. He didn't want to answer, but here in this Saarinen dining room, all white and open to the equally white light of the terrace, there was no way to pretend. It was better to face things head-on, and control them that way.

"I'm ashamed to say . . ." he ventured.

"You don't have to be ashamed of anything in front of me. I'm your mother, and whatever horrible things may have been said about me, nobody's ever said I'm not broad-minded."

There was a small silence, then Mauricio explained:

"Sometimes I went to Galerías Preciados . . ."

"To Galerías Preciados?"

"Yes, and to the other stores that sell records. I pretended I was going to buy records and I would take out the ones I wanted and put them on the turntable and listen to them with earphones or in the listening booth. I know all the record stores in Madrid, and some of them know me and let me listen to all the music I want, so long as I don't bother the customers. But the girl who let me listen to music isn't at Galerías Preciados anymore. She got married and went to live with her husband in Badajoz."

"That was sweet of her! Did you fall in love with her?"

"Come on, I'm too young for that. Besides, she was ugly."

"What was her name?"

"I don't know."

"Do you mean to tell me that you don't know the name

of a friend who was so good to you? You didn't carry her name written down in your pocket?"

"I don't remember."

"That's appalling. Did she like Ravel?"

"I don't know. I doubt it."

Paolo saw that Sylvia was about to get dramatic, and he intervened to placate her. "Leave him alone, Sylvia. You're bothering him."

She turned to her son. "Tell me—am I bothering you, Mauricio?"

"No . . ."

"Look . . . I have a record player here in the apartment that's just marvelous, stereophonic and all that, and I never use it. The truth is that music rather bores me. I don't know why. Maybe because I think it's so boring when people don't talk. And Ramón doesn't really like it either. I'm giving you the record player, Mauricio. You take it back to Madrid. I'll buy the records for you, however many you want . . . so Granny can see what kind of a boy you are. I'll buy you all of Ravel . . ."

"No . . ."

"What's it called, that thing you were whistling?"

"*Gaspard de la Nuit.*"

"I'll buy it for you tomorrow."

"Don't buy me *Gaspard de la Nuit.*"

"*Yes.* And everything else."

"No."

Sylvia suddenly turned red, and pushing her chair away from the table, she stood up and began to pace back and forth in the dining room.

" 'No' . . . 'no' . . . 'no'! I don't understand it . . . It's appalling that a boy your age doesn't have more interests . . . Ravel: the refined, the elegant. You aren't interested in anything freaky, anything modern, anything outrageous. Look at the way you dress. Tomorrow morning we're going right out to buy some decent shirts and a motorcycle . . . I want to see you involved in something more cheerful, something younger than Ravel; he's an old decadent, a closet reactionary . . ."

"All right. Buy me whatever you like . . ."

"Aren't you interested in *anything?*"

"No."

"Not even in the record player?"

"No."

"Or the records?"

"No."

"Why not?"

Silence. Sylvia and Paolo's eyes were fixed on Mauricio. Mauricio picked up his napkin and abruptly made a noose around his neck. With a macabre gesture, he let his head fall like a hanged man's on his chest, his tongue dangling. Sylvia ran to hug him from behind his chair and untie the napkin. Mauricio smiled his empty archaic smile.

"My poor son," said Sylvia. "You have to change. At the beach . . . you'll meet some normal boys and girls your age . . ."

He couldn't whistle to frighten his mother off, her torrent of words kept the music from coming out. But a color slide like the one in the coin-operated machine suddenly wiped out his mother and Paolo with forest lights as they began arguing about whether it would be a good idea to introduce him to so-and-so's children. . . .

"How do you get to Vallvidrera?" he asked.

They gave him directions, Sarriá, the cable car, and all the rest. Nothing they said had touched him. Sylvia, standing in front of him while he finished his dessert, realized that none of it interested her son. When he finished, he asked:

"I've cleaned my plate. May I leave the table?"

Sylvia's arms fell and all her tensions dissipated; it was as if she had been taken apart. She closed her eyes as she answered:

"Yes, Mauricio."

"Can I go out?"

"You know you can. Whenever you like."
Paolo got up and shook hands with him.
"Goodbye, Mauricio."
"Goodbye."
"And . . . congratulations," Paolo added.
Mauricio left. In the living room, Sylvia gave Paolo a dressing-down. Nobody ever explained anything to her . . . This whole Ravel business . . . did they think she was a stupid puppet just because she was a model? . . . Why Ravel? . . . She wanted to understand . . . And what was this "Congratulations" bit? Paolo answered patiently.

"Don't you realize? A boy of sixteen has to have . . . has to be . . . something very special to understand and like Ravel so much . . ."

"It's escapism."

"No it's not."

"Don't tell me you're a Ravel freak too!"

"I don't know."

"Aren't the baroque composers your specialty?"

"I don't know . . ."

"Now look, Paolo, you're a real magpie, so don't you go enigmatic on me and start talking in monosyllables like Mauricio . . . I'll die if you do. Frankly, I'm getting just a little bored with this tiny gift my husband sent me. He doesn't want to go to the beach and I'm going to have to stay in this godforsaken city every weekend this summer, which absolutely collapses me. I suppose I'll wind up taking him to see the Holy Family Church in my spare time."

"Let Ramón do that. He has such bad taste, I'm sure he admires that crazy wedding cake . . ."

Sylvia laughed. "You demolish everything, Paolo, even poor Gaudí! Don't let Ramón hear you blaspheming like that! Who can get me records of Ravel played by Casadesus?"

Paolo thought for a moment. "Raimunda Roig went through a Ravel period. She ought to have them. I'll ring her up if you want."

And while Paolo talked to Raimunda, it dawned on

Sylvia that Mauricio had asked her how to get to Vallvidrera, when only a short time before he had said he spent the whole morning there. She gave a little scream of terror. Paolo hung up on Raimunda, saying Sylvia was having an attack of hysterics, he'd explain everything afterward.

3

MAURICIO thought that maybe it would be better to look at Vallvidrera in the coin-operated viewer at the entrance to the zoo, since the abstraction of a slide would be more tolerable than seeing those woods invaded by the Sunday hordes. But the idea of riding in a cable car amused him. And the little car dangling from its string climbed the mountain between the pine woods and the cascades of honeysuckle and bougainvillaea. In his compartment, a young priest was trying to control ten restless little boys, all bursting with pride at being members of the Patufet Excursion Club and showing off their insignia. As the car ascended, the dark gray film that enveloped the city plain and the harbor was left behind, and they reached a level where the air was clean and the horizon and the sea were clear and vast. Getting off at the funicular station at the top, the Patufet Excursion Club left Mauricio entangled in their race out of the plaza, running like a bunch of chickens toward the fields.

There was something of the stage set about this plaza, Mauricio thought. It was as if a perfectionist director had taken the trouble to gather together in a small space all the elements necessary to re-create a Sunday outside the city: children on swings, couples strolling and drinking Coca-Cola under the friendly sun, agonizing Modernist façades resuscitated during the summer months under the languishing honeysuckle, well-bred dogs obeying their masters, well-

bred children minding their parents, clusters of teenagers
sitting on the steps saying hardly a word, humming bits of
tunes very different from what Mauricio knew how to
whistle. But this wasn't what most separated him from them.
It was rather that all of them were so eager to find something that would mark that day, arrest it in their memories,
keep them from losing it . . . keep the day from escaping
them: the Sunday fear that time is swallowed up like drops
of water in parched ground. That was why the children
were humming. That was why the girls were shaking their
long, straight hair. That was what all these people were
searching for. The yellow-jerseyed soccer players wanted
this to be the day they beat the team in lilac-colored jerseys.
The ladies with hairdressers' hairdos wanted to remember
this as the day that Mariana lost her first tooth, even at the
cost of blood and tears; the tooth would be treasured, just
as other people would look for other things to treasure, to
keep this Sunday from dying without being dignified by the
ritual of having "a good time."

Keeping his distance, Mauricio followed a group of girls
and boys who—he heard them say—were going to the
swamp. They would lead him, set him on the right track.
After that he could disappear if he felt like it. The road out
of the little town was dusty but comfortably shady, with
open views toward the forest-covered Vallés. Perhaps the
color slide hadn't lied about everything. But Mauricio soon
realized that, being so close to the city on the first true day
of summer, the place would be jammed with picnickers, and
what should have been velvety thickets would be littered
with papers, cellophane bags, plastic bottles, beer caps,
napkins, and grass crushed under the weight of stretched-
out bodies. But he was already there—at the suggestion or
command of the machine at the entrance to the zoo. He
didn't like what he saw. But he could erase these people and
their rubbish just by letting the music invade him, sup-
planting the insufferable world of this Mauricio with the
fine, fresh world of another Mauricio. After a frustrating

morning and a tiresome lunch with his mother, he was seeing one of the city's suburbs, Vallvidrera. The world of the
other Mauricio was better. But it didn't matter, it was a
question of substitution, giving way, walking, whistling,
looking, getting rid of everything that prevented him from
penetrating the very center of the music. Paolo, it was true,
had talked too much, but what he said wasn't all stupid.
The author of the text to *Gaspard de la Nuit* had changed
his given name, Louis, and in discarding it had adopted a
name that really fitted him—Aloysius. But Mauricio was a
long way from completing the substitution. Sometimes it
was so hard for him to invent what the other Mauricio had
invented—like the tremolos that he was whistling now.

"What are you whistling?"

"Nothing."

Afterward he realized he had answered before even
being certain the girl's question was addressed to him. But
he wasn't mistaken. In a group of boys and girls his age,
dressed in blue jeans, a girl with long, blond, heavy hair
parted in the middle waved to him to join them. They were
throwing a ball and running around. Mauricio smiled at the
blond girl; she threw him the ball and he picked it up,
becoming part of the group. They looked at him. But only
to accept, to have a good time, which was not what it was
all about. But why shouldn't he have a good time too? He
was still this Mauricio. He smiled again at the blond girl,
who threw the ball back to him, very high and wide now,
and Mauricio had to jump to catch it.

"Good catch!" they all shouted.

And Mauricio threw the ball again, to all of them. But
none of them caught it. It was caught by a boy passing by
who moved on after returning the ball, so that Mauricio
never saw his face before he disappeared, only his back.

"What's your name?"

"Rosemarie."

With them, it was easy to be Louis instead of Aloysius;
this Mauricio found it perfectly easy to follow where they

went, playing and laughing and spending a Sunday under
the trees. They weren't coarse or vulgar boys and girls.
Nothing marked them, neither coarseness nor lack of coarseness, they were generic not individual, all of them trying
modestly to have a good time. Mauricio asked them where
they were going.

"To watch the soccer game."

"Where?"

"There's a playing field a little farther down."

"There's always a match on Sunday."

"Who's playing today?"

"We don't know."

They didn't know anything, just as he didn't. Maybe just
as he was, they were also, each in his own way, trying to find
something or somebody on whom to unburden themselves.
The blond girl paired up with Mauricio without anyone's
taking it amiss. There was only one couple in the group,
with their arms around each other's waist. They didn't talk
to each other or anybody else, and they kissed from time to
time. The girl wore a broad-brimmed straw hat, and the
boy carried the picnic basket. When the ball was thrown to
them, they protested briefly, then tucked their noses in each
other's neck again. Other groups went by, adults or children
on their way to the playing field. The boy who had caught
Mauricio's throw was lost among all the backs. Now the ball
was rolling down the precipice, among the maidenhair and
gorse that grew around the trunks of the ancient pine trees.
Nobody seemed bothered by its loss, and they kept on
walking.

"How old are you?" Rosemarie asked Mauricio.

"Sixteen. How about you?"

"Fifteen. Where are you from?"

"Madrid."

"That's why you talk funny."

"Well, you do too."

Rosemarie laughed. "I don't talk funny, you do. I'm
Catalan."

A closed but not very deep circle of spectators was already clustered around the soccer field. The Sunday people had found this modest entertainment ready and organized to amuse them. The time allotted to the ritual of the game would be spent cheerfully, wasted with forethought. The teenagers in Rosemarie and Mauricio's group moved up to the first row. One of the boys, by the name of Esteban, handed a red apple to Rosemarie and offered another to Mauricio, who said no, thanks, and so Esteban gave it to Carlos. But perhaps, thought Mauricio, not all these looks would stay floating on the anecdotal surface of the afternoon. Why else had the machine at the entrance to the zoo tempted him to look inside? What was the reason for Jordi's impertinence, pulling his trouser leg so that he would get down and not satiate his curiosity about Vallvidrera, so that he would feel compelled to go up there and find out what had been suggested to him? If Jordi hadn't forced him to get down, he wouldn't be here trying to find out what the color slides had failed to tell him. Rosemarie didn't know how to look at things any differently from the way she did, almost not using her eyes at all, perceiving through her transparent skin, freckled around the nose. As she and Mauricio were pressed together by the screaming crowd, their warmths touched, but Rosemarie didn't seem to notice that they were touching. Maybe that was *her* secret language, just as Mauricio had his: *his* counterpart had crossed his path in the plaza at Vallvidrera, glancing at him—but not directly—as he had too; they hadn't recognized each other on the way to the soccer field with the group of friends, because he had soon disappeared among the backs moving off into the woods and now Mauricio couldn't remember what his back looked like, not even whether it was a back he was looking for . . . or not looking for. The contact with Rosemarie's body, as she suddenly became a passionate partisan of the unknown team in lilac-colored jerseys, was pleasant. He could say "Come on," and take her out into the woods. But Rosemarie didn't even realize she was touching his whole body. What mattered to her was the match, the game, the Sunday, the entertainment: not a language, whatever it was, not even the language of touch, and certainly not the language of looks that pretend never to see. Maybe he was being watched by unseen eyes on the other side of the field, hidden in the welter of faces, shoulders, backs, arms, hats, necks, hair, clasped hands, around the small, brown field opening between the pine trees, where twenty-two men divided into two groups were trying to humiliate each other according to established rules that would no longer apply when the allotted time ran out. Nothing, thought Mauricio. Maybe if I hint, if I do something . . . Mauricio from Madrid or Jaime from Tarrasa, it was all the same to Rosemarie . . . it would be too easy to get Rosemarie to give everything a girl her age could give, open and agreeable at the beginning, then defensive and wet-eyed until she had to say no and stand up. Nothing. The knowledge of what she was and would continue to be weighed on Mauricio with all the load of his mother's violations. . . . He had to get rid of this little pain—which could grow—along with the others that were warping him. It would be better to slip away and return to the plaza. But he didn't.

He asked himself why he didn't, while an argument over a foul went on and he stood on the edge of things. The tremolos, there in the depths, were beginning to organize themselves. His eyes, captivated by the loud, dusty fracas, accepted from somewhere a look that was not looking anywhere. Rosemarie was arguing heatedly about the penalty and he argued back just as fiercely, pressing his point of view as he tried to get closer to the center of the dispute. Now the tremolos were crawling up from the depths of the dark earth, a beetle, a black, glistening insect. It was impossible to make out the notes, which slipped through the clots of earth and pebbles but still wouldn't come into the light and were drowned in the argument over which Mauricio's point of view was beginning to prevail, but his attention was fixed on the insinuating notes and he had no idea what he was trying to convince them of. Rosemarie came over and this time yes, she actually leaned on him while the argument ended and the knot between Mauricio's eyebrows became blacker and more entangled, hiding the beetling look beneath. But it wasn't Rosemarie's body that kept him from leaving, although a few minutes earlier he had wanted to. The beetle was about to emerge into the sun. He scrutinized the spectators, who had rearranged themselves around the playing field as the match continued, now that the question of guilt in the foul had been settled. Boys, girls, people having a good time on a sunny Sunday, and those unidentifiable eyes looking at him . . . it was a glance he had never seen before and it stopped him from leaving just as he felt the urge to go. He was staying to have that hidden, meaningful glance look at him, to let the beetle's seemingly dark carapace be revealed, sparkling brilliantly in the broad daylight, to let the beetle formulate its own chromatic spectrum.

"What are you whistling?"

"Nothing."

It was the second time Rosemarie had asked. He didn't realize it, though, because his attention had turned to another level, not the one encountered this morning in the lady with the Jackie O sunglasses or the poor bastard in the brown suit. The notes were gloriously spanning the entire keyboard: the glance that had stopped him from leaving was looking at him just as he had always looked at the faces of strangers in streets and parks. How to trap it, without tying himself to it, without breaking it, taking infinite care to keep hold of that thread amid the tangled skein—that look which had insinuated itself for an instant through the crowd absorbed in its ritual game.

The match was over. Caught up in inexplicably ardent passions in their brief commitment to one team or the other, the spectators cheered, argued, laughed, slapped each other on the back. Rosemarie's group was the most boisterous, passing a wineskin around to celebrate, offering it to Mauricio, who drank too, while Rosemarie's eyes, focused on him, explored a dimension of Mauricio which the unidentifiable glance in the crowd was already undoing. Mauricio looked at his watch.

"I've got to go."

Rosemarie frowned. "Why?"

"It's late."

"It's barely six."

"I've got to go."

"Leave him alone."

"Leave him alone, Rosemarie . . ."

"Come on, Rosemarie!"

"Can't you see we're just small fry to the kid from Madrid?"

"Goodbye . . ."

"Bye, now . . ."

Mauricio was already gone; the words from the group didn't touch him. As he drew away, the possibility that had held him close to Rosemarie transformed itself into a momentary nostalgia for a patch of skin touching his skin, having no other outlet than that contact. Goodbye. He walked with long, slow strides, his hands in his pockets, whistling, his black eyebrows neatly drawn across his forehead like the wings of a flying swallow. Now that the group of teenagers was farther away, the short-legged beetle started to crawl toward the light again under the wide umbrellas of the pines. The whistling came out of the very depths of Mauricio's being . . . but now it was a struggle to form the notes, his breath scarcely brushing his lips with the modulations, until at last he achieved the intensity that would disentangle the whole thing and lead him to the look he had perceived in the crowd.

He moved a little farther into the woods. Today he wouldn't go down to the swamp: it was getting late. The crowds were beginning to leave, picking up the flowered tablecloth bought for the outing, picking up the nonagenarian grandfather in his undershirt whom they had deposited like a bundle in the sun (and now he was sunburned); they put him in the 600 with all the other foldable objects—chairs, containers, children—and drove off, leaving a stain on the flattened grass that was now a different shade of green, surrounded by cans and paper plates and chicken bones. How would the beetle take flight? After a few minutes of seeing no one, the beetle managed to slip out at full speed, and the tremolos began to resound under the trees festooned with ivy in the underwater atmosphere of imminent dusk. The people were leaving because they didn't like the peaceful light. They wanted sun—raw, yellow sun, the way it appeared in ads for dark glasses—not these curtains of half-light that billowed gently to allow the beetle to abandon its dark habitation in the center of the earth and begin its nacreous flight.

Better to go. He returned to the plaza in Vallvidrera. Now he couldn't find the revitalizing glance amid the crowd that pushed together to find a place on the cable car. He decided to go down the staircase, hundreds, thousands of steps, his long legs skipping them two by two, faster than the cable car—but no, the cable car left him behind, with Rosemarie and her group singing and waving to him without rancor, and they lost him as he accelerated his vertiginous race down the mountain until, exhausted, he reached the plain.

He walked back to the apartment house through the streets, whistling with all the simplicity and carelessness that Rosemarie might whistle a pop song. Going up in the elevator he felt happy, as if somebody had accompanied him right to the door. He could go back to Vallvidrera whenever he felt like it, on a weekday, when there wouldn't be such a crowd. He went into the living room, where his mother was talking to Ramón, and said hello. Then he lifted the white veil of the curtain to go out on the terrace: the air wasn't as transparent down here, among the plants. He walked to the railing and looked down eight stories. Accompanied, or followed? What was the difference? Down in the street, a policeman directed traffic. People went by, the usual people, or maybe not the usual people, it didn't matter . . . one couple, another . . . someone hailed a cab, a bicyclist went by; there was the back of a boy leaning against a lamppost, flipping through what looked like a comic book, his legs crossed, his toes resting on the ground; some teenagers like himself were coming home a little late. The beetle lit up, glittering, in its subterranean cave, but didn't move: someone was watching him from the street and knew that he was watching too and that the beetle was going to crawl up into the light and open its wings. The red light halted the cyclist. The teenagers went into an apartment building. The boy reading the comic book crossed the street as the light changed, and disappeared.

Mauricio heard music that erased his own: Casadesus's arpeggios emerging shamelessly not from himself but from his mother's record player. He turned, leaning against the railing: Sylvia's silhouette, uniting veils and transparencies like some deluxe water sprite, left Ramón sitting on the scarlet sofa, crossed the shadows on the terrace, and closed in on Mauricio, who saw her approaching not like the water sprite of "Ondine" but like a man-eating fish that flutters its transparent tail and fins before moving in for the kill.

"Mauricio . . ." she murmured.

To keep her from coming nearer and violating him definitively, he said, "Turn off that music."

Taken aback, Sylvia stopped in her tracks.

"I thought you liked it."

"I don't want . . ."

"But Mauricio . . ."

Avoiding his mother's outstretched arms, Mauricio crossed the living room and without hearing what Ramón said to him he went into his bedroom and locked the door behind him. Sylvia was about to run after him, but Ramón stopped her.

"Come here."

Sylvia let herself drop beside Ramón on the sofa and sat listening to the music for a moment. Then she threw herself into his arms, sobbing. The tears dissolved her make-up, erasing her eyes.

"What we have to do," he said, "is go to the country for a few days—just the two of us. I'll make you rest."

"How can we possibly go?"

"Why?"

"What about Mauricio?"

"We'll take him with us."

"He doesn't like the country."

"It doesn't matter. Just tell him we're going . . ."

"That wouldn't be a rest."

"He doesn't like anything."

"Not even Ravel, apparently . . ."

"He's a difficult child."

"His father didn't warn me."

And Sylvia began to sob again. "What a drag this is! I'm an utter wreck. It would be heaven to rest for a week without having to fix myself up or put on my face!"

Ramón tried to cheer her up. "Maybe we're making a mountain out of a molehill and it isn't that bad . . ."

"What?"

"Mauricio."

Sylvia sat up, drying her tears. "You're just like all men— let the woman take care of the dreary family problems— that's what we're for, we sex-objects . . ."

"I'd be delighted if you asked me to be *your* sex-object! The shocks it would save me . . ."

"You don't take me seriously."

"Let your husband take the responsibility for Mauricio. And stop crying! Mauricio has probably forgotten the whole thing by now and is dying of hunger."

Sylvia was dialing her husband's number in Madrid; when he answered, she jumped straight into an argument with him about just exactly what he meant by saddling her with Mauricio when she hadn't asked him to, when he had taken custody away from her to begin with on grounds of "desertion . . . I love him like any mother, maybe even more, because my position with him is so difficult. In fact, I *adore* him. But that doesn't mean I ought to *sacrifice* myself or stop everything just for his sake. It goes against all my principles, I'll wind up hating him. What do you mean, Mauricio isn't any trouble? Are you going to tell me . . . totally ordinary and *normal*? What about this *Gaspard de la Nuit* business? Ravel . . . piano . . . Don't tell me you've never heard him whistling it . . . Impossible . . . You're out of your mind, the child should be sent to an analyst. You and your mother think we intellectuals are all closet hysterics? Getting upset over nothing? Like *Gaspard de la Nuit*? . . . I see . . . I don't understand . . . anything . . . Ramón doesn't either . . . he says to say hello . . ."

Sylvia's conference with her husband went on until the music ended. Neither she nor Ramón, who was pacing back and forth on the terrace frowning, his hands in his pockets, was listening to it. Ramón could see Sylvia gesticulating wildly with the receiver in her hand. Finally she became so violent that he went inside, took the receiver out of her hand, and hung up. Sylvia fell into his arms, crying, repeating over and over that she would have to learn how to have a normal relationship with her son . . . not get angry . . . not be worried . . . treat Mauricio like the ordinary, normal boy that he was . . .

"It's late. Do you want something to eat, Ramón?"

"Yes. Fine."

"It's Sunday. That witch Mrs. Presen only came for a minute this morning."

"Let's eat out, then."

"With Mauricio?"

"Why not?"

"I'm terrified to ask him."

"I'll ask him."

"Do you think he likes movies?"

When Ramón invited Mauricio to have dinner out and

go to the movies, the boy accepted without any fuss. Mauricio chose the same movie as Sylvia had, and she patted herself on the back: young people had the same taste as they did. The show started early, so Sylvia made them a snack and then they went to the movies. On the way out, they all agreed that Lelouch was a sentimentalist with a good cinematographer, and afterward they went to the Tortillería to eat. Mauricio looked happy, or at least normal. Sylvia was proud to introduce him to two or three women friends who came over to their table: he wasn't just handsome, but very distinguished, refined, discreet, well-bred . . .

It was late when they left the Tortillería. But the night was so pleasant that they preferred to take Travesera and walk back to Ganduxer. Mauricio knew that somebody was . . . walking with him? following him? No, not "somebody," because he immediately identified the stare he felt on his neck as the one he had felt all day . . . felt for the first time in the depths of the color slides of Vallvidrera, which the machine had shown him. To turn around and look back now, of course, would ruin everything, put features on a sensation that was digging deeper and deeper into his feelings, opening a burrow right down into the center of the earth to let the sleeping creature out into the light, awake and shining. On the way home, as he talked to his mother and Ramón about the movie, he realized that the beetle was obeying that pursuing glance, and as it obeyed, it began to run timidly on its short legs, it lost its dark armor, until at last, the whole rest of the way back to the apartment, it displayed the blinding iridescence of the notes that pierced its rich outer shell: arpeggios, chords, tremolos, all flowed out, brilliant and full. And they would only go on flowing, Mauricio warned himself, if he could enter the building without looking back. Sylvia and Ramón were discussing their own affairs, leaving him alone, and now the melody wasn't hiding in the depths of his mind—rather he was bringing the triumphant chords out into the light. A whistle echoed him, tentatively trying "Scarbó": those difficult embryonic tremolos, the imprecise harmonies that had to be executed with the greatest precision . . . and because the other whistling needed it, Mauricio corrected it, to teach it that necessary precision. Mauricio didn't want to know who was following him down the street, echoing his whistling, man or woman, young or old, rich or poor, because all of these things were irrelevant definitions that drowned it just as his own drowned him. At the door to his mother's building, he didn't look back.

When he woke up next morning, he whistled just like any other teenager as he took a shower. The notes fell like light, slowly, well spaced, dropping through branches: the sildes seen in the park machine were as abstract and pure as the music, not violated the way it had been yesterday. The beetle called to him from Vallvidrera, but this morning he noticed he was whistling with the mistakes of the echo that had followed him from the Tortillería, along Travesera, to Ganduxer and his house.

He dressed and left the house early, making the trip up to Vallvidrera in an empty cable car. The operator, a Basque, thin and flexible as a knife, greeted him as if he were an acquaintance. From the deserted plaza, Mauricio descended the slopes, following the path to the swamp. Nobody. Everybody in the village was working, or, like his mother and Ramón down below in the city, fulfilling their obligations, becoming faceless in activities that erased their features. He, on the other hand, had the child's privilege of not doing anything, walking through the forest of Vallvidrera with his hands in his pockets, kicking pebbles. He passed the deserted soccer field on his way down to the swamp. He avoided the snack bar and made a trail through the trees to the other bank. There, he examined the eye of opaque water that was looking at him. He went a few steps up the hill among the pines and threw himself on the soft ground to look at the water from above. Nobody. Trees. Clear sky. And the music that generated and repeated itself until it cleaned him out completely. Nobody. It was the privileged silence of these mornings when adolescents do not go to school. Trees, stones, sounds had only natural structures that didn't depend on any formalizing intelligence. He opened his eyes, then squeezed them shut again. There was no order, either, to the spots floating behind his eyelids and the intolerable sound of his blood flowing . . . but no: listening attentively through that natural flow, he picked out a whistle that ordered these sounds for a few seconds. Mauricio opened his eyes. From behind a wall of gorse, farther up to the left, a thin, uncertain thread of smoke revealed another presence in the thick brush. The whistling that floated up with the smoke grew louder, still imperfect, but between the flaws it was possible to recognize Ravel. Mauricio stood up. Then sitting down again on the hillside in the layers of dry pine needles, he whistled higher and louder, correcting. The imperfect whistling repeated him, accepting the correction, and began anew. After some very bad measures, it stopped as if out of breath. Mauricio corrected, and it went on, improving but not yet exactly capturing the marvelous ambiguity of each note. It was hard, Mauricio knew that. It had taken him a long time to learn. The nameless girl at Galerías Preciados always laughed when she saw him arrive the moment the store opened in the morning. She would tease him about coming there instead of going to school, and then she would hand him *Gaspard de la Nuit* to take to a booth. She never asked him why he always wanted the same record . . . she was better than his mother, because she understood without needing explanations. Mauricio would put on the record, lift the needle to the right spot, and pursing his lips, begin to whistle. Until he learned it. But the most important thing about his apprenticeship wasn't memorizing the notes in the listening booths of record stores, but rather—once the essence of the music had soaked in—walking alone in the parks, through the Retiro, alongside the river; and while he walked with long strides between the trees, whistling with his hands in his pockets, he gained control of the music: the concentration demanded to learn it drove everything else out of his mind, and thus, although he could be walking on a crowded street or in a deserted park, he remained like a blank page, ready to receive something unknown which had to come from somewhere. And on those walks, his eyes, without actually looking, were searching for a relationship that wasn't a relationship, but a sign—in somebody, in a glance . . . but the men reading newspapers on park benches were always nearsighted, the ragged hobos he used to follow so often and so excitedly would sense him following them and run away or set up a confrontation that he would have to elude, the women never understood anything because they were thinking about their shopping lists, the girls always took everything the wrong way . . . And so Mauricio remained alone, locked in his well-starched blue shirts and his khaki pants, the prisoner of his name, address, father, grandmother, and a mother who was aloof and amusing but lived in another city and even so forced him to "be somebody" . . . He was only able to erase all that momentarily when he whistled and like a hunted creature took momentary refuge at the bottom of that burrow where, crouching and untouched, he could wait.

Mauricio stretched out again on the dead leaves. It was better not to watch the thin column of smoke. The whistling that was coming from behind the furze had absorbed all his corrections. So well, and so easily, indeed, as to give him the curious sensation that he was recording on an uncut disc, and that the other whistling, eager for everything he had, was absorbing everything of him . . . was actually *somebody*. But careful. Don't go any farther. Learn nothing more. Don't ruin things.

Stretched out there, surrounded by the music he was whistling, he had the sensation of falling asleep: a presence approached him in his sleep and stood watching him, as if to study and absorb him. When he opened his eyes there was nobody, but he felt he had seen his own face leaning over him. He began "Ondine" from the beginning, like a call, like a challenge . . . then he listened: nothing. But now he was whistling "Ondine" very imperfectly. This gave him a strange pleasure, as if he were being stripped naked. He listened again. The clean light of the forest, the rosemary and the furze—everything was quiet, and that was the way it had to be. He stood up, shook out his clothes, returned to the plaza in Vallvidrera, and in the cable car going down, he talked to the Basque.

4

HIS MOTHER wasn't home. Nobody was home. Only a note warning him: "I won't be home for dinner. Mrs. Presen left you something in the icebox. But I won't be very late. Kisses. Mama."

Mauricio had the apartment to himself for the rest of the afternoon and part of the evening. Nobody was coming. He took the phone off the hook and undressed because he was hot. Leaving his clothes in a pile on the floor, wandering naked through the apartment, he realized that by taking off his clothes, he had removed much of the weight that was upon him. He had the same sensation of space as in Vallvidrera, and the music, precise and perfect again, gushed forth like a spring that moistens the earth.

He stretched out naked on the scarlet sofa, going over and over the music he knew so well, concentrating to make it precise, make himself one with its very center so that all of him was erased . . . eight . . . ten hours stretched out on the sofa repeating the musical phrases that made him float, neither seeing nor hearing, outside time. Stretched out with his arms crossed behind his head, he existed only as a thin film of music separating nothingness from more nothingness. He didn't even see Sylvia until she came over and started to shake him violently.

"Mauricio!"

At first he couldn't react. Again she shouted. "Mauricio!"

He rubbed his eyes. Sylvia noticed that it took him a few seconds to recognize her—*her*, his mother, Sylvia Corday.

"Mauricio."

"Good morning."

"What's the matter with you?"

"Nothing. I was asleep. What time is it?"

"I don't know. Eleven p.m. Don't lie to me, Mauricio, you weren't asleep, you were whistling and you had your eyes wide open."

Sylvia sat down on the edge of the sofa, next to his naked body, supporting herself with one hand on the back cushions while she scrutinized her son with fear and affection, which he rejected.

"What's wrong?"

"Nothing."

"Were you smoking pot?"

"No."

"LSD? You have to be very careful with that."

"No."

"You were . . ."

"Resting."

"Why are you so tired?"

"I was walking . . ."

"Doing what?"

"Taking a walk."

"Where did you take a walk?"

"All around."

Sylvia closed her eyes. "I don't understand anything."

"Then don't try."

"If it had been pot . . . I would understand, at least I'd have a frame of reference. But . . . this . . ." She burst into tears.

Mauricio sat up. "Don't cry."

She let herself fall on his chest, embracing him. "Are you sick? What's the matter? I'd give anything to understand you . . . you must have some rare disease, whistling with your eyes wide open when you thought you were asleep."

"I wasn't asleep."

"Then explain to me."

"Explain what?"

Sylvia thought it over. "Nothing." She stood up brusquely and began to pace up and down the living room. "Nothing. You aren't anything. It's as if you were transparent, slippery. You don't have any personality, *that's* what's the matter. You're like an unconsecrated communion wafer."

When Mauricio smiled at that, she turned to attack. "You think it's funny, do you? In the real world you can't be like this, Mauricio. You have to be strong, you have to fight, have ambition, I don't know, you have to have an *angle*. You're too *fin de race* . . . even your appearance: look how thin you are . . . and that appallingly decadent music, yes, I know Ravel was a Great Composer, but that doesn't make him any less decadent . . . and it's as if it were your essence, the only personality you have . . ."

"It's not my essence."

"Well, what is it, then?"

"I don't know, a path . . ."

Sylvia sat down beside him. "A path to what?"

"I don't know. If I did, I wouldn't whistle."

Sylvia became tense again. "Are you aware how you reject me? One moment you seem to open up, but it never lasts more than a second, and then you snap shut again."

"I can't explain to you."

"I'm willing to give you everything. I've worked very hard, I've fought people's prejudices and ways of life that I think chain people down . . . but I don't understand you. If you lived with me instead of that reactionary father of yours, I'd take you to see an analyst: this must be one of those adolescent upheavals. But you have to fight your problems, Mauricio, not let yourself be devoured by them . . ."

"No . . ."

"I offer you anything you like—a summer at the most

amusing beach in Europe, a motorcycle, clothes, trips, money, everything—and you turn it down. Everything inside you is negative, hostile . . ."

"No . . ."

"Worse than hostile: you're apathetic."

While his mother was talking to him, Mauricio stood up and began putting on his clothes: his light-blue shirt, his khaki pants, his coffee-colored loafers. She had her elbow on her knee, her hand supporting her chin. She got up, her face dry and her eyes serious, watching him put on his other loafer.

"Do you want anything, Mauricio?"

"No, nothing, thank you."

"Good night, then. We've been working until now and I'm exhausted. Good night."

He looked up at her from where he was sitting. She was very tall, very narrow, very thin, and he had inherited the way she stood: crossing her long legs like a stork below the knees, steadying herself on the floor with the toes of one foot. Mauricio suddenly remembered the silhouette of the boy down in the street leaning against the lamppost: he had been reading a comic book in precisely the same pose . . . yes, on Sunday, before crossing the street with the light and disappearing. Remembering that silhouette, Mauricio realized he hadn't assumed that posture again from that moment on. He rose to his feet to try it, but it wasn't comfortable or graceful.

"Good night," he said.

Then, with a last great effort, he added, "Sleep well."

Sylvia stopped in the doorway. Turning around to look at him, she laughed.

Next day, Mauricio went back to Vallvidrera. The Basque in the cable car, all bone and energy and smiles, greeted him amiably. He was beginning to acquire a personality for the Basque, Mauricio thought. It would be a good idea to go up by another route the next time so this wouldn't happen. And as he disappeared into the forest, he felt he didn't even have to whistle because everything—trees, air, light—embodied the music.

He stopped. Amid the generalized music, a whistling took form. He listened: imperfect. It was yesterday's whistling waiting for him to finish the apprenticeship. Its timing was wrong. He followed the path with his hands in his pockets, moving very slowly. The chromaticism of the arpeggios was too exaggerated. As he walked through the forest, the whistling always kept ahead of him, hidden, or behind him, dodging in and out of the underbrush, closing in, moving off, all the time asking him to teach and correct. At last, after much walking and whistling, Mauricio descended to the edge of the swamp, and crouching among the rushes, he listened. At last the whistling was perfect from beginning to end, and he exclaimed:

"Good!"

But when Mauricio tried to whistle *Gaspard de la Nuit* as he went up the hillside, he couldn't: precision evaded the breath let out by his lips. Well then, he could at least listen to it inside himself, let it mark his steps on the wind . . . but no, nothing, it was as if the dry earth he was treading had swallowed every last drop of the music and no longer could give it back. That was when Mauricio smiled his archaic, triangular smile, more pronounced now than ever before.

He sat on the hillside to look down at the swamp from between the trunks of the pine trees. But now, it was no more than that: a swamp seen between tree trunks, branches, furze, rosemary, fennel, dried pine needles. Farther down, in the distance, near the swamp, a boy was squatting in front of a small fire, cooking his meal; near him, dry fallen branches, a huge, rough boulder. The smell of the food being warmed reached Mauricio's nostrils and he said, "Chickpeas."

He looked at the boy again. Next to him on a sheet of newspaper, the boy had spread out some slices of sausage and a loaf of bread cut in half, to make a sandwich. Here were more facts with which Mauricio, in his new silence void of anything to cling to, could identify the external world: there was a boy with black hair, and when the boy stood up, Mauricio judged by his figure that he was more or less his own age, although he couldn't see his face. The boy picked up a comic book, leaned his back against the nearest tree trunk, and while waiting for the chickpeas to warm up, he crossed his long legs below the knee in a pose that seemed peculiar to Mauricio, but he didn't recognize it. He tried to imitate it, leaning his own back against a tree and resting the point of his shoe on the ground, like the boy flipping through the comic book. Of course in the boy's case it wasn't the point of a shoe, but whatever it was that protected his feet—across the distance they looked like a pair of faded sneakers, because the boy was a street urchin. Only beggars and urchins eat chickpeas at eleven in the morning and satisfy their hunger according to invisible, personal schedules. The boy watched the smoking pot, threw the comic book on the ground, sat down and took his time eating the chickpeas, all the while keeping his back to Mauricio. After finishing his meal he stretched out face-up on the pine needle mattress, his arms crossed behind his head, and fell asleep. Mauricio waited awhile. Then he crept closer, hiding behind bushes and tree trunks, as if he were going to steal something, making no noise, right up to the place where the boy was sleeping. His breathing was deep and regular. He didn't move. Mauricio drew closer.

Yes. As he had guessed, a street urchin. Pants in tatters, his sneakers full of holes, his shirt frayed and filthy around the collar, the pot he had used to heat his chickpeas battered, the comic book coverless. Then Mauricio leaned over the boy to examine his face: it was identical to his own. Mauricio experienced no surprise. He had been expecting it: the flying swallow of thick black eyebrows joined over the nose, the archaic, triangular smile even in sleep, the still childlike sweetness of the oval face . . . and the body, the long legs, the frail chest, the delicate structure of the shoulders . . . All of this was his, too. Did the boy also have green-brown eyes that sometimes turned black when he scowled? Maybe. But what did that matter? The important thing was that now he wouldn't have to go on inventing shadows to frighten the people who violated him. He came closer. The boy's body smelled dirty, but not disagreeable: it would be easy and not unpleasant to acquire that smell. And his hair was perhaps a little too long, just the way his mother wanted his to be.

Leaning over him, like somebody taking a long look back across his whole life, he asked himself what he wanted from that creature he had been seeking for such a long time in streets and parks and who now was stretched out, in his power, sleeping at his feet among the bushes. Did he want to talk to him, embrace him, make friends with him, kiss him, ask him things, find out how and when and why, whistle together, kill him? Mauricio trembled a little because he didn't know what to do. Wake him up and ask him? No, that was the most repulsive idea, he couldn't behave like his mother, who in her efforts to express things only killed them. Mauricio leaned farther over this mysterious body that contained what was his: he smelled his breath, heavy with chickpeas and cheap sausage. Touch Him! . . . with the back of his hand he touched the softest part of the sleeping boy's neck, just under the chin. For a second, no more, he couldn't resist letting his hand rest there, and in that instant of physical contact he discharged onto the other boy everything that had been weighing him down. He pulled his hand back as if he had burned it and stood up. The sleeping boy moved slightly under the shock of trans- ference. His breathing became more rhythmic. Mauricio retreated a step, then another, fearful that the boy would wake up and their glances would cross, before the thing had been properly consummated. He hid behind some black- berry bushes, then moved farther and farther away: he saw the boy waking up gently and stretching. When he sat up he looked around as if he had seen a face hovering over him in his sleep. But he didn't see anybody. His dark brows hid his eyes. Mauricio disappeared into the forest that surrounded the swamp and soon he couldn't see the boy or the place where he had been sleeping.

On the opposite bank, which received the full force of the sun's rays, he sat down for a moment to rest. It was very hot. He took off his shirt, then felt an irresistible impulse to plunge into the water—yes, into the filthy ooze of the swamp. Taking off all his clothes, he did just that. He splashed around in the thick water for a while, refreshing himself, and then waded out to lie down, not in the sun but near the shrubs, to dry off. And with his hands behind his head, it wasn't long before he too fell asleep.

The shape of another boy emerged at once from the thick underbrush, as if he had been following Mauricio and knew exactly where to find him. He too crept surreptitiously forward, and for a long while observed the adolescent's precise contours, the taut skin over the arched ribs, all bone and softness like his own body, sleeping on the grass while the heat dried the water, leaving a film of swamp dirt on the skin, and a crust of mud between his toes.

Mauricio's sleep was not quiet. He tossed and turned, sighed, murmuring things, phrases, words, as the boy, listening carefully, was learning how to say them. While he watched his sleeping fellow, he whistled perfectly, but without realizing what he was doing. For a second he rested his open hand on Mauricio's chest, then ran to hide behind a nearby rock. There he took his clothes off. Leaving them in a small pile beside his comic book, he slipped into the water. Unlike Mauricio, he didn't splash around. Shielded by the reeds along the shore, he found one of the falls of clear water and there washed himself carefully, until he was clean and odorless, as Mauricio had been. When he emerged from the water, he stretched out behind a rock to dry off, and closed his eyes, perhaps asleep. When his eyes were closed, Mauricio came over, put on his shirt, his dusty, worn-out sneakers, his old pants, rummaging through the pockets to see what he could find. Nothing: a dirty handkerchief, seven pesetas, not even an I.D., a name . . . nothing. Realizing this, Mauricio ran like a thief who knows he has stolen something priceless, and disappeared into the woods.

As soon as Mauricio had gone, the boy opened his eyes. There, ten feet away, was the pile of Mauricio's clothes. He crept over to it: clean, light-blue shirt, coffee-colored loafers made of good leather, khaki pants from Galerías Preciados . . . they had once thrown the boy out of Preciados on suspicion. He dressed carefully and naturally. Although it was no longer early, the boy continued Mauricio's walk through the woods, whistling, then went up to the funicular station in Vallvidrera. The Basque asked him what he had been doing with himself all day long; the man had begun to think he had gone down on foot, maybe by way of Las Planas, or somebody had picked him up in an automobile. The cable car was almost empty. The boy's heart was beating fast as they descended to the city. Getting out, he didn't want to answer the Basque in more than monosyllables, for fear the man would hear a difference in his manner of speech. He hailed a cab and gave the address in Ganduxer. He paid and went up to the apartment. Opening the door, he thought he had better say as little as possible until he felt more confident.

"Mauricio?" That was unmistakably a mother's voice.
"Yes."

They were already in the dining room. Explain? Better wait until they asked him why he had come home so late . . . maybe they wouldn't ask at all. The other one must be Ramón, whose name Mauricio had murmured in his sleep.

"Hello." And he stayed waiting at the dining-room door. Ramón and Sylvia responded with smiles, hearing Mauricio say hello with a grin they had never seen. Then the boy went over to Sylvia and kissed her on the forehead. Since Ramón looked stupefied, he went over and kissed him too. Neither Sylvia nor Ramón said anything because they knew Mauricio and they knew any remark could set him off.

"Would you like some dinner, Mauricio?"

"Yes."

"Don't tell me you're hungry."

"Yes, I am."

Ramón and Sylvia looked at each other in surprise.

"We brought some pizzas," she said. "Knowing how little you eat, we thought it would be enough . . . But if you're hungry, it's no trouble to make you a pork chop and a salad."

"Yes, please, a salad."

He repeated the words as if to learn how to pronounce them the way they did. Sylvia went to the kitchen. Meanwhile Ramón sat talking to the boy, telling him about a new house he was building for some rich clients in Cadaqués, on a cliff. He would be glad if Mauricio and Sylvia would come with him one day to see it.

"Fine," said Mauricio.

Sylvia set the hot pizza in front of him.

"Did I just hear you say you'll come with us to the beach, Mauricio?"

"Yes."

Sylvia didn't answer; she was dumfounded.

"Could we leave tomorrow morning?" Ramón asked.

Sylvia thought it over for a moment and said, "The boy doesn't have any clothes. Luckily his hair seems to have grown . . . It looks great that way, Mauricio."

Ramón broke in. "Why don't you go shopping for clothes tomorrow morning and we'll leave in the afternoon. How's that?"

Sylvia turned to her son. "I'm going to buy you some hippie shirts, Mauricio."

"All right, Mama."

There was a moment of complete silence, in which the boy feared they had found him out by a mispronounced word or some other false step, but he saw that Ramón was looking in Sylvia's eyes, which were full of tears. Ramón covered Sylvia's hand with his own. She disappeared into the kitchen again.

"Mauricio," Ramón began.

"What?"

"Do you know that's the first time since you've been here that you've called her Mama?"

Ramón continued to look at the boy. Because he had to obey his impulses, the newcomer followed Sylvia into the kitchen, where she had put a pork chop on a plate for him. She had shredded some salad in a wooden bowl and was pouring a golden thread of oil over it, a thread that shook as she heard her son come in. But she didn't turn around, because she didn't want him to see her crying. He came over to her, hugged her from behind, and kissed her cheek. He was taller than she was, but not much. And then she let her whole weight fall on the boy's chest, and he took out his clean handkerchief and dried his mother's tears. Then he went back to the table.

Later, saying good night to his mother before he went to his room, he kissed her again. She covered his face with kisses and ran her perfumed fingers through the shock of black hair. As they parted, she told him to get dressed early so they could go out together to buy clothes. They would have a good time.

"Mauricio."

He turned round in the doorway.

"Yes?"

"Is there anything else your heart desires that your stingy father hasn't bought for you?"

"Yes."

"What?"

"A motor scooter."

"But just the other day I offered you one and you told me no."

"Now I want one. Gunmetal gray."

Sylvia laughed. "What awful taste, Mauricio. And how unlike you. But that's all right—it's funny. We'll buy it tomorrow morning. Good night."

"Good night, Mama."

And that night Sylvia listened while her son undressed in the next room, whistling *Gaspard de la Nuit* perfectly, and for the first time she found it beautiful, not terrifying.

5

MAURICIO, on the other hand, there in the forest, couldn't whistle correctly. He tried to, but it wouldn't come out, and he laughed: it didn't matter. The boy's clothes fit him perfectly, even the odors in the clothes blended pleasantly with his own smell. He couldn't believe his good luck: again and again he felt in the pockets for some identification, something whose presence in his clothing would define him in some way. Nothing. No I.D., no name, nothing to betray a habit or a preference: it was the blank page, the empty staff on which he could begin to write. A five-peseta piece, two one-peseta pieces, some ordinary paper napkins . . . he wasn't anybody.

Walking without whistling, and stepping gently on the forest grass with the rubber soles of his sneakers, like an animal on its own tracks, he moved through the trees in the night, still without whistling, no note to upset the tranquillity of his mind. Each move he made was perfect now: jumping over a ditch, climbing down a precipice, he was as precise as the notes had been before, but they had never moved him forward with the sureness of these sneakers. From the wooded mountainside he looked at the Vallés through the night: San Cugat, Tarrasa, and farther off a string of lights along the road that started a few yards away from his feet . . . and farther still Vich . . . and after that the Pyrenees, and on the other side France and Germany . . . and after them, the Russian steppes and Asia, where the wind buffeted ice and sand and caravans and unfamiliar races . . . all starting at the very feet of the boy he was now.

But he had to wait awhile. Curling up behind a bush, he soon fell asleep. He couldn't leave without seeing Mauricio once again. He had received so much in exchange for so little that at least he ought to wait and see that everything was going all right in the deal they had made, that the new Mauricio didn't need him anymore. And besides, he wanted to know what color the new Mauricio's eyes were anyway. Their glances had never crossed, as his had with so many people when *he* was Mauricio, following them through the streets, whistling some musical phrases which now he couldn't even produce by a composer whose name he didn't remember anymore. Before setting off for good, he wanted his eyes to meet Mauricio's and feel what the passers-by felt when a boy in khaki pants and a light-blue shirt followed them, staring at them, whistling.

He wandered around Vallvidrera all morning. He went over to the funicular station to see if the Basque would recognize him, but the Basque, who would joke with practically anybody, refused to return his glance, since it was no longer that of the distinguished young man. He walked back down to the forest and disappeared, heading for the swamp. He bathed again, let the sun dry him off, and lay down to sleep.

The sound of a motor on the road woke him up. A gunmetal-gray Vespa such as his mother had offered him and he had rejected, along with everything else, appeared. Driving it was a boy wearing a pretty yellow shirt. The boy passed him without a glance. That boy was Mauricio, and he was that boy who didn't look at him and whose face was radiant, the black high-arched eyebrows like swallows in flight, the skin clean in the wind, the archaic smile now a defense not against all the terrible things that he didn't want imposed on him, but against the dust and wind produced by speed. The ragged boy clambered up a hillside that had a broad view over the road: from there he could see all the

serpentine turns between the hills and woods . . . and he saw
Mauricio, dressed in a yellow shirt and riding a gunmetal-
gray motor scooter, hurtling down the road, taking the
curves at full speed, then coming back, making the motor
purr to test its efficiency downhill, shifting gears, testing the
scooter among the thickets and boulders, accelerating, brak-
ing just to see what it would do, flying down the road at full
speed and disappearing behind the hills, and coming back
again, climbing more slowly to a spot near those eyes that
watched him. He killed the engine and began to wipe the
scooter with a rag. He squatted down to examine its small
motor and its wheels, testing the flexibility of the handlebars
and adjusting the seat . . . all very carefully, as if it were
a jewel. And as he did this he whistled some musical phrases
that the boy watching him from the hillside didn't recognize.

The ragged boy climbed down the hill. He took the path,
passing very close to Mauricio. As he went by, Mauricio
raised his head and their eyes met. In Mauricio's glance the
boy saw a look of fear he didn't like. His own eyes were
clear.

Mauricio finished fiddling with the engine. He was sixteen years old. In buying him this motor scooter his mother
had promised that when he was eighteen and could get a
driver's license, she would give him a car: a Fiat 600 to begin
with . . . and then a mini, if he stayed with her to prove to
her husband's family that even a boy Mauricio's age could
suffocate in the monastic environment in which they were
forcing him to live. He had said, "All right, Mama."

"I don't know how you could stand life before, living
there . . ."

"I don't either, Mama."

Mauricio picked up speed as he passed a ragged boy
walking down the road. The boy heard him whistling the
usual music, which he no longer needed to whistle or hear,
ever again. Now he couldn't contain himself: he had to leave
Vallvidrera. If he stayed there, little by little he would

About the Author

José Donoso was born on October 5, 1924, in Santiago, Chile, into a family of doctors and lawyers. After three years at the Instituto Pedagógico of the University of Chile, he was awarded the Doherty Foundation Scholarship for two years of study at Princeton, where he received his B.A. in 1951. Mr. Donoso has taught English language and literature at the Instituto Pedagógico of the Catholic University of Santiago, Chile, and held an appointment in the School of Journalism at the University of Chile. In 1956 he was awarded Chile's Municipal Prize for journalism, and in 1962 he received the William Faulkner Foundation Prize for Latin American literature for the novel *Coronation*, which was his first work to be published in the United States. Mr. Donoso's other books include two novels, *This Sunday* (1967) and *The Obscene Bird of Night* (1972); *Charleston and Other Stories* (1977); and an autobiographical work, *The Boom in Latin American Literature: A Personal History* (1977). Mr. Donoso now lives in Spain, where he is at work on another novel.

A Note on the Type

The text of this book was set in Caledonia, a Linotype face designed by W. A. Dwiggins. It belongs to the family of printing types called "modern face" by printers—a term used to mark the change in style of type letters that occurred about 1800. Caledonia borders on the general design of Scotch Modern, but is more freely drawn than that letter.

Composed by Maryland Linotype, Baltimore, Maryland.
Printed and bound by American Book, Stratford Press, Saddle Brook, New Jersey.
Typography and binding design by Virginia Tan.